K.M. TOMKINSON

HER STOLEN FAMILY

ISBN: 978-1-7635268-8-4

Three Little Ducks Publishing

With thanks to my husband, Luke.
Couldn't have done it without you.

<u>Prologue</u>

November 18, 2016

Dear Diary,

Well, today is my seventeenth birthday…and after her threats this morning, I fear I won't see my next. If something should happen to me, hopefully someone finds this extract. Maybe then the world will know my story, and she'll be held accountable for everything she's put me through…

I was six years old the night she came for me. My mother woke me up in the middle of the night. I remember how scared she was, the fear in her voice as she shook me awake. "Get up, Claire, we need to go. Now!"

Foggy, I climbed out of bed, still semi-asleep, rubbing my eyes. I reached lazily for my slippers, but she yanked me out of bed before I could even touch them, dragging me toward the door. As she threw my coat over me with shaking hands, my father snatched one of my blankets and bundled it close to his chest. It was storming outside, the wind howling like a wounded dog, and even though it was almost summer, the air was unnaturally cold. I shivered, not from the temperature, but from a creeping sense that something was terribly, terribly wrong.

Somebody started pounding on the front door loudly—heavy, violent bangs—as if they were trying to break it down. The sound jolted me fully awake. "Mama, I'm scared," I whispered, and that's when my mother started crying, soft and quiet, as though she hoped her tears could escape without being noticed. She scooped me up in her arms, holding me close as we ran toward the back of the house, my father trailing behind us.

Suddenly, a deafening crash filled the air—the front door splintering as it ripped off its hinges and collapsed to the floor. I got a quick glimpse of a wild, ferocious-looking woman with flaming red hair, standing in the doorway like something out of a nightmare, before my mother yanked open the back door.

Before I knew it, we were at the bottom of the small hill in our backyard. Dad pulled aside some thick shrubbery, and they pushed me into the hollow between them. I huddled in a ball as they squeezed in beside me, all of us wrapped together, our breath fogging in the cold, rain-soaked air. My spine tingled when a sharp crack of twigs snapped nearby, indicative she was close. The strange woman with the fiery-coloured hair. Too close.

Without warning, my dad kissed my forehead, a swift, final gesture of affection. "I love you both," he whispered as he pushed us down before leaping out of the bushes, fists flailing wildly.

The woman's laughter rang through the air—cruel, unhinged— followed by the echoing sound of a gunshot.

I tried to squeal, but my mother clamped her hand over my mouth, smothering the sound. With the exception of the heavy rain, all was silent for a few seconds. Then something large rolled under the bushes and stopped at my feet. Lightning suddenly lit up the sky and there he was—my father. His eyes were open, but they were empty, and it horrified me to see them so glassy, so lifeless. Blood had soaked through his clothes already, and it pooled on the grass, sickeningly absorbing into my socks.

My mother whispered his name over and over, like a chant, before her voice broke into a loud, heart-wrenching wail. It was the first and last time I ever saw her properly cry, for at that moment another loud gunshot shattered the air, and she fell forward, collapsing onto her knees by my feet. Bleeding rapidly from her shoulder blade, she pointed silently toward the far end of the bushes, gesturing for me to run.

I hesitated for a second, watching her struggle to her feet and tackle the woman with one last war-cry-like scream, causing another gunshot to go off. I screamed loudly and tried to cover my head with my arms. Lightning flashed again, illuminating the immediate area and I saw a pair of bright green eyes staring at me through the hedge. Wavy, matted bright red hair hung over her ears. Strangely, I felt like I'd seen her somewhere before.

It was then I bolted. Being so young, I don't think I could process what was happening exactly, only that I needed to get away from the stranger. I dashed back up the hill, past the house and onto the path, the cement soon becoming sand. I had reached the beachfront.

Running as fast as my little legs could carry me, I stumbled, cutting my knee on a wet rock. Crying, I instinctually called out for my mother as I nursed my knee and brushed sand away from my mouth, tasting both salt and blood on my lips. An unexpected blow to the back of my head sent me sprawling forward into the sand again.

Despite me screaming and kicking wildly, someone snatched me up by the waist, jamming a hessian bag over my head as I thrashed. I remember thinking it had a funny smell to it just before my vision blurred and the world slipped into darkness.

When I woke, the sun was harsh, beaming down on me as I lay on the deck of a weathered boat. A pretty blonde lady crouched beside me, gently cleaning dried blood off my scraped knee with a sponge. Her smile was warm and comforting.

"Don't worry, you're safe now, little flower," she said, her voice sweet. "I rescued you from the beach last night after I scared away your attacker. It's nice to officially meet you. I'm Roxey Jenson."

I believed her. I thought I was in excellent hands.

Roxey handed me fresh clothes and itook me below deck to the "bathroom," letting me bathe alone in a giant bucket of warm, soapy water. Over the next few months, I grew attached to her, this kind, maternal figure who cared for me. Years passed, and she became the only family I knew.

My world would crumble once more when I was ten years old. That morning, excited for my birthday, I forgot to knock and burst into Roxey's room unannounced. I got more of a shock than either of us bargained for. She sat up in bed, startled, her hair no longer the soft blonde I had grown to love. It was red. A cascade of curly, tangled, fiery-coloured hair spilled down her shoulders.

My mouth fell open, my eyes zoning in on the bedside table beside her where a blonde wig perched neatly on a mannequin's head. Our eyes met and the combination of her brilliant green eyes and fiery red hair stirred horrible flashbacks in my mind. I saw my mother, father and then… her. It was her! Roxey was the one who'd killed my parents. Roxey, the woman I had trusted for years, my adoptive mother, was the murderer who had torn my life apart to begin with. She smiled wickedly. "Oops. Sorry, my darling little daisy. Remember me, do you?"

My throat burned. The weird thing was, I wasn't scared of her. Even though she had proved to me before that she was perfectly capable of murder, I wasn't afraid. No, I was filled with pure, uncontrollable hatred. I had lived with her on a boat in the middle of the ocean away from all other people for four years, trusting her every word. She kept me confined to the boat, convincing me the world was perilous and I'd be in danger if I ever went back to the land. That my parents' attacker would find me.

I can barely believe it's been seven years since that day, eleven years since she took me. Her ship is still my prison. Now I'm treated like her slave—have been since the day I found out who she was. She reminds me, often and in vivid detail, of what she'll do to me if I ever escape. It's the only thing she says that I do still believe.

Am I going to die here?

Chapter One

Claire's eyes snapped open, her heart pounding. To her dismay, the pair of glimmering green eyes from the nightmare she'd woken from were still there, hovering an inch from her face, livid and ferocious. Claire screamed involuntarily and received a sharp blow to her forehead with the handle of a long broomstick. Pain exploded in her skull as she jolted upright, ripping the blanket off her body. Roxey stood assertively, her face twisted in rage and her chest rising and falling with heavy, angry breaths. She raised the broom for a second time, but Claire jolted out of the way on instinct, throwing herself off the bed and dropping to her knees at Roxey's feet as a gesture of obedience.

As she stared at the floor, the dream played in her brain in a vicious loop. Her awful past hadn't stopped haunting her since the moment she'd found out Roxey was the one responsible for slaughtering her parents. It was always the same nightmare. No matter how the dreams began, they ultimately ended with her escaping onto the beach, helpless and alone, just like she had been thirteen years ago when Roxey took her.

When she'd stolen her.

Another thwack struck the back of her neck, harder than the first, jerking her back to the present. Tears welled up in Claire's eyes, and her vision blurred from the pain, but she bit down on her lip, blinked hard and forced herself to look up at Roxey with a forced smile.

"Having nightmares again, my darling daisy?" Roxey cooed in a fake, girlish tone, smirking all the while.

Claire clenched her teeth, swallowing her frustration. She couldn't stand Roxey's nickname for her.

Derived from the first time she'd called her little flower; it had eventually morphed into Claire being as delicate as a daisy in the wind.

"Yes, unfortunately," she replied, her words strained. Roxey clicked her tongue three times in a slow, familiar rhythm of disdain before letting out a quiet, unsettling giggle. Claire hated her fake, spine-tingling laugh. Roxey began to circle her, eyes glinting with a dark thrill, much like a hungry shark preparing to attack its prey. "Tell me darling," she hissed, "what time is it?" The tone of her voice had changed; it was now cold and harsh.

Claire's heart sank as she glanced out the window at the brightening sky. "Around seven-thirty, Mother," she muttered, a wave of despair washing over her.

"Clever girl," Roxey breathed, her lips curling into something far from a smile. She leaned in dangerously close. "Now, remind me, darling, what time are you supposed to get out of bed?" She backed off and resumed circling Claire, her expression growing fiercer as she waited for a reply.

"I… I slept in, I know—" Claire began.

But Roxey cut her off, snapping, "I believe six-thirty was the correct answer. Yes, you slept in. Whilst you've been dreaming, the rest of your family has been waiting in the kitchen for you, their beds empty, yet unmade. You are an hour behind on chores and now it's time for breakfast!" She stopped abruptly and bent in front of Claire, almost nose to nose to ensure she breathed the last sentence directly in her ear. "You are a disgrace, child." Finishing her rant, Roxey turned on her heel and swept out of the room.

Claire exhaled shakily, shivering as she forced herself up off the ground, quickly smoothing over her bed and opening the window to chase out the stifling tension.

A few months after Claire's tenth birthday, Roxey, as if finally unleashed, began collecting young women from a nearby island she frequently sailed to. Although she phrased it, "expanding her family." She took only women, displaying an intense aversion to men, often cursing them with a passion Claire didn't understand. Through the years, Claire had watched helplessly as young women boarded the ship, oblivious to Roxey's twisted intent until it was far too late. Some Roxey enticed aboard with flattery, manipulating them by playing the hero, but the rest she abducted, knocking them unconscious just as she had with Claire. It just depended on how easy they were to coax.

Each woman was assigned a bed and a daily chore to take care of, lightening Claire's workload marginally. As Roxey's personal servant, Claire was initially expected to manage the duties that resembled those of a nineteenth-century housekeeper. Not only waiting on Roxey hand and foot, she was made to clean the ship from top to bottom on the daily, only stopping to cook and serve their meals. Once Roxey had delegated enough chores to the others she'd recruited, Claire became responsible only for general upkeep in the bedrooms. She also had to serve all the meals, as for some reason, waitress was tacked onto her job description.

Eventually, once her numbers exceeded the bed capacity, Roxey *"rewarded everyone"* by upgrading from her overnight cabin boat so everyone could live more comfortably. Somehow, she acquired a small, but spacious, ship complete with below-deck bedrooms, a decent sized kitchen, and a functioning bathroom. From the outside, it resembled a traditional pirate ship, the original owner having renovated the lower interior levels only to match modern standards. Roxey even managed to transfer her whole crew onto it whilst out on the water, ensuring no one had the chance to escape. She made one rule painfully clear: nobody would ever leave the ship. Except her.

In the beginning, Roxey used to rely solely on threats to control her crew, but when Claire was fifteen, she witnessed the brutal consequence of defiance that would see Roxey tighten security. In a desperate escape attempt, Sierra, a seventeen-year-old Roxey had abducted not long after Katalyna the year prior, bore the consequences of Roxey's follow through. Sick of being trapped, the girls decided to escape and snuck onto the deck in the dead of night. When Roxey caught them in the act, Sierra panicked and threw herself overboard. Roxey, in a chilling display of power, fished a terrified Sierra out with a net, dragged her back on deck, and stabbed her in front of the entire crew. She made everyone sit and watch Sierra bleed to death on the deck and called it "a teachable moment." No one dared test Roxey again.

Even so, Roxey took precautions from then on, locking her "family" in a steel cage below deck whenever she docked for supplies. Later, she installed an elaborate tripwire alarm system, rigging every inch of the ship with sensors to catch anyone who dared to get too close to the edges. As if that wasn't enough, she even bought a vicious guard dog, a beast she named Rumble, to patrol the ship's corridors at night. The loyal Neapolitan Mastiff would monitor the cage when Roxey was in town and, if the alarm sounded, was trained to maul anyone who was not within the cage or in a bedroom.

Pushing down the gloomy feeling lingering in her chest, Claire decided to delay making the girls' beds until after breakfast. She dressed quickly and climbed the narrow staircase leading to the kitchen; it was the only room on deck. Roxey had converted the former captain's quarters into an impressive kitchen, opting to sleep in the former kitchen instead—a larger, more secluded room by the stairwell below. This was so the family could enjoy meals with a view, she claimed. She ran a tight, unrelenting schedule, requiring everyone to gather for every meal, every day, without exception.

Claire pressed through the swinging double doors and was immediately greeted with a delightful aroma. Around the long, narrow wooden dining table, the stitched family sat patiently, the room abuzz with the soft murmur of conversation. Bonnie was busy at the stove flipping perfectly golden pancakes onto a growing stack, amongst other perishables. Claire had always liked Bonnie. She was grounded, kind-hearted, and easy to get along with. As Roxey's newest recruit, brought aboard just a year earlier, Bonnie had seemingly adapted more easily than the others to their strange and stifling life, considering the plans she had for her life before her entrapment.

When Claire was twelve, while cleaning Roxey's quarters during a docked stop, Claire stumbled upon a hidden diary tucked beneath the bed. Since Roxey was in town buying supplies, back when she still trusted her girls to roam the boat freely, Claire knew she had the time to read it. Flipping through the pages, Claire's stomach churned as she realised what it was. Each entry chronicled in harrowing detail how Roxey lured her victims aboard. It was a grotesque trophy case in written form, with meticulous notes on their lives, their vulnerabilities, and the manipulations Roxey used to get them on the boat. Claire would read entry after entry every time a new girl was taken.

As Bonnie bustled over the cooktop, Claire recounted Bonnie's tale in her mind, picturing it like a streaming video. The journal entry Roxey added a few months ago, told the story of an ambitious culinary student, dreaming of a career as a chef aboard luxury cruise ships. She had longed to travel the world, blending her passion for food with the thrill of adventure. Upon completion of her degree at twenty-four, that dream was cruelly stolen when Roxey posed as a potential employer, inviting Bonnie to a "trial day" for a live-in chef position. Overwhelmed with excitement, Bonnie eagerly accepted, not realising what she was walking into. On the appointed day, she nervously showcased her culinary talent for Roxey's all-female "crew." After a flawless meal, Roxey sealed the deal, offering her the "job," then informed her that she would never be leaving. The struggle that followed ended with Bonnie locked in her new room for several days, before emerging ready to perform her role with a quiet resilience the others didn't possess for a long time after their capture.

Roxey was perched on her self-designated throne at the end of the table as always. She lounged with confidence, a cheerful smile on her face, one hand lazily stroking Rumble who was humbly guarding her feet.

"Blecch," Claire muttered under her breath as she watched Roxey converse with Tayla and Serenah, who sat either side of her, listening intently like they were her best friends. The rest of the girls sat in their designated seats as always, looking as bored as ever. Katalyna, Josie and Daphne were in order on Serenah's side, whilst Emerald was forced to sit beside Tayla on the other, the seats parallel to her empty and waiting for Claire and Bonnie. No one was permitted to sit opposite Roxey at the other end of the table. Roxey's act of playing "queen of the family" made Claire's skin crawl. She pushed back a feeling of disgust deep in her stomach and walked over to the stove. Bonnie promptly handed her a serving tray piled high with breakfast goodies and leaned in close, her voice barely audible over the chatter.

"Start serving, lovely," she murmured with a quick wink. "She's in one of *those* moods this morning."

Claire mustered up a small smile and took the tray,

balancing it carefully as she approached the table with a selection of bacon, eggs, sausages, pancakes, jam, cream, maple syrup, and two jugs of orange juice. Her nerves hummed as she walked steadily toward Roxey; the last thing she wanted to do was make her angrier. She was almost there when out of the corner of her eye, she saw Tayla, Roxey's smug little favourite, flash her a horrible grin and discreetly stuck out her foot. It happened too fast to stop. Claire tripped over Tayla's foot and tumbled to the ground. The tray flew wildly from her hands, and in an instant, everything was airborne. Soft cooked eggs went sliding, creating a slippery mess whilst pancakes cartwheeled through the air and sticky streams of syrup splattered across the walls, mingling with jam and cream in an explosion of chaotic colour, creating the worst art gallery there ever was.

The jugs shattered on impact, sending a waterfall of orange juice pooling across the floorboards, which was now running across the floorboards, straight towards Roxey's feet. She stood up so suddenly it made the table shake, her serene smile disappearing in an instant. She placed her hands on the table, shoulder width apart as if steadying herself. The room fell deathly silent. Everyone froze, eyes darting nervously between Roxey and the wreckage.

As she glared at Claire, her eyes blazed into deadly balls of fire, like she was trying to melt her into the ground. Claire, sprawled on the sticky floor, swallowed hard. She scrambled to her feet, heart pounding, and stood stiffly, bracing herself for an inevitable punishment. She dared a glance around the room, noting with dismay that a particularly large pancake had glued itself to the ceiling, dripping syrup in slow, menacing drops. Another was sliding down the wall directly behind Roxey's head like a mocking exclamation point to the disaster.

Roxey's eyes flicked to the mess on the floor, walls

and ceiling, then back to Claire. Her chest heaved as she inhaled deeply, a futile attempt at regaining composure. She shook her head and strolled toward Bonnie without a word, the heels of her favourite boots clicking dangerously on the floorboards. Roxey's silence was more terrifying than shouting could ever be. Bonnie stood frozen by the stove, her expression unreadable as Roxey approached her. Ignoring the way she instinctively flinched, Roxey snatched the metal-headed egg flip from Bonnie's trembling hands.

Claire stood rooted in place, head bowed, fists clenched at her sides as Roxey turned her attention toward her. Despair swirled inside her. She barely noticed the syrup oozing down her arm or the way her legs stuck to her syrup-coated jeans. All she could do was wait, dread pooling in her chest as Roxey closed the distance between herself and Bonnie with measured steps. The only sound in the room was the relentless drip of juice from the table, and the faint, mocking *plop* of the ceiling pancake finally hitting the floor. She stopped inches from Claire, the egg flip glinting coldly in her grip. Claire's heart thundered in her chest, but she didn't dare back away.

"Hold out your hands," Roxey whispered, her voice low but laced with venom.

Claire swallowed the lump rising in her throat and reluctantly stretched out her hands, holding them mid-air in front of her. She closed her eyes, bracing for what she knew was coming. A few seconds later, Claire let out a strangled cry as the first blow landed with a sickening crack, the sharp edge of the utensil colliding with only the fingertips on her left hand. The searing pain radiated through her hand like fire but before she could fully process the agony, the second hit came—harder this time—clobbering the tips of her other hand. Tears blurred her vision, but she refused to let them fall, refused to let Roxey see her break.

Satisfied, Roxey pegged the utensil back at Bonnie with a force that sent it clattering onto the counter. "Everybody get out of my kitchen!" she bellowed, her voice cracking like a whip. "Go. Move!"

The room erupted into chaos as chairs scraped loudly against the floor, and the girls scrambled to obey. Claire turned to follow, cradling her throbbing hands against her chest, but before she could take a single step, Roxey's iron grip closed around her arm. Claire winced, the sharp sting of Roxey's nails digging into her skin. "Not you," Roxey hissed, her breath hot against Claire's ear. "You don't get to just walk away."

Chapter Two

As Tayla left the room, she cast a smug glance over her shoulder before practically skipping out the door. Soft giggles trailed after her, fading as she disappeared. Once the room was empty, Roxey's fury erupted.

"Get this place cleaned up!" she snapped, her voice reaching an octave that was usually reserved for extraordinary circumstances. Without waiting for a reaction, she stormed out in a huff, the doors swinging wildly in her wake.

The moment Roxey was gone, Claire crumpled to the floor, tears spilling silently down her cheeks. She reached for the smeared food tray, clutching it to her chest as if it could somehow hold her together. How Claire hated Tayla. Then again, so did most of the others. Tayla was the one person Roxey genuinely seemed to like, and that gave her a certain power over everyone else. The awful part was, Tayla had never used to be a bitch, not when she'd first come aboard, anyway. She'd morphed into what she was under Roxey's influence.

Claire's knuckles whitened as she squeezed the cold tray tighter, remembering the morning Roxey told her she would soon have a sister for company, and later that day dropped an unconscious Tayla on the deck. Claire was almost eleven at the time and knowing how scared Tayla would be when she woke up, crouched beside her and held her hand, waiting to ease the transition.

When Tayla finally awoke, it was to the sound of creaking wood as the ship battled a change in the wind.

"You're okay," Claire said softly, though she knew that statement was far from true. Before Tayla was able to get a grip on her new surroundings, Roxey strutted over, wearing an old lady face. Claire was too afraid to ask why at the time, but later learned it was one of the ways she altered her identity on land. Roxey peeled away her rags, tugged off a grey wig, and removed the mask that had concealed her true skin. Claire remembered the words that drove Tayla into a fit of despair.

"You're part of my family now. Welcome to *The Siren's Hearth.* You'd better learn to love it here, because you aren't leaving."

That's when Tayla broke. At first, she cried endlessly, panic driving her into a fragile, frenzied state. But after a while, Tayla's absolute fear of Roxey started to drive her insane. It was like she couldn't quite cope with what had happened, the isolation from land. Or her family. And Roxey noticed. Like a predator sensing weakness, she worked to break Tayla down even further, feeding her lies until reality blurred. Bit by bit, Tayla became some sort of brainwashed puppet, convinced she'd grown up on the ship with Roxey, believing the false memories planted in her head. By the time Tayla's transformation was complete, Roxey had moulded her into a cruel reflection of herself. She wasn't just Roxey's favourite—she was her double. An utter cow.

After a few minutes of uncontrollable sobbing, Claire forced herself to pull it together. She wiped her face with trembling hands and began cleaning up the breakfast mess. Her fingers throbbed like crazy, relentlessly pulsing as if her body had just realised the extent of their injury. Wincing, Claire gathered the scattered dishes, salvaging what she could. The unbroken crockery and ramekins clinked as she stacked them in the sink, each sound biting at her nerves.

As she worked, Claire pondered why Roxey was so disgustingly evil. What made her so utterly devoid of empathy or humanity? Despite her apparent craving for a "family," she was some kind of a hollow shell—cold, cruel, and incapable of love. There had to be a reason, some dark truth that explained Roxey's behaviour, and Claire wanted to know what that was.

She grimaced as she bent down, sweeping the shattered remnants of ceramic and glass into her hands. As she dumped the sharp fragments into the bin, a sharp pain jolted through her foot, and she lifted it to discover a large piece of glass lodged deep in her skin. Claire wrenched the glass out, causing blood to trickle in between her toes. Feeling too worn down to care, she wiped the foot over with a cloth and the glass wedge quickly joined the other broken pieces in the bin. Claire returned to cleaning as if nothing had happened. It wasn't strength that kept her going—she felt none of that. It was spite. The only thing stopping her from stabbing herself in the neck with a stray shard of glass was a suppressed desire that one day she would find a way to get off the boat, start a new life and become a free woman. And once the world knew what Roxey had done to her, done to all of them, she'd get everything she deserved.

It took more than half an hour, but Claire finally finished scrubbing the kitchen until it gleamed. She stepped back to double check, before leaving the spotless room behind, heading downstairs to make a start on tidying the bedrooms. Thankfully, even with nine women aboard, there were only five rooms to clean. Everyone shared a room except for Roxey, who, unsurprisingly, reserved her own space. Unfortunately for Claire, her assigned roommate was Tayla.

Moving methodically, Claire worked her way through each room. She smoothed out the beds, vacuumed floors, cracked open windows to let in fresh air, and gathered piles of dirty laundry into a basket. Washing the clothes, however, wasn't her job—that responsibility belonged to Katalyna. The eldest woman on board beside Roxey, and the only mother. Whilst tidying Katalyna and Josie's room, Claire picked up the picture Josie kept tucked neatly under her pillow. Unfolding it carefully, like she did every day, she stared at the faded image of a young Katalyna, standing beside an old car with a radiant smile ear-to-ear across her perfectly shaped jawline. The picture was a relic of a life Katalyna no longer had, and possibly the only photo any of them possessed. Claire often wished that she had a photo of her family.

Poor Josie, she thought, gazing at the photograph. Josie had never seen the city, never even set foot on solid ground. Katalyna had given birth to her on the boat, so her entire existence had been confined to its creaking walls and uneven floorboards. Though Roxey had written all about Katalyna's background in her journal, Katalyna herself had told Claire the full story—as most of the girls on board had done. A confidant to everyone, Claire was an empathetic listener and respected the details of their former lives. The story of Katalyna's life before Roxey was a tale she had not even told Josie yet. Claire tucked the photograph back where she'd found it, swallowing the ache rising in her throat as she thought about how Katalyna was tricked aboard.

Years ago, before Katalyna was taken, she was like any other woman in her twenties, trying to survive a life in the big city. She juggled double shifts to scrape by each week, determined to build something better for herself. Her parents had disowned her as a teenager when she came out to them as a lesbian, leaving her to fend for herself. Eventually, she moved to the heart of the island to start a simpler life. To celebrate her twenty-sixth birthday, her girlfriend took her out to a bar and unbeknownst to her, someone spiked her drink. Her girlfriend found her hours later at dawn, slumped and barely conscious in an alley outside the club. Katalyna said she remembered nothing about the night.

Weeks later, intense, relentless nausea drove her to the doctor. The diagnosis he gave shattered her. She was pregnant. Her doctor explained the grim reality: she must have been sedated and raped at the club. Katalyna was devastated, yet, after days of agonizing over the decision, she chose to keep the baby. She spent months trying to track down the father, desperate for answers, but her efforts came to nothing. A supposed private midwife she'd been seeing during her pregnancy suggested ocean therapy as a way to relax and offered her a room on her so-called holiday boat, gifting her a "babymoon." With no reason to refuse, Katalyna accepted.

As the week of her due date arrived, she went down to the beach to board the boat, expecting to be home before the baby arrived. Roxey greeted her with warmth, offering a cozy bedroom and plenty of reassurances. Before Katalyna's arrival, in order to ensure their silence, Roxey sealed the other girls at the bottom of the boat, forcing them to stay out of her recruitment plan.

The next evening, Katalyna unexpectedly went into labour. Roxey delivered the baby herself, and Katalyna named her Josephine. Exhausted but relieved, Katalyna planned to leave as soon as she regained her strength. Roxey encouraged her to stay one more night to rest before heading home. Katalyna was grateful, until the next morning. When she stepped onto the deck, the shore was gone. During the night, Roxey had left the dock. The boat was adrift in the open ocean, never to take her home again. Claire remembered the fight that went down between them, in which Roxey won by threatening Josie's life. She promised to toss the infant overboard if she ever caught Katalyna attempting to leave.

Josie was five now, a quiet child who, despite never knowing life off the ship, could sense that something was wrong. She saw the cracks in Roxey's so-called "family," the way punishments came swiftly and cruelly for any perceived wrongdoing. Claire could tell Josie was unhappy. She had no friends, no proper education, and no real childhood. Josie had never even seen a boy; she only caught glimpses of them when the ship was near enough to a shore. Josie would point at them in awe, like they were animals in a zoo. Katalyna had told her many stories of the city, using the memories of her almost twenty-seven years of life on the land as bedtime stories, describing the busy streets, colourful parks, and brainstorming the things they would do if they could go back. Claire frequently heard them both crying together at night. All she could say was, at least they had each other. The rest of the women were torn from their families long ago. Still, Josie was the most unfortunate. Claire might have been raised aboard *The Siren's Hearth* also, but not from birth, as Josie had reminded her many times.

After finishing the other girl's rooms, Claire made her way to the captain's suite. She hesitated briefly before knocking politely on the door. When there was no answer, she turned the handle and entered cautiously, dragging the vacuum beside her. The room was dark, as the curtains were still drawn tight over the windows. *Typical*, Claire thought, suppressing a sigh. Roxey couldn't be bothered with even the simplest of tasks. Shaking her head, Claire crossed the room, tugging the curtains open and cracking the window. Sunlight immediately flooded the space, illuminating the stark contrast between the immaculately kept furniture and the oppressive energy that lingered in the air.

As she moved to the bed, Claire carefully straightened the dishevelled blankets and fluffed Roxey's pillow just the way she liked it, causing a crumbled-up piece of paper to fall out of the pillowcase.

Claire frowned, glancing instinctively toward the doorway. The coast was clear. Against her better judgment, she reached down, picking up the paper and unfolded it. She stood very still, skimming over what looked like a threatening note. It was ripped, and the writing was formed in a messy, nearly illegible scrawl, which Claire could barely make out. She quickly checked over her shoulder again and took the time to decipher the words, her fingers tightening around the paper as she scanned it again, as if the words might change.

Roxette,

I know you're keeping her prisoner on your ship. How could you? Run all you want, I know you're good at it, but I will catch up eventually and when I do, you'll regret it. I want my daughter back.

Chapter Three

Claire's body went rigid, and she held her breath for so long she began to feel faint. Even after she forced herself to take a breath, her mouth still hung open in disbelief. She was too stunned to close it. Moving her thumb in an effort to close the paper, she noticed the bottom half of the page was torn, straight through part of a sentence.

My wife would never have—

With trembling hands, Claire folded the note, her fingers pressing so tightly it crumpled slightly in her grip. She felt a weird sensation forming in her gut. Was it panic? Her mind raced with questions. What did this little note mean? Was someone out there truly searching for one of them, for one of the girls? The thought was both electrifying and terrifying. She wondered if she should tell the others. The room seemed to tilt as a wave of dizziness washed over her, and suddenly, she recognized the feeling clawing its way up from the depths of her gut. It wasn't panic burring in her stomach–it was hope.

Claire froze as footsteps echoed nearby, closing in. As fast as she could move, she shoved the note back into the pillowcase, slammed it down on the bed and dashed for the vacuum. Her foot caught on the uneven floorboards, sending her sprawling. Pain shot through her palms as she scrambled to get to her feet, grabbing the vacuum just as the door handle twisted. The captain burst in like a storm, slamming the door so forcefully a sharp gust whipped her hair over her shoulders. Her bulging eyes locked onto Claire, narrowing as they flicked to the slightly askew pillow. Claire stood silently, feigning innocence as she slowly lifted a hand to fix her hair. It didn't work.

"Get out! Out of my room, you stupid child! Out,

out!" Roxey's voice cracked like a whip, her fury almost tangible. She took a menacing step forward, and Claire didn't wait for another warning. She darted past Roxey, her feet skimming the floor as she shot into the hallway. Behind her, the door slammed shut almost catching the back of her head. Claire paused to catch her breath, her mind racing. *Does she know? Did she somehow figure out I read the note?*

Fear mingled with exhilaration as the weight of her discovery pressed on her. She wanted to run and tell someone—*anyone*—but it was too risky. If Roxey overheard, Claire knew the punishment would be swift and fatal. And if she were gone, what chance would the others have of finding out there was someone out there looking for his daughter? Claire was still reeling with emotion, unsure how she was supposed to go about her average day now. That tiny scrap of paper had ignited something in her—a flicker of hope, which had been lying dormant for years. It reminded her there was a world beyond this ship, a life she had nearly forgotten existed. Freedom. Safety. Choices. If someone out there was searching for one of them, maybe others were, too, they likely just hadn't gotten as far. And what if this determined parent didn't make it at all? Roxey could have already "stopped" them. Claire shuddered, clenching her fists; they hadn't been forgotten. For some reason, it had never occurred to her that the girls' families might be looking for them. Perhaps they were even registered in a missing persons database. If she could rally the girls, maybe as a team they could manage an escape this time. Each and every one of them could go back to land. Maybe it was time.

Claire racked her brain. What day was it? Tuesday. Her heart sank. Friday was the only day Roxey docked the ship to run errands and pick up supplies. That meant three more days of waiting, strategising—and hoping she didn't slip up. Roxey ran the supply runs with military precision, and the system was ironclad. The crew's requests went on a list pinned to the fridge, but Roxey rarely granted anything beyond the bare essentials. Bonnie would meal plan and was usually the exception. Her requests for ingredients were always approved, though she kept her list practical—except for the hair dye. Bonnie's vibrant streaks of blue, and green through her maintained bubble gum pink hair were her one indulgence, which for some reason, Roxey allowed. But heaven forbid anyone want something silly like a chocolate bar once in a while.

In the last year or so, shortly after Bonnie had joined the family, Roxey had started taking Tayla into town, like a statement that reeked of distrust toward the others. Roxey claimed it was Tayla's twenty-second birthday present, apparently a make up for not having done anything special for her twenty-first.

Every Friday, the routine was the same. Roxey would don her blonde wig, then spend an hour or so doing both her and Tayla's makeup, completely altering their appearances. Tayla would either leave the boat looking as though she were a drag queen fresh from the stage, or an eighty-year-old woman. After they were disguised, they'd proceed to lock the rest of the crew in the ship's makeshift dungeon—a rusted but strong, caged structure on the bottom floor of the ship's belly, and would dock, heading into town for a few hours to shop. The girls had tried countless times to break free, but the key locked iron gate didn't budge. Opening it wouldn't have made a difference anyway, Roxey was carefully consistent with activating her security.

Though the women hated being cooped up in the cage, it was the only time they got to talk to each other without fear of Roxey overhearing. The women even tried to reclaim control in their own way, dubbing it the "weekly goss meeting," pretending it was their decision to gather to make themselves feel better.

Claire was suddenly faced with a decision. Should she talk to the girls now so they had time to prepare an escape plan or wait until Friday and tell them during the goss meeting, giving them a whole week to prepare? She winced. The thought of staying silent for another week was unbearable. But sharing her excitement too soon carried its own risks. If Roxey caught wind of it, she'd ruin any chance of escape—and Claire doubted she'd live to try again.

Claire wanted to confide in even just one person before the goss meeting, but first, there were chores to finish if she wanted to live long enough to escape. With a sigh, she headed down the dimly-lit hall, arms full of the dirty laundry she'd piled in the hall from earlier. The "laundry room" was hardly deserving of the title. It was a cramped corner tucked behind the bathroom, just big enough for one person to stand in at a time. A battered washtub dominated the space, and it was Katalyna's domain. She was tasked with handwashing every item of clothing each morning, and have it dried and folded by the afternoon.

As Claire stepped into the corner and saw Katalyna hunched over the tub, she had to clench her lips together. She almost blurted out the secret then and there. If anyone would share her excitement, it was Katalyna. She'd be thrilled to know that someone out there might be searching for one of girls. Claire faultered at the thought of telling Katalyna what she'd discovered now. What if someone overheard them?

She must have been left with a weird look on her face because when Katalyna looked up, frowning as she pushed clumps of damp, naturally pigmented red hair off her lightly freckled face she asked, "Honey, are you alright?" Her soft voice was laced with concern.

Claire nodded, her mind scrambling for a reply. All she managed was a smile, dumping the washing pile on the floor and getting out of there as quickly as possible before she opened her mouth. As she slipped back down the hall, guilt gnawed at her. Katalyna had a way of sensing when something was wrong. She was the ship's quiet nurturer, the first to notice a tear, a sigh, or a small change in behaviour. Claire felt certain Katalyna knew she was hiding something, but she couldn't share it yet. Not until she was absolutely sure it was safe. She needed to present her idea in the dead of night, to ensure they weren't being listened to.

As Claire darted back into the hall, she collided headfirst into Emerald, sending her frail body stumbling sideways and causing Claire to smash her own shoulder into the doorframe. Trying not to swear, Claire rubbed her shoulder and blurted, "sorry, sorry!"

Emerald said nothing for a moment, brushing her messy, sandy blonde hair off her face, then smiled and pulled Claire into a hug. "I'm sorry about what happened to you at breakfast," she said. "I saw Tayla trip you. What a bitch."

Claire's lips twitched into a grin as she pulled away. "It's in the name," she replied, her voice laced with playful sarcasm.

In unison, they broke into a singsong chant, "It's in the name, in the name it is! Britches are bitches." The familiar inside joke made them both dissolve into giggles. It was a relatable phrase that had bonded the girls over the years, used whenever someone called Tayla a bitch. Her last name was Britches, so it suited her perfectly. A couple years ago, Claire had initiated the joke as a way to cheer Emerald up, not long after she had been dragged aboard.

Emerald's arrival on the ship had been one of the hardest to watch and to hear about. Unlike some of the others, the ones lured aboard by Roxey's manipulation, Emerald had been drugged and taken like Claire and Tayla. Not unlike Tayla, she'd had an extremely difficult time accepting what had happened to her and nearly got herself killed on the spot when she woke up on the deck. She'd been in her second-to-last year of high school, the top student in her grade. Her parents, relentless in their expectations, had pushed her to excel in everything, from academics to mastering five languages. Emerald had bent over backward to please them, even as their criticisms cut her deeply whenever she fell short of perfection. The day of her final exam had been a breaking point. Overwhelmed by pressure, she'd stepped outside for fresh air. A teacher she didn't recognise approached her, offering her a chocolate bar with a kind smile. Grateful for the gesture, Emerald accepted it, unaware it was full of sedative. Moments later, the world spun, and she collapsed.

When she woke two days later, it wasn't to the comfort of her home, but to Roxey's cruel explanation of her new life. Emerald had fought tooth and nail— screaming, crying, and refusing to obey—even going as far as to punch Roxey in the face. But, like all the others, she eventually had to give up. Claire had been the first to befriend her, offering support, which Emerald accepted. Over time, their bond had grown with Emerald becoming one of Claire's closest friends, given they had so much in common, and Emerald was only a year younger.

"It's okay Emmie," Claire replied as the laughter faded, "Tayla can do what she wants. Trust me when I say things are going to get better."

Emerald frowned, her expression doubtful, but Claire left her with a smile and a reassuring tap on the shoulder, smiling to herself as she got back to her chores.

Later, when the clock ticked well past midnight, unable to sleep, Claire decided to sneak out of her room.

She was now in the right frame of mind to go and talk to Katalyna. Since she was the mother of the group, Claire knew she could bounce her feelings off her about her discovery and ideas to plan to escape. Claire cracked her door open, peering into the dimly lit hall. Rumble's glowing blue eyes were nowhere to be seen, and the dog's distinctive snore rumbled faintly in the distance. Claire's heart hammered as she tiptoed into the hallway, her bare feet silent on the cold wood. She darted into the next bedroom, slipping inside and shutting the door behind her.

The second the door clicked, Katalyna sprang into action. She sat up in bed like a shot, gripping a wooden spoon in both hands, poised as though she'd been preparing for this moment her whole life.

"Whoa, whoa!" Claire jumped back, throwing a hand up in surrender. Her other hand shot up to her lips in a shushing gesture. "It's just me, Kat. It's Claire!"

Katalyna squinted through the shadows, the moonlight filtering through the window casting just enough light to illuminate Claire's face. She relaxed instantly, lowering her makeshift weapon and exhaling a breath. "Oh, honey, what in the world—" she whispered, but the words were cut short as she leaned forward to wave Claire over. Her elbow knocked a hairbrush off the edge of the bed, and it hit the floor with a loud *clatter*. The sound was like a trigger. A low, menacing growl rumbled from just outside the door.

Chapter Four

Katalyna pressed a finger firmly to her lips, her wide eyes urging Claire to remain silent. Claire didn't need the reminder; she barely dared to breathe let alone make a sound. Her entire body had seized up, every muscle tense as she prayed Rumble wouldn't catch her scent or decide to bark. Every second felt like an hour as she listened to the low, raspy sound of the dog's breath just outside the door.

Finally, the tension broke with the rhythmic click-clacking of his claws down the hall as he shuffled away, retreating to his patrol bed.

Katalyna let out a quiet breath, her shoulders dropping as she turned to Claire with a mixture of relief and exasperation. "Claire, honey," she whispered fiercely, "are you crazy? If she catches you in here at this hour, she'll have your head on a stick!"

Claire grinned, the first genuine smile she'd felt in what seemed like months. She climbed onto the end of Katalyna's bed, keeping her voice low but steady. "I'd say remind me again what I'm living for, but I think I finally have a reason to give a crap." She leaned in, her words sharp. "Kat, I've decided I'm getting off this boat. And I want you to help me convince the others to come with."

Katalyna's blinked and her diamond-blue eyes widened larger than Claire knew a person's eyes were capable of. Her hands shot to her cheeks, clasping them as though she were trying to tear the skin off her jawbone. Claire's heart twisted at the sight—she knew this was how Kat reacted when stress overwhelmed her. For a moment, she was silent, searching Claire's face as though trying to gauge just how serious she was. Still silent, she snuck a glance at Josie. Watching the little girl breathe deeply as she slept, her orangy-red locks peeking over the blanket, seemed to calm Katalyna down.

Finally, she reached out, her hand resting gently on Claire's arm. "What on earth gave you the idea that any of us are ever getting off this ship?"

Claire leaned forward and wrapped her arms around her, pulling her into a quick, tight hug. Katalyna froze in confusion, and frowned when Claire pulled away, clearly expecting an explanation. "I was cleaning Roxey's room this morning," Claire began, steadying her voice, "and I found half a letter stuffed inside her pillowcase. It was from someone who said they want their daughter back. He addressed Roxey formally by name, Kat. He said he knew she was holding his daughter prisoner on this boat."

Katalyna raised her eyebrows momentarily, but her frown deepened as Claire continued.

"The second I read it, I had an epiphany. I'm done with her. I'm done with *this*. There is more to the world than the walls of this stupid ship. I want to reclaim my life. But I don't want to leave without you guys. Every single one of us deserves to get out of here and I think we'd have half a chance if we did it together. Properly. You know that as much as I do, we've just never had a good reason to really try. Can you imagine what the girls will think when they find out one of their parents is trying to get them back? That there is still someone out there who gives a damn about us?"

Kat appeared deep in thought for several minutes, her expression now unreadable. Then she sighed and shook her head. "Oh, honey," she said, her tone empathetic. "I know how fantastic that sounds. But do you realise how unrealistic it is? The idea of us getting back to land? It's wonderful to think someone knows Roxey has their kid, but you don't know the rest of the story. I say let him or her come to us if that's what they want to do. Then it'll be their fault when they get killed. You can't expect me to convince the girls to risk their lives on a tiny glimmer of hope that *one person's* family is still looking for them."

Claire's smile faltered, replaced by a pang of disheartenment. She truly thought Katalyna would be just as excited as she was, that she'd jump at the chance to plan an escape.

"Never mind," Claire said quietly, standing up. "Maybe you're right. Sorry I woke you." Claire got up to leave, her mind churning over Katalyna's words. The more she thought about it, the more she reiterated to herself that she didn't agree. Kat was wrong—but Claire also knew she might be wrong too. Convincing everyone to escape together was risky and possibly selfish, but withholding the truth wasn't right either. Claire had already made her decision. The moment she'd read that note, she'd known she was leaving. Friday would be her last day aboard the *Siren Hearth*. The others deserved to know why, though. And they had the right to choose for themselves whether to stay or go. Claire couldn't make that decision for them.

The next morning, Claire made a point to wake up on time and power through her chores, finishing a solid half-hour earlier than required. She wanted to spend her morning free time—a precious hour allocated between eleven and twelve—in solitude, plotting an achievable escape plan. Each day there were two scheduled free periods, one hour in the morning, and a longer downtime between three and five in the afternoon. She was so deep in thought that she didn't notice Serenah sidling up to her, encapsulated in her own little world instead.

"Hey, you wanna play poker?" Serenah asked, bending enough that she needed to place her hands on her knees for support.

Claire didn't respond, staring blankly at the ground as she traced the notches in the wood grains with her finger. It wasn't until a portion of Serenah's mousy brown hair fell directly in her line of vision that Claire realised she had been asked a question. She let out a grunt, not with it enough yet to form actual words.

Irritated, Serenah cocked an eyebrow and squatted just above Claire's eye level. "You seem unusually distracted today, Claire. Everything alright?"

Shaking herself out of her trance, Claire bobbed her head in response as she looked up. The sun caught Serenah's eyes, reflecting a beam of golden-brown light at Claire's face and forcing her to squint. "Yep, I'm great. I think I just wanna be alone right now. Sorry."

Serenah shrugged, clearly unbothered, and wandered off to ask Katalyna if she wanted to verse her instead. Even if Claire weren't preoccupied, she didn't really feel like playing poker with Serenah anyway. She had a reputation for being sneaky and always found a way to cheat. Serenah played to win, even if it meant using tactful distractions or loopholes. And she got nasty if she lost.

Still, Claire tried not to hold it against her. Serenah's tough skin was hard-earned, forged by a rough upbringing even before Roxey got her claws into her. From what Claire understood, however, she'd brought most of it on herself by falling in with the wrong crowd and rebelling against her parents every chance she got. Claire didn't know if she was just trying to seem cool when she arrived, but Serenah had bragged a lot about sleeping around after losing her virginity at thirteen. She claimed to have thoroughly enjoyed all the attention she got from boys, drawing attention easily with her hefty bust and slim lined, shapely curves.

Serenah had given Claire a basic rendition of how Roxey tricked her aboard. It was the same night her parents had kicked her out, the final straw because she stumbled home one night half naked and drunk at age fifteen. After sleeping the night on the beach, Serenah woke to Roxey posing as a cruise ship captain, kindly offering her a place to stay. With nowhere else to go, Serenah accepted. By the time she realised it wasn't a cruise ship at all, the dock was a distant memory, and Roxey didn't have to pretend anymore.

Back then, it was just Tayla and Claire on board, and Serenah spent most of her early days bullying them, taking out her anger and frustration on the only people she could. She got nicer over time, enough for Claire to tolerate her, but the two had never grown close.
It didn't help that Serenah's closest friend on the ship was now Tayla. Of course, it made sense. They were both as selfish as each other, and the two beauty queens of the ship. Tayla was the picturesque blonde-haired, blue-eyed doll cliché. With her perfectly tanned, sculpted figure, she was a natural beauty who may as well have stepped straight out of a magazine. And Serenah, equally as gorgeous, who's caramel skin practically shone in the light with her Latina glow and perfect cheekbones. It was hard for Claire to trust someone who found kinship in Tayla, but after six years, Serenah had mellowed enough that Claire didn't outright avoid her anymore.

Still, as she watched Serenah saunter off, Claire felt a pang of relief. Today wasn't the day for poker, and Serenah wasn't the person she wanted to confide in. She needed time to think, to plan, and to figure out how to turn her faint glimmer of hope into an actual path to freedom.

Tucked in a secluded corner of the deck, Claire crossed her legs as she leaned against the cold wall. It was now eleven, and she watched her fellow shipmates as they gathered, free for just a brief time from their ridiculous chores. Their laughter and chatter seemed authentic, but Claire's keen eye caught the stiffness in their movements, the lethargy that spoke of lives stuck on autopilot. She knew the feeling all too well. Every day was a monotonous cycle. Free time meant exchanging a few words, playing a round of cards, or maybe dust off a battered board game or book. Rinse and repeat. Other than the weekly newspaper Roxey brought home for the girls, the only concession to modern life was Roxey's laptop, a forbidden relic none dared to touch.

Once a fortnight, on Sunday evenings, Roxey would decree a "movie night," selecting a film and gathering everyone on the deck to watch it "as a family." She would alternate between fictional television and educational documentaries, always emphasising how kind she was to still teach them about the way civilisation on land operated. Beyond that, technology was strictly off-limits. Roxey's tight control ensured no one glimpsed the world beyond the ship's confines, keeping them tethered to her warped version of reality.

As Claire sat, a random memory of sand between her toes—its warmth from the sun, its texture—clouded her mind. She closed her eyes, tilting her head as she struggled to recall the sensation clearly, and the longing it stirred in her cut deep, a dull ache in the pit of her stomach. More determined than ever, she straightened and forced herself to focus. Sierra's mistake had been jumping overboard in a panic. They hadn't really planned anything in advance, thus why they'd been caught. In a way, Claire was grateful for her learning curve. She had to form a careful plan this time, and there were now three critical barriers to overcome: escape the dungeon chamber, outwit Rumble, and disable or bypass the alarm.

Claire figured that escaping the cell might be straightforward in theory. All she needed was to nab the key after the cage was locked. Simple, right? She grimaced as the doubt crept in. *Maybe not so simple after all.* How was she going to pull that off? And then it hit her—she wasn't. Her gaze settled on Serenah. Claire trusted her instincts. Serenah could manage to pickpocket the key; she was clever and quick enough for the task.

As for Rumble, Claire's stomach twisted at the thought. She loved animals, but Rumble was a problem they couldn't ignore. Killing him was out of the question, he didn't deserve that for simply being Roxey's pooch. But incapacitating him? That might work. Perhaps Bonnie could whip up one of her creative concoctions, something potent enough to knock him out or make him sick for long enough to neutralize him. Or maybe stuffing him full of a cocoa filled substance would work. She'd seen a movie before where the family dog got ahold of chocolate and became so sick it couldn't move.

Then there was the alarm system. Claire's knowledge about how it worked was frustratingly limited, but she knew Roxey kept a digital beeper that alerted her if it was triggered. The trip wires sent a signal of some kind and were controlled by a program on the computer. Emerald, though…she was sharp, quick with learning gadgets and plotting ideas. If anyone could figure out how to disable or bypass the alarm, it was her. Claire nodded to herself. The plan was coming together in fragments, but one thing was clear: she couldn't do it alone. To pull this off on the coming Friday, she'd need the girls all filled in and ready. The only way forward was to tell them everything in advance, and three days planning was more than enough.

Suddenly careless about being overheard, Claire pulled herself up, brushing the dust off her pants. During their free periods, Roxey was below deck, doing whatever she did on her laptop to make money remotely. Practically skipping, Claire made her way over to Bonnie and Emerald who were sitting mid-deck playing marbles in the sun. They exchanged wary glances as she approached, clearly alarmed by her sudden burst of enthusiasm.

"Okay, you're *way* too happy. Spill," Emerald chirped, while Bonnie cautiously leaned away, as if Claire might explode.

"Get on the edge of your seats, ladies," Claire whispered conspiratorially, her excitement barely contained. "I have something to run by you."

Emerald leaned in, curiosity lighting her deep hazel eyes like bulbs.

Claire's voice dropped lower, charged with urgency. "How would you feel if I told you we're getting out of here? I have a plan to escape this damn ship. And I'll need your help if you want to come with me."

Before they could respond, a sound froze her mid-thought—two sharp, deliberate clicks behind her. Claire's heart plummeted as a voice sliced through the air.

"You're going *where?*"

She turned slowly to find Tayla, arms crossed, smirking with the satisfaction of catching someone in the act. "Did you say…escape?"

Claire's mind raced, her expression carefully neutral. "Nope," she said lightly, forcing a laugh. "You clearly walked into a conversation at the wrong time and misinterpreted. I said nothing of the sort."

Tayla's smirk deepened as she tilted her head lazily. "Sure. Right." She called over her shoulder, her voice ringing out. "Oh, Roxey! I think there's something you should know!

Chapter Five

Without thinking, Claire's arm shot out, striking Tayla hard on the shoulder with the back of her palm. "You are such a nasty little bitch," she hissed.

Tayla didn't flinch; instead, her lips curled into a smug, callous smirk so similar to Roxey's that it made Claire's blood boil.

Roxey thundered up the stairwell moments later, her imposing frame cutting through the little groups' tension like a knife as she marched over. She planted her hands on her hips, radiating irritation that Tayla had the audacity to summon her. "This better be important," she snapped, her body language heavy with displeasure.

Tayla tilted her chin in mock sincerity. "Sorry to bother you, Ma'am," she began, her voice projecting innocence. "But I thought you might like to know what I just overheard. It seems Claire and her little friends here are planning to escape the boat."

Roxey's expression darkened, her face shifting to a dangerous shade of red. Claire stiffened, bracing for the inevitable repercussion. But what happened next left her stunned. With a sharp crack, Roxey's hand connected with Tayla's cheek, silencing her mid-gloat. Tayla stumbled slightly, her face frozen in shock, a pink welt blossoming where Roxey's hand had landed.

"Foolish girl," Roxey spat with a venomous snarl. "You summon me like some common dog for *that*?" She straightened, her eyes narrowing as they swept over the group. "No one is leaving this ship. No one *can* leave this ship. And you should all know what happens to anyone stupid enough to try."

Staring Tayla down, Roxey gestured toward Claire and Tayla flinched, bowing her head, appearing to fear she was going to get slapped again. The faintest hint of a smirk played on Roxey's lips as her gaze flicked to Claire. "The girl's brainless sometimes but give her a little credit," Roxey said. "Claire knows better." Her words echoed in Claire's mind, a chilling reminder of how wrong things could go if she did decide to go through with her plan. Roxey turned her back to them to address the entire deck, and Claire seized the moment to shoot Tayla a smug look. But as Roxey began to speak, her voice carrying with practiced authority, the smirk faded from Claire's face.

"Now, listen to me, girls," Roxey declared, spreading her arms wide in a theatrical gesture. "I've said this before, and I'll say it again, so there's no confusion. This is your home now. *I* am your provider, your protector. Everything you need is here. You all have jobs, food, shelter, entertainment, and most importantly, love." Her gaze swept over the group, her expression softening into something disturbingly maternal.

"We don't need the land…or the people on it," she continued, her tone lowering into a more firming conviction. "Especially men. They just cause pain. I'm trying to keep you safe from all that. In fact, I've been spending a lot of time lately developing new ideas—a system for growing our own food and crafting our own supplies. A life where we'll never have to return to the land for anything at all. Just imagine that! How wonderful will it be never to have to spend another day locked in the dungeon room while I shop? You know how much I *hate* doing that to you, my beautiful girls."

Roxey held her arms open as though embracing them all and looked around slowly, her sickening smile lingering on each girl, one by one. Her words hung in the air like a poison cloud, and Claire scanned the deck, gauging the others' reactions. Most were frozen, their expressions distant and unreadable. Only Tayla looked mildly pleased, her smile faint but unmistakably painted on her lips. Little Josie, perched on her mother's lap near the boat's edge, seemed oblivious to the speech at first, her face locked on the distant horizon. However, even though they were on the opposite side of the deck to her, Claire swore she saw a tear roll down Josie's lightly freckled cheek. Katalyna quickly wiped it away, glancing around nervously to ensure Roxey hadn't noticed.

Roxey took a step forward, her voice lowering as she switched her tone to reflect the seriousness of what she was about to say. "Let me remind you," she said, each word cutting through the stillness, "that your lives belong to me. From the moment you stepped on this deck, willingly or not, they have been mine. And if I ever hear a whisper—just one *whisper*—about escape again, there will be consequences." She paused, letting the weight of her words sink in. "I will not hesitate to claim your life permanently with your death."

Claire's stomach churned as she noticed the subtle, nervous glances exchanged among the girls as they absorbed what Roxey had just reinforced. The word *escape* was taboo, a dangerous spark that had been uttered only three times during her years aboard the ship. The first was when they had attempted to escape with Sierra, a memory that still haunted Claire. The second was a few years later, when someone dared to bring it up whilst recounting it to the newcomers on board. They were caught praising Sierra's bravery and punished harshly for supporting her. Thankfully, Roxey hadn't overheard the part of the meeting where they had joked about the possibility of attempting again since their numbers were larger. And now, for the third time, it lingered in the air like an unspoken curse.

Appearing satisfied with her little speech, Roxey let her eyes sweep over the group one final time, daring anyone to challenge her. Then, without another word, she turned sharply and marched off the deck, descending the stairwell to the ship's belly. The weight on Claire's chest eased as Roxey's presence disappeared below deck.

Feeling like she could finally breathe again, Claire inhaled deeply and tried to remember what she had been saying to the girls, but quickly remembered why she had known it was a bad idea to talk about such a thing during the day. She glanced back at Tayla, who was now pouting and rubbing her reddened cheek. Tayla shot Claire a glare before turning on her heel and walking away in a huff.

As Bonnie got up in preparation to leave, Claire realised it was almost time for lunch and instantly felt guilty. Thanks to her, Bonnie now had a smaller window to prepare a quick meal. Thankfully, lunch was the simplest meal of the day, to allow appropriate time for the afternoon's chores.

Before Bonnie could walk away completely, Claire whispered urgently to her and Emerald, "To be continued. Can both of you meet me in the kitchen at midnight?"

Without waiting for their reactions, she turned to leave the deck, as did everyone else at the same time. As she weaved across the deck, Katalyna suddenly blocked her path.

"You *told* them, didn't you?" she whispered with exasperation, her eyes darting around to ensure no one overheard.

"I did not, actually," Claire replied coolly, meeting Katalyna's pale stare with unwavering confidence. "That's later. Midnight. I'm organising a meeting in the kitchen. Please come. And tell Serenah if you see her before I do."

Katalyna tilted her head, giving Claire her unmistakable *seriously?* look. Claire simply shrugged and powered on. There was no time to argue, Katalyna would just have to get over it.

Claire pushed past her and slipped into the kitchen, scanning the room quickly to ensure they were alone. Spotting Bonnie at the counter, she tapped her on the shoulder and leaned in close. "Got anything with cocoa?"

Bonnie narrowed her eyes suspiciously and nodded toward the pantry. When Claire reached into the cupboard and snapped a few squares of cooking chocolate off a freshly opened block, Bonnie frowned, opening her mouth as though about to protest, but Claire cut her off with a cheeky smile. "Hopefully this will shut down one alarm system for a bit," she explained cryptically.

Bonnie chuckled under her breath, shaking her head as she continued buttering some bread, but not pushing further.

Claire felt a flicker of confidence surge through her and skipped out onto the deck to head downstairs. At the neck of the stairwell, she bumped into Daphne as they both tried to squish through at the same time. Daphne immediately recoiled, her dark skin flushing bright as she mumbled a string of four apologies, each quieter than the last.

Claire held up her hands to stop her. "It's fine, really. No harm done."

Claire didn't know what her deal was. She knew nothing about Daphne—none of them did, really. Daphne had been aboard longer than Emerald, yet she remained a mystery, barely speaking to anyone and keeping to herself. She seemed shy, almost painfully so, and never engaged in the camaraderie the others occasionally shared. The other girls had opened up over time, sharing small snippets of their lives before the ship, their fears, and how they were taken. But Daphne had stayed silent, speaking perhaps less than ten sentences the whole time she'd been with them. All Claire knew about her came from Roxey's "capture journal."

"Logan's girlfriend. He spoils her and provides money for her constant shopping habits. Disgusting. Lure her to the beach by pretending to be selling the boat. Will come aboard easily."

The entry was short, impersonal, and devoid of the obsessive detail Roxey usually noted about her captives. It left Claire with more questions than answers. Claire didn't know who Logan was, but she'd always wondered why Roxey cared so little about documenting Daphne's backstory. Everyone else had almost a whole page written about them. Except for Sierra, who's page had never been written.

Breaking the silence, Claire decided to take a chance. "Hey, I don't know if you're interested, but we're all meeting tonight in the kitchen. It's kind of important. You're welcome to join us."

Daphne's face remained unreadable for a several moments, like she was trying to decide if Claire was telling the truth or dicking with her. Finally, she gave a small, almost imperceptible nod. Feeling a sense of accomplishment, Claire grinned and darted down the stairs, a bubbling warmth filling her chest. Was it happiness? Relief? She wasn't entirely sure.

That evening, as the clock crept toward midnight, Claire lay in bed, her nerves wound tighter than a coiled spring. The borrowed alarm clock from Bonnie glowed faintly on her bedside table, its quiet ticking mocking her impatience. Determined to stay awake, she snapped a rubber band against her leg every time her eyelids began to droop. A soft thump echoed in the hallway. Not loud enough to wake anyone, but noticeable to those already awake—like Claire. About two hours beforehand, she'd fed the chocolate she'd taken from the kitchen to Rumble, hoping the effects of slight poisoning would render his guard duties useless for the night. Thus, allowing them to conduct a meeting in the kitchen without fear of being caught. Claire suspected the chocolate had finally done its job.

By five minutes to midnight, Claire couldn't wait any longer. Slipping out of bed, she crept across the floor toward Tayla's half of the room, carefully glancing over the mound of blankets she'd cocooned her body in. Claire waved a hand in front of her face, watching her eyelids for any sign of flinching. Tayla was usually a heavy sleeper, so, convinced she was truly asleep, Claire tiptoed to the door and peeked into the passage.

There, in the dim glow of the hallway light, Rumble lay curled in a heap, whimpering, his chest rising and falling steadily. Relief mixed with guilt as Claire stepped over him. The concoction had worked, but she hated involving the dog in any of this. To make it worthwhile, she truly hoped everyone was going to show for their meeting, but had a feeling there would be at least a few too scared to face the consequences of getting caught.

Surprisingly though, Roxey was generally a heavy sleeper so Claire knew if they stayed quiet they wouldn't have to worry about her. She hoped the others would consider this useful fact.

Upon entering the kitchen, she stopped short in surprise. Every single girl she'd invited was already seated at the table, their hushed whispers dying away as she entered. Emerald shot her a reassuring smile and tapped Katalyna on the shoulder. Katalyna turned to face the doorway, her hands fumbling nervously in front of her. Claire hesitated as she took point at the head of the table, her heart pounding. All eyes fixated on her. She had to get this right.

"I don't know if any of you have guessed why I called this meeting," Claire began, her voice steady but quiet.

"I know we usually save our vent sessions for Fridays, but this is... so much more than that."

The girls leaned in, their expressions turning serious, but intrigued.

"I can't think of any way to ease into this so I'll just say it," Claire continued, pausing for a breath. The words she planned to blurt out—*It's time to go home*—caught in her throat. Instead, she found herself starting with something else. "I found something important in Roxey's room this morning. A little piece of a note thing she'd torn up." Her attitude shifted, carrying a sense of importance. "The thing is, someone from the land gave it to her. I don't know when, and I don't know how, but what I do know is that someone out there is looking for one of us. Well, one of you."

A collective gasp filled the room. The girls glanced wildly at one another, their expressions a mixture of shock and disbelief.

"It was from a parent," Claire went on, her voice firmer now. "He mentioned a wife, and told Roxey he knows she has his daughter. Any of you who still have a father out there—it could be *you* he's looking for."

The realisation rippled through the group like a wave. Gauging the positive reaction of the girls gave Claire the courage she needed to jump right into the true reason she'd called a meeting. "The second I saw that letter, something clicked inside me," Claire said, her voice rising with certainty. "I'm done. Ladies, I've decided to go home. Whatever that means for me."

The room fell utterly silent, the weight of her words sinking in. "This Friday," she declared, "when Roxey goes to town, I'm getting off this ship. I'm going back to land. But I want you to come with me. If we work together, we can all reclaim our lives."

Chapter Six

For a moment, no one spoke. The girls' reactions were varied, but not as horrified as Claire had anticipated. Bonnie's jaw dropped, her wide eyes reflecting shock. Katalyna buried her face in her hands, shaking her head in quiet dismay. Emerald and Serenah exchanged uneasy glances, while even the darkest pigments of Daphne's cocoa skin had almost turned a startling shade of white. A tense murmuring followed, rising into a quiet buzz of discussion. Claire had to rap her knuckles on the table to reclaim their attention, her voice cutting through the noise.

"Please, just hear me out," she urged, her voice structured but imploring. "I've given this a lot of thought. First, let me reassure you—we're not going to end up like Sierra. We weren't prepared last time; we were too impulsive. It was reckless of us to think we could scale the side of the boat, and Sierra made a bad decision in the heat of the moment."

Katalyna raised a hand, her expression pleading. "Isn't this just another bad decision in the heat of the moment, Claire?"

A ripple of agreement spread through the group, Serenah rolling her eyes before adding, "She's got a point. If one of our dads is looking for us or whatever, I say we let him find us! Why not just wait for him?"

Claire braced herself against the growing pledges of concurrence. "No," she said, shaking her head firmly. "Not a good idea. What if it takes him years? What if it's already been years? I don't remember seeing it before, but that note could be ancient, for all we know. And even if he does find us, the moment he climbs on the deck, he's dead. He'll just become a missing person like anyone else who crosses her, and we'll be back to exactly where we were before. Nowhere."

She scanned the room, keeping her stance strong, her words pressing into the silence. "No. We're not waiting for him to find us. We're going to find him. In the end, though, that concerned parent is just one reason to have hope. If he's come looking, what's not to say there are others? How do we know others haven't already tried and she's taken them out before we knew about it? It's up to us now to let the world know we're still here. What's not to say they do, but they just can't find us? Together, we can take Roxey down. Once we're off this ship and ashore, she won't have the same power over us."

Her voice steadied, strong with a clarity even she didn't know she had. "If we plan this right, if we use our strengths and stick together, we can make it happen. Girls, think about it. I don't know about you, but I don't want to spend the rest of my days here. What kind of life is this?" She paused, letting her words settle. "I want you to take a moment and think about what you had before all of this. Really think about it. Can you honestly tell me you wouldn't give anything—*everything*—for the chance to get it back? Tell me, in the absolute worst-case scenario, that you wouldn't lay down your life for a chance to escape Roxey and truly live again. I would, and I don't even remember my old life."

The room fell into a heavy silence as the girls sank into deep thought. It wasn't unanimous, not yet. Claire could see the hesitation lingering in some of their eyes. But she had planted the seed, and she could feel it growing. This wasn't just a meeting anymore; it was the first step toward freedom. Moments later, Claire noticed a shift—small, hopeful smiles began to appear, even on Katalyna's dimples. Her earlier disapproval seemed to be melting away.

Claire seized the moment, delivering passionate encouragement. "Kat," she said, leaning forward, "aren't you tired of telling your little girl stories about *your* childhood? Don't you want her to have her own. Not *this*, a real one? To go to school, play in the grass, meet a boy someday?"

She turned to Serenah. "And you—you want to see your parents again, don't you? To show them the strong, mature woman you've become? To have a chance to prove to them how successful you can be?"

Claire tilted her head toward Emerald, her tone softening, though she tried to keep up the sense of determination. "Same as you, Em. What would you give to take that final exam you worked so hard for? To show not just your parents, but the world, what you can do with your beautiful brain?"

Casting a quick glance at Daphne, unsure what her motivation was, she simply said with a smile, "You used to love shopping, right? What would you give to hit the stores in the city again?"

Finally, she looked at Bonnie. "Bonnie, I know you love to cook and all, but didn't you think you would have seen everything by now? Travelling the world, waking up every day with the thrill of being somewhere new, meeting all kinds of fascinating people? Isn't that the life you imagined?"

Claire's voice grew even more resolute as she addressed them all. "This is what we all want. What we *deserve*. I love you all so much, and the only thing I'll ever thank Roxey for is bringing us together as a family. But that's exactly why we have to do this—because we love each other enough to fight for something better. I don't even have family waiting for me, I just want to start my own life. Some of you have so much more to fight for, so do it. Make an effort."

Katalyna's eyes welled up with tears as she kicked out her chair and threw her arms around Claire, pulling her into a bear hug. One by one, the others followed suit, their emotions spilling over. As they formed a group hug, Claire knew, even before anyone said a word, that they were with her.

"So," Bonnie asked eagerly, "what kind of plan have you come up with so far?"

Claire pushed through the crowd, and everyone backed off so she could answer, sitting once more around the table. "Alright, the first thing we need to think about is the obstacles. Serenah, do you think you can somehow get the cell key *after* they lock us in the cage?"

Serenah scoffed, rolling her eyes. "Duh. Tayla's the one who usually locks the door. I can pickpocket that dumb bimbo any day."

Claire widened her eyes, nodding slowly with a forced smile. She wondered what Serenah called her behind her back, if that was how she spoke about her closest friend. "Easy then. The hardest part is going to be knocking out the security system. Emmie, do you reckon you can disable the alarms?"

All eyes turned to Emerald, who shrank a little under the sudden pressure. "Um… I don't know. Maybe…"

Claire cut in, her voice warm with encouragement. "You absolutely can! We believe in you, right, ladies?"

An array of nods and murmurs of support filled the room. Emerald's lips curved into a tiny smile. "Okay. I'll try."

Claire grinned and laid out the framework she had so far. "Okay, here's how it'll work. Friday morning, before Roxey and Tayla leave for town, I'll slip Rumble some chocolate again to make him sick. As proven tonight, it does work, it just takes a bit to kick in. That'll work well though, because he won't feel it until after they've gone and they won't suspect a thing. Once Tayla locks us in, Serenah will quickly pinch the key. After they've left and we're out, Emmie will disable the alarms. Then, we can use the emergency lifeboat to make the trip to shore."

Katalyna piped up, her expression sceptical but thoughtful. "Mm, just to throw a spanner in your little works there—what the heck are we supposed to do once we get to shore? We won't have anywhere to go and we're going to need a place to hide that she can't connect to any of us. We'll have no money, no way to buy food. Even cheap, shady hotels require payment upfront or at the very least a credit card to have on file."

Claire was stumped; her mind went blank. She hadn't thought that far ahead. For the first time since concocting her escape plan, uncertainty flickered in her eyes.

Serenah waved a hand to catch their attention, a wry smile playing on her lips. "Uh, hello, we're women. Making easy, shady money is about as simple as breathing. Do you know how easy it is to walk into a strip club and start earning, no questions involved?"

Claire's eyebrows shot up. "Seriously?"

Serenah shrugged nonchalantly. "Don't ask."

Claire hesitated for a moment, then nodded. "Fair enough. I guess that's one problem solved. If we get stuck we can make some quick cash to pay for a hotel room and some food. So, how's everyone feeling about the plan so far?"

A few of the girls nodded hesitantly, while others murmured indistinctly, avoiding her gaze. No one seemed to want to say one way or another how they felt. Claire sighed softly. "On that note, let's call it a night. We've got three days to smooth out the details. Just remember not to breathe a word out in the open about the plan in the meantime unless you're real careful. If

Roxey or Tayla catch wind of what's coming, it's over and we will all suffer ungodly consequences."

The girls waited, tense and still, for Claire to rise. She stood and motioned toward the door, and only then did they begin to move. One by one, they shuffled out, quiet and subdued. Left alone, Claire sat on the edge of the table and stared at the empty room, her thoughts spiralling. Roxey had turned them into sheep—silent, obedient, waiting for her every instruction. It felt awful to be at the head of that now.

Friday couldn't come fast enough. Every second leading up to their plan felt agonizingly slow, as though time itself was dragging its feet. And then, suddenly, it was here.

Claire took one last look around her bedroom, expecting to feel sentimental somehow. But the feeling wasn't there. Whilst serving breakfast, Claire's heart pounded as she managed to sneakily slip a sizeable chunk of chocolate into Rumble's bowl. Katalyna created a distraction, giving Claire the perfect opening. Once breakfast was over, Roxey had the girls' line up as usual, and Tayla herded them single file down the narrow corridor to the ship's lowest level.

As they reached the cage, Roxey left to prepare the travel boat, leaving Tayla to lock them in. The skeleton-headed key glinted in Tayla's hand as she secured the lock, twisting it with an audible *click*. She smirked at the group through the bars, clearly revelling in her power. Claire watched, trying not to laugh as Serenah leaned casually against the bars, meeting Tayla's smirk with one of her own. Tayla narrowed her eyes suspiciously, but turned away, shoving the key into her bum pocket with exaggerated force.

Serenah didn't hesitate. Gradually, she extended her hand, her fingers inching toward the pocket where the key was concealed. For a brief, electrifying moment,

Claire thought she might succeed—until Tayla's arm shot out like a snapping turtle's jaw, her hand locking around Serenah's wrist.

"Did you really think it'd be that easy?" Tayla sneered, her grip tightening. "Who's the dumb bimbo now?"

Serenah stuck out her other hand, slipping it under Tayla's arm. It appeared she was trying to pry her captured wrist free, but Tayla flung her arm back into the cage with a derisive laugh. Claire's heart sank as she looked around at the others, their faces mirroring her own despair. The plan was unravelling quickly.

Tayla stepped out of Serenah's reach, grinning triumphantly as she assertively put her hands on her hips. "Yeah, I listened in on your little meeting in the kitchen the other night. I wanted to see if you idiots were actually stupid enough to try it. Apparently you weren't kidding." She strutted across the room and pulled a rickety chair from a pile of useless junk that had gathered dust for years. Proudly perching herself on it, she folded her arms and stared into the cage with a smug glare.

Almost ten minutes passed, and Claire began to worry that Rumble would collapse before Roxey left the ship. Finally, just when the tension became unbearable, Roxey stormed into the room, clearly irritated she had to come retrieve Tayla.

"What's taking so long?" Roxey snapped.

Tayla, visibly nervous, hesitated before answering. "I had to keep an eye on them, they were getting ideas, Ma'am. I'm almost certain one of them tried to steal the key from my pocket. I felt fingers brush my jeans."

Roxey's expression softened, a flicker of worry passing over her face before it hardened into anger. "Well, maybe if you used your brain and didn't put the damn key in your pocket until walking away from the grabby little fingers behind the bars, that wouldn't be an issue, would it?" She turned to the girls, shaking her head in disgust. Pacing slowly in front of the cage, she let the silence stretch, her heels clicking ominously against the floorboards.

Finally, she stopped and spoke, the words rolling off her icy tongue without mercy. "I would've hoped we wouldn't have to revisit this lesson, but seeing as we are starting to become a little defiant, I suppose we need to touch base on it again. You are *never* going to leave this ship, not a single one of you. Seeing as we haven't learnt yet…I'm left with no choice." She leaned closer to the bars, her voice dropping to a venomous whisper. "When I return from town, one of you will die. It seems we need a reminder of what happens when you get these *silly* ideas."

Chapter Seven

The cage echoed with gasps and hushed murmurs as the women grappled with the grim, impossible decision before them. Claire hung her head, fighting back tears, the guilt weighing heavily on her. It was her fault, her plan that had brought them to this moment, sending one of them to their death. Claire made a snap decision: she would ensure it was her. No one else deserved to pay the price for her defiance.

Roxey turned to Tayla, who instantly sprang to her feet. "No, dear, I'm going alone today. Unfortunately, you'll have to stay behind and watch them."

Tayla hesitated, disappointment flickering across her face, but she nodded and sat back down.

"Foolish girl, stand up!" Roxey spat, visibly spraying saliva in Tayla's direction. "I'll still need your assistance to lower the bloody travel dingy into the water, won't I?" Shaking her head, she laid a final glare at the caged women before storming out, Tayla trailing close behind.

As soon as they were out of earshot, Claire let out a held breath and burst out, "I'm so sorry, you guys. I'll provoke her and make sure she takes it out on me—I never wanted any of you to get hurt because of this!"

"Would you shut up for a second?" Serenah snapped playfully, pulling the skeleton-head key from her sleeve and holding it up triumphantly. A collective gasp of relief filled the cage.

"Wait…you got it? How?" Claire whispered, disbelief etched across her face.

"A simple trick," Serenah said, a sly grin spreading. "When she grabbed my wrist, I slipped my other hand under hers and swiped it. While she focused on keeping me from reaching into her pocket, I passed it right under her nose. I told you I could fool the bimbo, didn't I?"

Before Serenah could say another word, Claire threw her arms around her neck in a fierce, but awkward, hug. "You saved me. You saved us all."

Serenah pulled back; her expression building irritability. Emerald leaned over. "No, Claire. You're the one who's saving us, let's be clear. We're just going to help make sure your idea sticks."

Tears welled in Claire's eyes, but she quickly wiped them away when Serenah crossed her arms with a disapproving look on her face. "Right then," Claire said. "Unlock it now before Tayla comes back! The door can just sit closed. Hopefully she won't notice it's unlocked until we burst out. Then we'll swarm her."

Serenah nodded and made quick work of jamming the key into the lock. With a satisfying click, the mechanism released, and she tested the door with a small push. It swung open briefly, just enough to confirm their freedom, before they quietly closed it again. Claire's eye began to twitch as she fought the urge to bolt. They weren't safe yet, but knowing the cage was no longer holding them back awakened something deep inside her, a powerful feeling she'd never really explored before. Excitement.

Tayla returned shortly after, slumping into her warden appointed chair with a miserable expression. She stared at the cage like the women inside were some dull exhibit at a zoo.

"What's your deal anyway?" she muttered in an annoyed manner. "Where'd this sudden idea to leave the ship even come from?"

"I thought you heard our little meeting? Don't you know?" Claire sniggered.

"I only caught bits and pieces through the door," Tayla admitted with a huff. "I wasn't able to get close enough to hear all the minor details."

"Well," Claire said, leaning casually against the bars, "I found a rather interesting torn up letter in Roxey's room. From someone on the land." She paused to gesture with her head. "Why don't you come over here, and I'll whisper to you exactly what it said? Some of the others don't know the full story, and I'd rather keep it quiet."

Tayla hesitated, eyeing Claire suspiciously, but must have decided she still held all the power. She strutted over to the cage, keeping her distance slightly. Claire stayed planted by the door and leaned in, strategically waiting for Tayla to mimic her action.

With lightning speed, she grabbed the gate and shoved it forward, slamming it into Tayla's face. The force sent her sprawling backward, clutching her forehead and letting out a wail of pain. Claire took the opportunity and launched at her, tackling her to the ground as the other women rushed through the gate to help. They swarmed like bees, grabbing Tayla's flailing legs and pinning her down.

"Check the junk pile for some rope!" Claire shouted over the commotion. Bonnie and Katalyna darted to the mound of random, discarded items stored in the corner, frantically searching for anything to bind Tayla.

"There's nothing useful in here!" Katalyna called out in frustration.

Meanwhile, Tayla and Claire wrestled with each other until Claire managed to come out on top, sitting on Tayla's back and wrangling both her hands together.

Emerald's voice cut clear through the chaos. "Uh, hello? Stick her in the cage!"

For a split second, everyone froze, glancing at one another before breaking into action. Serenah gripped Tayla's wrists firmly, helping to keep her in a face down position as Claire scrambled to get off her body. Emerald and Bonnie scooped up Tayla's legs, whilst Kat was considerate enough to lift her head off the ground to prevent it from dragging as they began hauling her toward the cage. Out of nowhere, Tayla let out a sharp, piercing whistle. The sound was a trigger, and Claire immediately recognised the ominous shuffle of heavy paws above them. Her stomach tightened in dread. Rumble was coming.

"I thought you were going to take care of him!" Emerald's panicked shout filled the room.

"I *did!* I thought it would've kicked in by now!" Claire shot back, her voice tinged with frustration and fear.

The thundering sound of Rumble's growls and claws scraping against the floorboards echoed through the tiny room as he got closer. Claire's breath caught as the dog reached the top of the stairwell, his shadow looming before them like a nightmare brought to life. He barked and Daphne shrieked, hightailing it back into the cage. Katalyna was quick to pull Josie in too, slamming the door shut behind them. Just as Claire braced for the worst, Rumble whined, losing concentration. His paws slipped on the edge of a step, and his bulky body tumbled down the stairs. The air filled with the deep thuds of his descent, ending with him in a graceless heap at the base. Rumble threw up violently, letting out a tear-jerking whimper. His eyes fluttered shut after a weak, gruff sigh.

"Guess you lose, Tay," Claire shrugged, trying to mask her relief with confidence.

"What did you *do* to him?" Tayla squeaked.

"Just a little dose of chocolate," Claire replied casually. "He'll survive."

The tension in the room eased as Rumble's threat dissipated, and the group resumed their efforts to wrestle Tayla into the cage. Daphne and Katalyna left the comfort of the cage to assist.

Tayla kicked and thrashed with wild desperation, her screams bouncing off the walls. "Okay, wait!" she yelled. "Stop! You don't have to leave me behind! Take me with you!"

Claire paused mid-motion, gesturing for the others to hold up. "Excuse me?" she asked, narrowing her eyes.

"Please," Tayla begged, her voice cracking. "If you leave me here, she'll probably kill me."

Claire glanced at Emerald and Serenah, like she was hoping to read their thoughts. Serenah let her eyelids drift back dramatically, and Emerald shrugged.

Inserting her opinion, Katalyna spat dismissively, "who frickin' cares?"

Claire nodded slowly. "I agree. Why should that bother us? If it were the other way around, you'd serve any of us up without a second thought."

Tears brimmed in Tayla's eyes, her voice trembling as she fought back sobs. "You don't think I want out of here too? It's called survival. I worked hard to become her favourite and act like her little bitch, because for the most part—it keeps me safe! But every time I step on land, it's like torture—God, I miss it. I want my life back, just like you! You won't leave me here to die, will you, Claire?"

Claire hesitated, she had a point. As much as she loathed Tayla, there was a painful truth in her words. She looked down at Tayla's tear-streaked face, searching for sincerity.

"Are you kidding me?" Emerald snapped. "You can't trust her!" She threw her hands up in frustration as Claire loosened her grip on Tayla's wrists.

"Maybe not," Claire admitted quietly, "but morally, I can't condemn her either." Her voice hardened as she locked eyes with Tayla. "You get one chance, Tayla. One. Double cross us and I'll kill you myself." She released Tayla's arms with a forceful shove.

Tayla rolled away quickly, scrambling to her feet and brushing herself off. "Fine," Tayla said, nodding sharply.

Emerald crossed her arms, glaring at Claire. "I hope you know what you're doing."

Tayla rolled her eyes. "Get over it already." She turned to Claire. "Well, what now smarty pants?"

Claire replied, fuelled with determination, "Now, we shut down the alarm system so we can lower the other lifeboat undetected. I don't suppose you know the password to Roxey's computer, do you?"

Tayla shook her head quickly. "Not a clue."

"It's fine. I've got it covered anyway," Emerald interjected confidently, motioning for everyone to follow her. The group crowded toward the stairwell, but Katalyna raised a hand, halting them.

"Hang on a sec," she said. "Maybe we should split up. Half of us should start carrying the lifeboat to the deck and get it back up on the levy ropes."

"True," Claire agreed, glancing toward the corner of the room. "Daphne, Serenah, Bonnie—do you think you can lug that thing up to the deck?"

The three nodded eagerly, moving to the dusty pile where the lifeboat was hidden among the rest of the debris. Originally, the ship had two dinghy lifeboats, but Roxey only needed one for her weekly trips so had cut the other off the levy ropes She'd stashed it in the dungeon room, amongst other items she deemed unnecessary, to avoid temptation.

With the group split, Serenah and the other two dug into the rubble to free the lifeboat, while Claire,

Emerald, and the rest of the girls tiptoed past Rumble, who was still sprawled on the floor in a deep, cocoa-induced slumber. They followed Emerald up to Roxey's bedroom. Emerald carefully pushed the door open and took a huge breath as she surveyed the room. Working up the courage, she crouched down, pulling Roxey's laptop from under the bed. Sitting cross-legged on the mattress, she opened the device and fished a small container of flour from her pocket. When Claire frowned, Emerald flashed a proud smirk.

"This morning," she explained, "I rubbed a tiny amount of oil on Roxey's doorknob. When she used the laptop to turn on the alarms, her fingers would've left oily residue on the keys she pressed for the password. Since the alarm program is activated with a mouse click, the only keys she should've touched are the ones in the password."

She lightly sprinkled the flour across the keyboard, holding her breath as the white dust settled. A moment later, she tilted the laptop and gently shook it. Sure enough, a few keys retained a faint residue where the powder had stuck.

"Gotcha," Emerald muttered, a triumphant glint in her eye. "Alright, ladies," Emerald said, her voice steady but tinged with urgency, "what password could she use with the letters A, E, R, C, H, L and the numbers 1 and 9?"

"Craehl?" Katalyna ventured a guess, frowning.
"Lercha?" added Emerald.
Tayla just shrugged, biting her lip and looking more nervous by the second.

Combinations whizzed through Claire's head, none of them feeling quite right. Then it hit her. "The number is 91," Claire said, confident in her realisation. "As in 1991, the year."

Emerald punched the numbers into the password bar, visibly deep in thought as she moved the cursor back to the front of the box. "Why 1991?"

Claire shrugged, racking her brain for a simple explanation. She remembered flicking through Roxey's journal the first time. The first half of the diary's pages had been torn out, but one of the dates remained printed in a corner. March 27, 1991. But she hadn't told any of the others the journal existed. "I don't know. Just figured 2019 isn't until next year so it had to be the other way around."

Like she'd been stuck with a red-hot poker all of a sudden, Emerald gasped. "It's Rachel! The only word that fits those characters is Rachel."

"Who's Rachel?" Claire asked, watching as Emerald swiftly keyed in *Rachel91*.

Emerald shook her head as the laptop unlocked. "I don't know, but it made sense—and it worked."

"Probably another woman she killed in her past," Katalyna muttered, glancing over Emerald's shoulder as she navigated Roxey's desktop.

Emerald scrolled quickly, her fingers flying over the mouse pad. "Everything's locked individually," she murmured, frustration creeping into her voice. She clicked on the folder labeled *Security Systems* only for a new prompt to pop up—a request for a four-digit pin code.

Claire leaned over. "Try 1991," she suggested, pointing to the keys.

Emerald keyed it in, then shook her head as a bright warning message flashed on the screen: *2 attempts remaining. Alarm will activate upon passcode failure.*

Chapter Eight

"Wait, none of the other letters have powder residue. Doesn't that mean she only used 9 and 1?" Claire pointed out.

Emerald's eyelids fluttered, like she couldn't believe she hadn't noticed that detail, and pressed the keys with swift precision. "Of course! Bloody thing. It was set up to *look* like a four-key passcode on the screen even if it only required two numbers. Another stupid layer of security. Okay, I'm in. I'm about to shut down the alarm system."

"Hang on," Claire interjected, grabbing Emerald's hand as she turned to look at Tayla. "Will Roxey get an alert on her remote when the system crashes?"

Tayla shook her head. "No, I don't think so. Since the command is coming from the control centre it should just switch off. She won't know unless she checks it."

Claire hesitated to release her grasp on Emerald's wrist. "Don't worry, she won't open the app until she's done shopping," Tayla reassured her. "We've got maybe two hours to get back to land and disappear."

"Let's move, then," Emerald said, frantically moving the mouse. She clicked a few times, giving the program the final go-ahead to disable the alarm system.

"Deactivation applied," a motorised voice announced, "your alarm system is now disabled."
A low buzzing noise reverberated through the walls of the ship, setting everyone on edge. For a tense moment, it seemed everyone in the room held their breath. Claire's skin prickled, her body caught in a swirl of excitement and fear, the two emotions so entwined, it was hard to determine which was stronger.

A loud clunk from above indicated that the other girls had managed to successfully shift the spare lifeboat from the ground level to the deck. At the sound, Tayla left the room without hesitation, and Emerald followed soon after, tossing the laptop carelessly onto Roxey's bed as she flitted into the hallway. Katalyna gestured for Josie to come, and she fell into step behind her. Claire stopped when she reached the doorway, sweeping a glance across the room. She realised that with any luck, she'd never have to see it again, and an involuntary smile crept across her face.

By the time Claire reached the deck, most of the girls were already working to position the lifeboat onto the pulley system, hoisting it into place. "I can't believe this is actually happening," Claire murmured as she stepped up beside Katalyna, her voice a flat monotone.

"Me either," Katalyna replied, clearly doubtful. "In a lot of ways, I still don't think this is a good idea." She leaned forward and wrapped her arms around Josie's shoulders, both of them watching Serenah circle the little boat, clicking giant buckles into place. Claire didn't blame Katalyna; her scepticism was warranted at this stage. They were still stuck on the boat; anything could go wrong.

Claire's mind filled with unease. She truly hoped Roxey didn't have any hidden booby traps none of them knew about. *Please, no,* she silently pleaded. They were so close now. As the lifeboat creaked into position, Claire's thoughts strayed. She couldn't quite remember what a lawn felt like beneath her feet, but found herself yearning suddenly for the sensation of her toes sinking into soft, cool blades of grass.

A memory flooded her, vivid and bittersweet, a reminder of a world she hadn't touched in so long. An image of her mother's face clouded her brain, sitting beside her in fits of laughter as they enjoyed a picnic in the park. And there she was, in the background. Roxey. Claire could see her figure looming in the short distance, watching her play, ruining her flashback. But Claire could remember now, the prickly feeling of grass brushing her skin. She couldn't wait.

"It's ready!" someone called out.

Claire snapped out of her daydream, her focus shifting to the girls gathered at the edge of the ship. They stood proudly, admiring the lifeboat now suspended beside the hull over the water, ready and waiting for its passengers. No alarms had blared, no sudden shouts or footsteps echoed from below deck. For the first time, Claire felt a flicker of certainty, a signal they were truly safe to leave. "Let's do this!" she shouted.

Cheers erupted as the group huddled by the ship's railing. Yet, despite the excitement, no one moved. It was as if an invisible barrier held them back, a shared fear that placing even a toe outside the perimeter might trigger a catastrophic event.

Claire took a deep breath, knowing she would have to go first. If anyone needed to prove this escape was possible, it was her. They were waiting for her. Without another thought, she climbed overboard, gently placing her feet down and swiftly sitting on the seat at the bow. Her face instinctively tightened, bracing for an explosion, a siren, or even the sting of a bullet piercing through her chest. But nothing happened. The lifeboat rocked gently as she stood up, arms shooting triumphantly into the air. Cheers erupted once more, louder this time, the sound breaking the tension like sunlight through storm clouds.

One by one, the others followed, forming a single line as they each climbed into the boat, their hope solidifying with every step. Aside from Katalyna, no one carried anything but the clothes on their back. It seemed none of them had any possessions they cared about on board. But Kat brought a small bag she'd strapped to her hip, the weight of its contents hidden beneath her quiet composure.

"This is it," Claire called out, gripping the pulley rope once everyone had found a place to sit. She tugged with all her strength, but the line wouldn't budge. Before frustration could take hold, Serenah stepped in to help, her arms straining against the rope. Bonnie joined them moments later, using her weight to jolt the chain into motion, and together, they managed to lower the lifeboat. The boat hit the water with a soft splash, dipping as it mimicked the rhythm of the ocean. Josie let out a squeal of delight as a small wave licked the side, shooting her in the face with a cupful of icy droplets. Laughter rippled through the group, Katalyna's the most prominent, her heart clearly swelling at her daughter's joy. Claire crouched, pulling out four splintered oars from beneath the seats.

"Let's move!" she urged, quickly organising the group into pairs, each team grabbing an oar. They rowed with everything they had, their muscles burning as the boat surged forward, aimed for the sandbank in the distance by the mainland. A knot burled in the centre of Claire's stomach, her thoughts darkening despite the progress. *This is too easy,* she thought. A strange, irrational vision flashed through her mind—a giant octopus with Roxey's face rising from the depths to drag them under. She forced herself to shake it off.

"Keep going," she whispered to herself, her grip tightening on the oar. She couldn't let fear win now. They were so close. Were they actually going to make it? Fortunately, reaching the shore didn't take as long as Claire expected. They began to pull the boat in on the side of the island farthest from the buildings, hidden behind a row of large, decorative boulders. The area seemed deserted, eerily quiet. Claire told herself it was likely an unpopular spot and forced herself not to wonder why. A nearby destination marker declared the section of beach as "Ibis Isle," a point that didn't spark in Claire's memory at all.

As soon as the boat touched the sand, she vaulted over the edge, splashing into the shallow water. Serenah had done the same moments before her, and together, they dragged the lifeboat onto the beach. A flock of Ibis ran backward as they approached, watching with beady eyes as they dropped the weight of the lifeboat onto the wet sand. Seeing the birds up close, Josie refused to get out of the boat, instead clinging to her mother's leg in fear. Katalyna patted her head, whilst Serenah waved her arms ferociously, shooing the hungry birds away.

"Bloody hell, I see why this place is called Ibis Isle," Serenah remarked.

Claire nodded, her eyes sweeping over the flock of at least fifty. She hid her fear but understood why Josie was scared of them.

"We made it…" Emerald murmured, ripping off one of her shoes and dragging her toes along the sandy bank. "We actually made it." She sounded pleasantly shocked.

"Not yet we haven't," Katalyna said firmly. "We need to get as far away from this beach as possible."

"Well, Tayla should be able to help with that, right?" Emerald stepped in front of Tayla. "You're here every week, which way do we go?"

Tayla's cheeks flushed a light shade of pink. She looked around nervously, as though expecting someone else to answer for her. "I, well, we don't usually come ashore here." Folding her arms assertively, she rolled her eyes. "Anyway, I don't decide which direction we go. Roxey changes the route all the time." She tilted her head at Serenah, as though silently pleading for backup.

"Okay, does anyone else maybe remember their way around the city?" Serenah asked, glancing over toward the distant buildings. "Come on guys, you know

Tayla's too self-centred to pay attention to her surroundings. And too dumb to learn directions."

Tayla shot her a glare, pursing her lips in a statement of irritation.

Emerald sniggered, holding back laughter.

A few mumbled responses followed, but Bonnie spoke clearly. "I remember the main strip," she said, pointing toward the buildings by the boardwalk. "There's a cluster of motels that way, I worked at a few of the kitchens. Uh, Pelican Paradise, I think the area was called. It's a tourist trap, though. Very busy."

"That's probably a good thing," Katalyna pointed out. "If we stick to the crowds, she'll never find us."

Josie, oblivious to the worries the adults faced, was happily squatting with her toes pushed deeply in the sand, her fingers tracing lazy patterns. It took several minutes of coaxing from Katalyna that it was time to leave, but eventually, the group abandoned the lifeboat and started toward the motel strip at Bonnie's lead. The walk along the endless stretch of beach felt both surreal and exhausting. Claire initially relished the sensation of sand beneath her feet, the memories of its texture flooding her mind, but quickly grew tired of trudging through it. It didn't help that she was beginning to feel lightheaded, and the world was starting to sway. Katalyna had to help Josie up several times, making the trip four times longer than it should have been. Her legs kept collapsing underneath her, sending Josie face first into the sand. The poor girl had no chance fighting the rocking motion her legs were so used to. Claire was afraid to admit it, but she suffered the same intensifying sensation and was grateful for the breaks. The constant nausea was overwhelming, and she was becoming increasingly dizzy.

When they finally stepped onto the boardwalk tracking beside the road, relief washed over her. The beautiful island's city displayed before them—Poseidon's

Point. A vibrant, chaotic world teeming with life. It was massive. Claire stood in awe, her eyes sweeping over the traffic, the clusters of people, and the towering buildings. The heart of the island was larger than the eye could see, and seemed to stretch on forever. It was a world she didn't recognise, her memories of life on land overshadowed by the trauma of her parents' deaths. She realised, in many ways, she was no better off than Josie, rediscovering the world as if for the first time.

Glancing down, Claire caught sight of Josie's wide-eyed wonder. The little girl's eyes darted in every direction, mesmerised by every detail. Her jittery awe was contagious, and Claire couldn't help but grin. Nearby, a family of four sat at a picnic table overlooking the water, enjoying the salty breeze. They were eating ice cream cones, and their youngest—a boy not much older than Josie—caught sight of her. The little boy smiled, and an excited Josie squealed loudly, tugging on Katalyna's arm.

"Mummy, look, it's a boy!" Josie cried, her voice full of amazement as she bounced on the spot. "A real boy, see? Can I go touch him?"

Katalyna giggled, happy tears glistening in her eyes, but the boy's mother stiffened. She placed a protective hand on her son's shoulder, her expression wary.

"Er, we should keep moving," Claire murmured, studying the family. It was the father who caught her focus, the sight of a fully grown man so close was oddly nerve-wracking. Katalyna nodded in agreement, and their group quickened their pace along the road. Claire was glad to keep walking, the motion helping settle the dizziness she faced from no longer being out on the water.

"Ugh, can we stop, I think I'm gonna throw up," Emerald announced, stopping suddenly and grabbing onto a nearby railing. "Why are my legs so weak? And the land shouldn't be rocking, right?"

Bonnie chuckled. "It's called sea legs, lovely. Until your brain gets used to being stable, it'll continue mimicking the feeling of ocean waves. Honestly, I'm surprised Josie's upright."

Supporting Josie's steps as she held most of her weight, Katalyna raised an eyebrow. "Don't speak too soon."

"Oh, I recognise that bar!" Bonnie exclaimed, pointing at a small building across the road by the corner.

Serenah let out a fake laugh. "Funny, I recognise the building opposite it."

Claire followed her gaze, her eyes landing on the dancing neon sign of a strip club. She raised an eyebrow. "Huh. You seem to know an awful lot about strip clubs, Serenah. Weren't you, like, fifteen when Roxey collected you?"

"Yep," Serenah replied with a shrug. "So? It was a great way to get free drinks. And money. I snuck in a few times with my tits on display and coaxed the guys tipping the dancers into give me a share. They just thought I was one of them." She stared into the distance with a satisfied smile on her face, as though reminiscing on her happiest memory. "I thought I was so done when the owner caught on. But, as it turned out, the owner was just as dodgy. When he found out how young I was, he didn't kick me out—he encouraged me to perform. That is, until he went and hired a new bouncer who actually checked IDs and he threw me out." She chuckled dryly, her tone sorrowing. "That was the night I went home still drunk and my parents kicked me to the curb. The night Roxey took me in." She took a moment to reflect on her regret. "Look, judge if you want," she continued, a rude edge in her voice, "but you know we're gonna need quick cash to get started out here. And that's where we can get it."

Claire didn't know how to respond, choosing to simply nod. No one else ventured a comment either, and as the group ran out of boardwalk, crossed the road—except for Tayla. She stood rooted in place, staring wide-eyed at a huge billboard above a building a few doors down from the bar. Claire doubled back, gently touching her shoulder. "Tayla, what's wrong?"

Tayla wiped a tear from the corner of her eye and shook her head. "Nothing's wrong. I mean, nothing bad anyway." She pointed at the billboard, her voice trembling with emotion. "It's just…that's new. That's my dad."

Claire looked up at the billboard, attempting to stand still as her body swayed involuntarily. It featured a man underneath the slogan in a pristine white lab coat, standing proudly in front of a dental office. His dazzling smile and perfectly straight teeth gleamed like polished diamonds. "Wow, you have his exact smile. Ohh, that's right. Your dad is a dentist, huh?" Claire said with a nod of acknowledgment, faintly remembering Tayla describing her family years ago.

Tayla nodded, licking her immaculate teeth. "A highly sought-after one, too. It's almost impossible for new patients to get an appointment, his waiting lists are that long." She looked back up at the advertisement, studying it. "I used to have a job too you know," she hummed.

Claire smiled softly. "Really? I don't think you've ever told me that before."

Tayla grinned. "Yep, I used to work as a waitress at a café down the road from dad's office. Didn't need to, of course, our family's quite wealthy. I just liked it." Her smile faded. Loathing her a little less, Claire gave Tayla's arm a reassuring pat, losing herself in thought as she stared at the giant sign. "Once we know we're safe from Roxey, we can go and find him, if you want. That's the point of all this."

Tayla's face lit up with a hopeful grin. "Gosh, I would love that." But her joy didn't last. Her expression quickly crumbled, fear spreading across her features. "Oh, no. Claire, I did something bad," she whispered.

Claire's heart sank. "What? Tayla, what did you do?" Before Tayla could respond, the sharp ping of a phone notification broke the tension.

Tayla fumbled into her pocket and pulled out a small mobile phone.

"Tayla," Claire urged, "why do you have a phone? Who's messaging you?" Then, as though giving her a hint, her mind replayed Tayla's recent words. "That's new," Claire repeated out loud, coming to a nasty realisation. "You know exactly where we are, don't you? If you recognise that billboard as 'new.'"

Tayla's bottom lip quivered as she stared at the phone's screen. Her voice came out small and trembling. "This is the start of the main strip. No matter which beach you start at, you'll end up here. As she left, Roxey gave me this"—she held up the phone—"because she thought you might be able to pull off an escape. When we got off the dingy…I turned on the GPS and sent her a message to let her know we're on land and…our location was available. She'll be here soon I imagine.

Chapter Nine

"Tayla!" Claire shrieked, "what were you thinking? How could you?"

Tayla flinched, her eyes wide with panic. "I'm so sorry! I wasn't thinking. I mean, I was, but I was thinking she's gonna find us anyway and I wanna live. So, I was still playing the obedient girl she could trust." Her words came in a rush, her voice cracking under the weight of her distress. "Oh, what are we going to do? I don't want to go back to the ship now, Claire! I wanna go home." Her outburst had drawn the attention of the others, their heads snapping toward the commotion, intriguing everyone to come jogging back.

Emerald grabbed Claire's shoulder. "Did I just hear what I thought I did? Tayla told her we escaped?"

Claire's chest heaved with the force of her anger as she nodded.

Serenah, listening, turned to the girls as they circled, asking "Roxey's coming?"

Claire could feel the group's collective dread begin to rise.

"Claire, what do we do now?" Emerald asked, her voice wavering.

With snakelike reflexes, Serenah snatched the phone from Tayla's trembling hands and pegged it at the ground. The device shattered on impact, but it appeared that wasn't enough to vent her fury. She stomped on it repeatedly, her boot grinding the pieces into the dirt. "Now we need to decide whether Tayla ends up like the phone!" Serenah hissed.

"Too right. What the hell is wrong with you, Tayla?" Claire spat, flinging her arms around wildly as she began to rant. "I spared you, bought your sob story, let you in on our escape, and this is how you repay us?"

Tayla shrank back, her arms crossed defensively over her chest like a straitjacket. Claire glared at her, teeth clenched, unable to understand Tayla's decision to betray them. Deep down, though, Claire knew she shouldn't be surprised. Tayla had never shown any loyalty to them, why would she start now? *This is my fault,* Claire thought bitterly. *I'm too nice. Too trusting.* Tayla stammered, her lips moving soundlessly, her face streaked with thickening tears as she struggled to produce words.

Claire was left in utter shock a few seconds later when Katalyna marched up to Tayla and, without a word, punched her square in the nose. The sound of the impact was so intense, Claire practically felt it through her own face. Serenah let out a loud gasp, whilst Emerald clapped her hands over her face, her eyes drawn wide with amazement and perhaps a smidge of satisfaction.

Tayla staggered backward, clutching her nose as a scream of pain escaped her. She doubled over, folding herself nearly in half, tears streaming down her face as she absorbed the blow.

"Oh, don't be so dramatic, honey," Katalyna scoffed, shaking out her hand and rotating her wrist as though stretching it out. "You're lucky that's all I did, considering how you've just probably screwed us."

Tayla straightened slowly, her eyes red and watery as she rubbed her nose to check if it was bleeding. She looked at Katalyna like a scolded puppy, her usual resting bitch face completely replaced by shame.

"Well, now that's settled," Bonnie interjected, reaching out to wipe a single droplet of blood from under Tayla's nose, "I think we ought to make a move, girls."

"Absolutely correct," Katalyna said, her voice icy. "The problem is, where can we disappear in a hurry? We've been robbed of the one thing that may have helped. Time."

As though choosing to break the tension at the right moment, a group of runners came jogging down the path, separating around their group. The runner who brought up the rear barged into Serenah's shoulder, initiating a flared reaction. She rotated her head, glaring as he passed, only to be met with a cheeky smile. She relaxed her posture, returning a similar grin. Katalyna rolled her eyes and pulled Josie closer, wrapping a protective arm around her until the joggers were a good distance away. Her wary eyes reflected the tension in her face. Exchanging glances with Claire, they looked around at the silent group.

Serenah, attempting to focus, turned back to the others after the jogger was out of sight. "Mmm. Okay. For starters, we can forget going anywhere near Pelican Paradise now, Roxey'll definitely search everything on the main strip."

"We could go to the bus station and leave the island!" Emerald suggested brightly.

Serenah rolled her eyes and shook her head. "Moron. That's the first place she'll look for us once she's done here."

Claire nodded in agreement. "Serenah's right. Sorry, Em. We need to hide out somewhere unexpected. Somewhere she wouldn't think we'd go."

It was Daphne who surprised everyone by offering a viable suggestion. She hadn't said a word since they'd made it to shore. Her voice was so quiet, they almost missed it. "I know of somewhere we can blend in. There's no way she'll risk doing anything to us in a place that full of people. We can easily wait it out there for a while." She hesitated, as though unsure if anyone was listening, then added, "About a block from here, there's a huge park right across from a big shopping complex. I used to shop there religiously. Every time, I'd tell myself I was going to have a picnic in that park someday…" She trailed off, her expression tainted with a wistful sadness. "Obviously, I never got the chance."

Claire scanned the group's reactions. They seemed receptive, even hopeful. "Makes sense," she said. "Lead the way, Daph. Let's get outta here before she shows."

Daphne nodded, pointing down the street by tipping her head, and everyone turned to follow her.

"Woah, where do you think you're going?" Katalyna snapped as she flung an arm across Tayla's chest. Tayla glared and retaliated by pushing Katalyna back, sending the two into a girlish brawl, shoving and swatting at each other.

"Enough!" Claire shouted, stepping between them and breaking the scuffle apart.

"Oh, come off it, Claire, you're not seriously going to let her come with us after what she's just done, are you?" Katalyna said, her voice laced with sheer disbelief.

Claire clenched her jaw as she considered the options. Her stomach twisted at the thought of abandoning Tayla, but Katalyna wasn't entirely wrong. Finally, she exhaled sharply. "Well, we can't just leave her here, can we?" Claire said firmly. "If we do, Roxey will take her frustrations out on her. I dunno about you, but I'm not about to condemn her to death for a mistake."

"Better her than us," Emerald muttered, folding her arms and shooting Tayla a cold glare.

Claire turned to face Tayla, narrowing her eyes. "Last warning, Tayla. The only reason I'm choosing to give you another chance is because I saw the fear in your eyes when you realised what you'd done. I've never seen you scared of Roxey before. But you screw us again and I *will* tie you to a chair and leave you to be devoured by the wolf," she remarked sternly.

Tayla nodded meekly, wiping her still-teary eyes. Satisfied, and hoping she'd made the right call, Claire turned back to Daphne. "We really have to go now."

It took longer than Claire had hoped to reach the park Daphne was set on. Apparently, Daphne's idea of a "block" was much larger than Claire imagined. Though, in a way, Claire was grateful. The elongated walk helped sort her brain out and the rocking motion finally calmed, taking some of the dizziness away. And as they turned the final corner, the sight that greeted them made the journey worthwhile. The crowded park stretched out before them, outlined by exquisite, meticulously maintained gardens. A massive playground dominated the central space, its climbable jungle gym towering above the other equipment, but it was the landscaping that blew Claire away. The whole place was truly something else. It was, in fact, overwhelming.

Everywhere Claire looked, families bustled about, children's laughter filling the air. It was busier than she'd imagined for a weekday, but looking around, she realised most of the children were toddlers. Or at least, younger than school aged. Seeing so many different people in one place, taking in the smell of the bark and the grass; it still felt like a dream Claire was about to wake up from.

Josie hung off Katalyna's arm, so jittery she couldn't keep still. "Can I play on that, Mum?" she squealed, pointing to the jungle gym.

Katalyna hesitated, her grip tightening around Josie's palm briefly before letting it go. "Sure, honey. Go ahead. I'll be sitting on that bench in front of the hedges, right over there, okay?"

Before Katalyna had even finished talking, Josie kicked off her sandals and bolted, her tiny feet kicking up little clouds of dust. Claire and the others laughed, watching the girl's uncontainable joy as she swatted away the puffs of dirt that choked her air supply.

Before anyone else had even taken a step, Josie suddenly halted, her tiny body going rigid like an unexpected obstacle had stopped her. She turned on her heel and came flying back, a huge smile on her face, though her voice reflected concern.

"I do like the feeling of the grass," she babbled. "But there's so many people on the ground, Mummy!" Her wide eyes darted around the bustling playground as she tugged on Katalyna's jacket. "And babies are *so* small! How fast do they move? I don't want to step on them. Can you come with me?"

Katalyna expressed a warm, maternal smile. Without hesitation, she reached down and took Josie's hand. "Of course, honey. Let's go together." Hand in hand, they made their way toward the jungle gym. Josie's earlier worry seemed to melt away with each step, her face lighting up again as they approached the towering equipment.

The rest of the group made their way to the bench Katalyna had first indicated, settling in beside each other. For a moment, it felt almost normal—just a group of women watching their friend's child play with her mother in the park.

"Do we really think we're safe to just sit out here?" Claire asked quietly once they were seated. She couldn't help but move her hips and jitter, fighting off invisible ants in her pants as anxiety riddled her brain.

Serenah groaned and leaned back against the bench. "Ugh, can we just enjoy the view of grass and the sound of happy strangers chatting for, like, five minutes without thinking about Roxey?"

"I'd love to," Bonnie cut in flatly, "but I agree with Claire. "While it's awesome to have even gotten this far, it will be so much more enjoyable and worth it once we are properly free. When we don't have to worry about her being on our tail anymore."

Serenah sighed dramatically. "Would you take a look around? She can't touch us here. Not unless she wants, like, two hundred witnesses."

"Yeah," Claire countered, "but we can't just live here for the rest of time, can we, Serenah? We're going to need somewhere to sleep tonight."

Emerald nodded. "Exactly," she chimed in, "we have to find a safe place to stay."

"And to eat," Bonnie added, rubbing the pudgy parts of her belly.

Claire held up one of her palms to control the flow of conversation, but Tayla ignored her gesture. "Wait, what do you mean somewhere to sleep tonight?" Tayla asked. "Don't we just go home after a couple hours?" Her general attitude was full of sass, but her eyes betrayed how worried she was.

Serenah sniggered, wiping a fake tear from the corner of her eye. "Yeah, give that a go, Tay. Either you or your parents will be dead before you cross the threshold."

Tayla frowned, and Claire shot Serenah a look of disapproval.

"What Serenah means," Claire said, attempting to lighten the tone, "is that, at least for now, we have to stay together to keep everyone safe. Going home prematurely is probably not the best idea. We don't know yet how Roxey is gonna react to our '*escape*.'" She used air quotes around the word escape, then turned back to address the group as a whole. "Right then. First things first," Claire said calmly, "Where do we go once we leave here? We're gonna need food and accommodation."

Rejoining the group mid conversation, having left Josie to play happily now that she had gotten used to the park, Katalyna sat beside Claire at the end of the bench.

Her gaze fixed on Josie, who was now scaling the jungle gym like a determined little explorer. She glanced sideways at the group. "Remember just after we left the main strip, there was that stubby little coconut shaped motel we passed on the way here? I think it was called the Coconut Palm?" She searched their faces, but no one made any effort to respond. "Anyway, I saw about four security staff out the front of it. There was a sign out the front saying some surfer dude was going to be signing autographs in its convention room later today. There'll be cameras and shitloads of people. I vote we go there, stick to the crowds. You reckon?"

Claire nodded; semi convinced. Across the bench, Emerald and Bonnie exchanged a look, but didn't argue.

Katalyna tried to get Daphne's attention, since she had remained silent and appeared absent from the conversation altogether. "Hey, Daph, did you catch that?"

Daphne didn't respond, and Katalyna was met with the side of her face as she continued to look at the ground.

Katalyna shook her head but didn't press her, instead glancing back at the others. "We're all agreed then?"

"Agreed," Claire said firmly.

Serenah pulled her legs out from under the table and stood up, gently lifting herself onto the tabletop to draw everyone's attention. "Since you insist on discussing this now…okay. Here's my counter. We'll meet at the Coconut Palm *if and only if* we get split up at any point. It's a good anchor, easy to find." She let her head fall to the side lazily, rolling her eyes at Katalyna. "*However*, we wouldn't want to get a room there, though. It'll get way too pricey, especially for such a large group. I reckon we head back to the edge of the island, but toward the other side. Find an off-grid, unknown motel." She paused to fold her arms under her bust, pushing her chest out as a handsome guy walked past their table, his eyes lingering on her. After she'd maintained his attention and flashed him a smile, she continued, "we're only going to be able to afford a one-star room for starters. But, more importantly, if we can get out of the main city area, she shouldn't be able to track us."

Pointing to a nearby light fixture saddled with a security lens on the corner of the park, Serenah added, "there's too many cameras surrounding the populated tourist hotels. She'll find us easily in here."

Tayla, whining, added her opinion to Serenah's suggestion. "A one-star motel room? I can't wait." She allowed her eyes to roll back, showcasing her irritation. "But I guess it's better than the park bench we've currently booked. In case you've all forgotten, we don't have any money at all," she pouted. "Cheaper or not, finding accommodation won't do us any good if we can't pay for it, Ree. Shouldn't we go to the police or something? Report Roxey and get her arrested?"

Serenah turned up her nose as though Tayla had said something disgusting. "As if they'd believe us. You do realise how ridiculously made up our whole story sounds, right? Besides, we have absolutely no evidence against her. Don't worry, we'll have money soon." She smiled and ran a hand up the side of her right hip, shaking her bosom gently. "I can easily make enough tonight to pay for a week-long stay with this body."

Tayla smiled, but Emerald's fierce glare was enough to wipe the smile from Serenah's lips. "No offense to your brilliant money-making scheme, *Ree*, but I don't think we can wait here until the early hours of tomorrow morning for you to come back from the strippers with fat pockets."

Bonnie nodded in agreement, gesturing to the incoming afternoon sun with her hand. "I don't want to go all night without food either. Start thinking of another idea, how can we make some quick cash *before* nightfall?"

Serenah pursed her lips, her eyes subtly scanning their surroundings. Claire observed the way Serenah's eyes lingered on a nearby pram parked two benches over. Two women, each cradling infants of different ages, were deep in conversation, oblivious to anything outside their bubble. In the storage compartment under the pram, a pink purse peeked out from a nappy bag, its bright colour pulling Serenah in like a beacon.

Claire's chest tightened as she realised what Serenah was thinking. "Oh no," she hissed quietly. "Serenah, don't do it. What a way to draw attention!"

Serenah gave a casual shrug, her expression infuriatingly nonchalant. "Look, either I grab a card or two, and we use it to check into a hotel before dinner, or you lot can wait it out in the park half the night while I earn some cash at the club. Maybe Roxey catches up, maybe she doesn't. What's it gonna be?"

Claire sighed and fell silent, frustration bubbling up but finding no escape. She glanced around at the others, hoping for backup, but none of them spoke. They all knew the reality of the situation. There weren't any good options if they wanted to get out of the open.

Josie climbed off the jungle gym and skipped all the way back to Katalyna, a smile still planted on her worn-out face. "Mummy, I'm hungry," she complained.

"I'll take that as you'd like to eat before two in the morning," Serenah said with a smirk as Katalyna pulled Josie onto her lap. "Don't worry, I won't get caught."

Claire looked up as the enormous town clock mounted above a nearby building began to chime. It was already two o'clock. Her stomach growled as if on cue, a sharp reminder of how long it had been since they'd last eaten.

Serenah bent down and whispered something to Tayla. She nodded, and they rose from the bench, moving with a practiced calm toward the two mothers sitting a few feet away. Claire watched, impressed, as Serenah masterfully inched closer, her movements so casual they seemed effortless. Step by step, Serenah positioned herself near the pram, timing her actions with precision. In a swift yet subtle motion, she pretended to stumble, her foot knocking the side of the stroller just enough to send a baby bottle tumbling to the ground.

"Shoot, I'm so sorry about that!" she exclaimed, crouching down with exaggerated concern. Her body arched forward, strategically blocking the view of the pram's storage compartment. Claire saw Tayla move quickly, her hand darting into the open nappy bag to swipe the pink purse sticking out.

One of the mothers smiled kindly and took the bottle from Serenah, her attention fully on accepting the false apology. By the time Tayla stepped back with the purse tucked securely into her back pocket, the whole interaction seemed like nothing more than an innocent accident. Both girls returned to the group, giggling and exchanging hi-fives triumphantly.

Claire breathed a sigh of relief—until the girls halted, their faces dropping in horror. From behind her, a voice she knew all too well cut through the din of the park.

"Excuse me, ladies, I believe there's been some kind of mistake."

The voice, a sound she never wanted to hear again, sent an ice-cold jolt down Claire's spine. She turned, her heart pounding, to confirm Roxey standing directly behind her, arms folded fiercely, and her face contorted with fury.

Claire's body went rigid with fear, every muscle locking up as Roxey's piercing green eyes swept over them. How had she found them so quickly?

"You girls have a lot of explaining to do when we get home," Roxey breathed, her voice very low and dangerous as she flashed the group a knife hidden in the lining of her jacket.

Chapter Ten

Strangely, Roxey's threat gave Claire strength. Summoning every ounce of courage she had, Claire took a slow, measured breath. Unsure of the outcome of her next move, she balled up her fist, and without a second thought, drove it hard into the side of Roxey's jaw. She stumbled sideways, dazed, giving Claire an opening to shove her into the nearest hedge.

"Girls, run!" Claire shouted, her voice carrying across the park. The group dispersed like someone had thrown a stick of dynamite at their feet, sprinting mindlessly in different directions. Claire's heart hammered even harder as she sprinted across the park, her feet sinking slightly into the soft grass. She glanced over her shoulder, relieved to see Roxey still struggling to extract herself from the dense hedge.

Josie's shrill voice rang out from somewhere behind her, and Claire's stomach dropped—if they lost Josie, Katalyna would never recover. She turned sharply, catching sight of the little girl weaving between playground equipment, having lost grip of her mother's hand during the commotion.

Claire noticed Katalyna struggling to lift herself up off the ground, apparently having tripped over a low piece of play equipment. "This way!" Claire shouted, waving frantically as Katalyna managed to pick herself up and ducked under a swing, grabbing Josie around the waist.

From the edge of the park, Claire spotted a directional sign for the Coconut Palm hotel in the distance. She hoped the others would remember they had agreed to use the tourist destination as a meeting point and that Roxey wouldn't follow them there.

Close behind her, Claire heard at least a few of the girls' footsteps pounding the pavement as they veered away from the park and back toward the hotel they'd passed earlier.

"Faster! We have to get out of sight before she catches up!" Bonnie urged, her voice strangled in panic.

Claire glanced over her shoulder, and her breath caught in her throat—Roxey had quickly freed herself from the bush and managed to stay within close quarters of their group. She was weaving through the crowds also, her eyes locked on them with murderous intensity. Thankfully, the girls sprinted across the street seconds ahead of a large city bus, which halted Roxey in her tracks and obscured them from her view. The bus, looming between them like a wall, bought precious seconds as Roxey was forced to wait for it to pass.

The coconut shaped hotel was close now, the street sign for it shone like a beacon of safety.

"Almost there!" Claire called back, her lungs burning with each stride. They reached the entrance, the large revolving door spinning slowly as guests came and went.

Katalyna pushed a frightened and confused Josie through first, the rest of them following quickly, tumbling into the quiet, air-conditioned reception. They'd made it to safety. For now. Panting, Claire scanned the area, her eyes darting between the faces of the girls with her. A quick headcount sent a jolt through her. They'd lost Emerald, Serenah and Tayla in the scramble.

"Crap," she muttered, her breath shaky. "She probably saw which hotel we went into, and we've lost half the group. We have to get out of sight." Holding her stomach to relieve some of the pain from a stitch, her head bounced freely like a bobblehead as she searched for a place to hide.

Across the lobby, Claire spotted a pair of plump, brown, comfortable looking couches and motioned for the girls to follow her. The snobby-looking man at the front desk stared down his nose at them, wary, as they casually hastened across the room. Claire ignored him, trying to lose his attention as she led the group. For a hotel that was soon to be teeming with guests, the reception area was annoyingly quiet.

"Get down behind these chairs," Claire whispered sharply as they reached the couches. The girls crouched low, their breaths coming in shallow gasps as they huddled together, barely concealed. As Claire squatted, horrible memories flooded her brain. Vividly, Claire recalled the last time she huddled in a group, trying to conceal herself from Roxey. Pangs of pain, or perhaps fear, shot through her chest.

"Do you think she saw us come in?" Bonnie's panicked whisper bounced off the girls.

"I don't know," Claire replied, keeping her voice low. "But we have to wait here for the others. We have no hope of finding each other if we get separated here. At least we sort of agreed on a meeting point before Roxey showed up." A knot tightened in her stomach as a chilling thought surfaced: What if Tayla had tipped Roxey off? Roxey finding them at the park had been far too easy. It was a navigable island, sure, but there was no way she could have pinpointed that specific location so fast. *Did Tayla have a second phone or another way to contact her?*

Bonnie peeked around the side of the chairs and scanned the rounded room. "I know we have to wait for everyone, but if we stay here too long, she'll find us," she murmured, her voice tight and barely a whisper.

Claire cast a nervous glance at Josie, who trembled as she clung to Katalyna in a manner eerily familiar to Claire, trying to stifle her sobs. Claire squeezed Katalyna's arm, her eyes reflecting a quiet urgency.

"Don't worry, if Roxey finds us before the others do, we'll split. I'll distract her, try to lead her away from you guys. Kat, take Josie to the bathrooms or something and climb out the windows. Bonnie, you and Daphne head for the back exit. We'll regroup back at the park," she said, her voice steady despite the fear churning inside her. "If I don't make it back within the hour, head for the edge of the island. Follow the plan. Maybe the others will do the same."

Katalyna shook her head at first, but reluctantly agreed when she looked down at Josie's terrified expression. Silently praying for a miracle, Claire held her breath, bracing as her eyes darted back to the lobby entrance. Just then, the glass doors revolved, and an array of familiar faces caught her eye. Emerald, Serenah, and Tayla slipped inside, wide-eyed and breathless, their hair blown back into a frizz from the desperate sprint. Relief surged through Claire as she waved them over whilst trying to stay low and out of the public's line of sight. They quickly hustled over and ducked behind the pair of chairs.

Emerald clutched at Claire's arm, her voice barely audible as she steadied her breathing. "We lost her, I think. We took the long way around, hid behind a bus stop trying to shake her."

Claire nodded, feeling a sense of calm for just a moment. Until a loud voice echoed from across the room.

"Nope. She's here," Claire whispered. Her heart sank as she caught sight of Roxey talking to the concierge. She moved with a calculated, deceptive calm, masking the violence that Claire knew lurked just beneath her composed surface. Roxey was a master manipulator, and her friendly demeanour was just as terrifying as her rage. She seemed to be asking questions, her eyes flitting across the floor like a hawk circling prey.

"Stay low," Claire hissed, motioning with her hands. She could feel the thudding of her heart in her throat, each beat screaming at her to jump up and throw Roxey off the others trail, using violence if necessary.

The blabbermouth concierge gestured toward the hallway furthest from the reception desk, right beside the couches the girls were hiding behind, and Roxey's face split into a satisfied smile as she turned to look in the general direction he pointed.

"She knows we're here. He told her which way we went," Katalyna whispered, her face pale as she locked eyes with Claire. They were out of time.

Roxey had stepped away from the concierge desk and was scanning the lobby. Her eyes narrowed in concentration as they swept across the floor dangerously, scanning the furniture, her lips pressed into a thin line. Claire knew they couldn't stay hidden much longer—Roxey would comb through every inch of the area eventually. She took a steadying breath and silently motioned to the others, her face screwed up in concentration as she tried to recall the lobby's layout from what she saw when they came in. "We have to move. Any ideas?" she whispered urgently.

Serenah subtly gestured with a nod. "There's a guest hallway just to our left with a line of elevators at the end."

Katalyna frowned and shook her head. "Elevators in places like this are usually only able to be activated by guest keycards. We won't be able to use them."

Serenah shot her a snotty look. "Yes, but where there are elevators, there are usually janitorial exits. I never said we should go up and trap ourselves more."

Claire raised a hand between them and waved it like a flag, cutting through the brewing argument before it could escalate. "Enough. We don't have time for bickering." She poked her head ever so slightly above the couch. Roxey was slowly examining the hallway at the end of the front desk. "We've got to move now," she hissed. "Let's slip out before she turns back this way and spots us."

She tapped Bonnie on the shoulder, who was closest to the end by the hallway, and signalled for her to take the lead. They edged along the floor, trying not to kick each other in the crawling conga line. Roxey had gotten closer now, her boots echoing sharply against the marble floor, and her expression had shifted to one of razor-sharp intent. Claire clenched. Just a little further, and they'd be able to drift out of sight.

With stealth, they slid into the hallway, racing to the end and disappearing around the corner, feeling like they were suddenly invisible and free. Claire spotted the staff door Serenah was talking about and yanked it open, holding it back as each girl darted through. As they entered an alleyway filled with huge skip bins full of garbage, it was like they were able to breathe again, and Serenah even burst out laughing with joy.

Seizing her chance to confront Tayla, Claire grabbed her by the shoulder and spun her around. "Tayla, did you contact Roxey again? She found us at the park way too easily. Was that your doing?"

Tayla threw her hands up in surrender. "Woah, no way. I meant what I said, I'm not working with Roxey anymore. Besides, I don't even have anything else on me to contact her with anyway. She only gave me the one phone." Claire studied Tayla's face with narrowed eyes, searching for any hint of deception. Finding none, she relaxed and nodded slowly, trusting her genuine demeanour.

"What now?" Bonnie asked quietly.

Claire took a shaky breath. "We stick to our original plan. Head for the island's edge, find a little motel outside the city. Maybe Serenah was on to something with the street cameras."

For a moment, silence blanketed them, each of the girls lost in thought. But then, almost in unison, they began to move as a tight-knit group, following each other like a herd. Their footsteps were nearly silent as they walked, eyes scanning the alleyways and intersections as they crossed blocks. Every shadow cast by another human felt like a threat, every distant voice like Roxey's. The closer they got to their destination, the more their pace slowed, weariness settling in. They weren't used to walking such a long distance to reach an end.

As the afternoon sun slid from the sky, Josie came to an abrupt stop, plopping onto the gutter with her arms crossed, tears spilling down her cheeks. "Mummy, I'm *really* hungry now," she whined.

"I don't think we're too far now, even crap motels usually serve meals," Serenah said reassuringly, though her tone carried more hopefulness than certainty.

Katalyna sat beside her child, stroking Josie's arm. "We have to find a place to eat before we find a place to sleep," she said firmly, addressing Serenah, but glancing at the group for support. "It's well past lunchtime, she can't wait much longer, it's not fair."

Claire checked their surrounding options, trying to catch sight of a restaurant, fast-food joint or even a street vendor they could purchase food from.

But it was Bonnie who spotted a tiny twenty-four-hour bakery wedged abnormally between a tattoo parlour and an adult bookstore. "Food!" she exclaimed happily, pointing.

Like zombies drawn to sustenance, they picked up their pace, trudging toward the little shop. Accustomed to a regimented meal schedule, Claire's stomach growled the moment she could smell food, and the sight of the bakery's offerings made her mouth water.

Bonnie took charge, selecting a variety of pies for the group and nearly emptying the bakery's hotbox in the process. Both Claire and Josie watched the ordering process with fascination.

"So, you get to see what you want first and pick it out and everything?" Josie asked in awe. "I'm so glad we came out to the world, Mum. It's so much better than our bad home."

The woman behind the counter raised an eyebrow at Katalyna as she packed the pies into takeaway bags. Serenah tapped one of the stolen credit cards against the payment terminal and the girls grabbed their food. They settled at the outdoor tables, devouring their long-awaited meal.

Yet, as Claire nibbled her pie, unease gnawed at her. Sitting out in the open, she felt like a target, a duck sitting on the water during hunting season. Still, she tried to savour the rare moment of peace in the wide-open world. When Josie pointed, mouth hanging open, at a pair of burly tradies who strolled into the bakery, Claire couldn't help but laugh.

The wide-eyed little girl whispered loudly to her mother, "Holy moly, those big boys are *huge*."

Claire nodded at her with a silly smile on her face, trying to shake the feeling that she was being watched.

Then, Daphne's voice cut through the group, claiming her attention. "I…I know where we are. And I know of somewhere close by we could go that Roxey definitely won't find us," she murmured, casting a glance down the street. "There's this old motel. I stayed there once after…well, once before." Her voice trailed off, but there was a certainty in her voice. "It's pretty run-down, but that's the point. The owners keep it off the grid, no modern updates. It's behind the campgrounds, opposite the boat dock at the end of this street."

Claire considered her suggestion. The shady motel Daphne pitched didn't sound that great, but surely Roxey wouldn't be able to find them there if it was as outdated and hidden like she'd said. She gave a quick nod. "Sounds good to me. Why didn't you mention it earlier?"

Daphne's cheeks tinted pink with a faint blush as she shrugged. "I only just remembered it when I figured out where we were. And…well, everything happened so fast after Serenah stole that purse."

At the mention of the theft, Serenah's hand reflexively went to her back pocket, checking for the stolen purse. She let out a small sigh of relief when she felt it still tucked safely there.

"All right," Claire said, standing up. Looking out onto the street, her stomach twisted with unease again when her eyes met with a stranger's across the road. He didn't linger, turning away immediately when Claire noticed him staring. She narrowed her eyes in suspicion, hoping perhaps it had been a coincidence. "Right, let's head to the motel," she announced. "We'll figure out the next steps in the morning."

It wasn't until they'd gotten to the end of the street and the faded sign of The Seawitch Motel came into view that the knot in Claire's stomach loosened. The motel looked abandoned at first, showcasing cracked windows and peeling paint. Daphne guided them around to a side entrance, bypassing the flickering front lights. They made their way up a narrow staircase, passing patches of faded carpet and paint chipped walls, until they reached a room at the end of the hall. The door creaked loudly as Serenah took charge and pushed it open, revealing a dimly lit, musty-smelling room.

The space was empty aside from two rickety beds, and a chunky dresser by the door. A pair of heavy curtains hung limp over the dusty, broken window, shielding the area from the little sunlight left outside.

"It's not much," Daphne said, biting her lip and flicking on the light as she entered first, "but it's a roof over our heads for at least a night."

Claire placed a hand on her shoulder, offering a small smile. "It's perfect." She gestured for the others to come inside, shutting the door behind them and securing the flimsy lock. The sense of finally being in a closed-off space, however dank, seemed to melt the fear in the room, and most of the girls sank onto the beds to rest a moment, their bodies heavy with exhaustion.

Katalyna peered out through the ancient curtains, her voice barely above a whisper. "Do you think she'll come looking here?"

"No one's even working the front desk," Serenah replied with a scoff.

Daphne nodded. "The place was empty when I stayed here too. I doubt Roxey would even consider a place like this. You just leave a pair of shoes in the hallway outside the door to let them know you took a room. They leave a piece of paper out for you to fill in credit card details. It's pretty much the shadiest motel ever. Full of affairs, I'd say. I only stayed here because it was all I could afford when I needed to get away from…well, when I needed a place to stay once."

Claire narrowed her eyes. Was Daphne finally giving away a piece of her past? She considered pressing for more but decided against it. Instead, she took a deep breath and allowed herself a brief moment of calm. She offered a small, reassuring smile. "Alright then, let's just breathe for a moment before we start figuring out this mess we're in. Cause, eventually, we're going to have to find a way to stop running and get our old lives back."

With a sigh, Claire jumped bum first onto one of the beds and leaned back, feeling the rough, scratchy fabric beneath her.

"Why can't we just go home?" Tayla suggested again. "I mean, back to our parents. For those of us who still have a home, that is."

Claire looked at her with disbelief, thinking of a way to answer politely, but Serenah didn't hold back.

"Because, dummy," she snapped, "you don't think that's one of the first places she will look for us? She killed Claire's parents to get her on the boat, don't think she won't do the same to yours. Honestly, how are you not getting this?"

Tayla flashed Serenah a dirty look, crossing her arms defensively as she glared at her. The tension between them hung heavy in the room, considering they weren't usually a pair to fight.

After an awkward delay, Emerald spoke up. "What if we just go to the cops?" she proposed. "Isn't it their job to stop people like her? They would surely help."

A knock on the door interrupted the rising heated discussion, sending a pang of panic through Claire's chest. She looked around as her stomach clenched. Every single one of the women had frozen in place. *It couldn't possibly be her*, Claire told herself in complete disbelief. No one moved a muscle as the hardy knuckles rapped the door again.

"It could be staff?" Serenah whispered, unconvincingly.

After a third knock, Claire edged forward with a sigh and pulled open the door cautiously. It wasn't Roxey standing before her, but a man. A man with a gun holstered to the belt on his jeans.

Chapter Eleven

"Evening, ladies," he greeted with a friendly, yet authoritative tone. "Sorry to disturb you. Name's Sergeant Henry McLaren." He held up an official looking badge pulled from the pocket of his jacket, and Claire's initial apprehension wavered slightly. "Mind if I come in for a moment, Miss…?"

Struggling to speak, Claire swallowed an uncomfortable lump in her throat, however, the tension melted the more she studied the un-uniformed supposed police officer standing in the doorway. It was still so strange to her, seeing a full-grown male up close. The facial hair of his five o'clock shadow alone was an odd concept, and she couldn't help but stare. She could understand Josie's awe at how different men were to women.

The cop appeared to be in his mid-twenties, with rough, chestnut brown hair that just peeked out from behind his ears. His eyes were a warm, unique hazel colour, and a reassuring smile curved at the corners of his mouth.

Claire nodded before she realised her body was moving on its own, stepping aside to let him enter. "Claire. It's just Claire," she finally replied.

Serenah, however, moved closer to the doorway, glaring at him suspiciously. "How did you find us?" she demanded, her voice low and wary. "Why are you here?" Her posture was rigid, and she clenched her fists by her sides as if preparing for the worst.

Unaffected by her rudeness, Sergeant McLaren lifted his hands, keeping his palms open and non-threatening, as he stepped into the room. "Sorry if I've upset you, I'm not even on duty. I mean, technically, it's my day off. But, I was at the park," he explained. "Saw you and your friend over there"—he nodded toward Tayla—"take that woman's wallet. I was going to intervene until I saw you"—his eyes shifted back to Claire—"punch that woman in the head, and the lot of you flee. The situation intrigued me."

Claire blinked, caught off guard. There was something undeniably genuine about the way he spoke, as if he truly cared about their well-being. But she still felt uneasy.

Serenah sure wasn't buying it. "So, what, you just decided to follow us?" she challenged, her voice harsh. "That doesn't sound like normal cop behaviour to me, '*Sergeant McLaren*.'" She made exaggerated air quotes around his title.

He turned to face her, his expression earnest. "Well…yes and no," he replied. "You did steal, Miss. But I admit, curiosity got the better of me, and honestly, something looked…unusual…about the whole thing." He scratched his nose, taking his time to continue. "Anyway, after she basically mowed me down to chase you, I followed the angry redhead and lost her at the Coconut Palm Hotel. So, I went back to the park to get some details from the woman you took the purse from. It was easy then to track you once you used one of her cards to purchase food at the bakery."

Claire crossed her arms, her defences up. "Wait," she said carefully, suddenly uneasy. "We're… safe here, right? If you could track us this easily…" she trailed off, flashing a glance at Serenah, whose face mimicked with concern. "Can she?"

The cop's face softened as he looked at her. "Er, I wasn't followed. Wait, are you girls in some kind of trouble?" He glanced around at the other girls, their stances fearful, but his eyes lingered on Katalyna, who had retreated into the corner to shield Josie behind the second bed. Turning his head back to Claire and Serenah, he added, "I'd like to help, but I can only do that if you're willing to trust me."

Bonnie's shoulders relaxed slightly at his words, but Serenah's tension didn't waver. "Trusting someone who says they're *here to help* hasn't really gone so well for us before," Serenah sneered, folding her arms defensively.

Claire caught the edge in Serenah's voice, and whilst she agreed with her, she couldn't help but wonder if they were better off talking to the cop about their situation before dismissing his offer entirely. Like Emerald had said, what would be so wrong with getting help from the authorities? It was their job to detain criminals, after all.

The handsome lawman didn't flinch under Serenah's scrutiny. Instead, he studied her for a moment, then accepted her resilience. "Fair enough," he said. He shifted his weight, resting one hand lightly on the side of his belt, causing most of the girls to flinch as his gun moved. "Look, I don't know what's going on here, but if I didn't know any better, I'd say you ladies were on the run. Now, I don't have to know why, and you don't have to accept my help, but unfortunately, I do need to ask that you hand over the stolen purse." He held out his hand. "Turn it over and I'll leave you be. No formal charges."

Claire nodded and gestured to Serenah, who reached into her pocket and removed the wallet with sass. She took a slow step forward, seductively locking eyes with the Seargeant for what seemed like an endless pause. Then, without breaking eye contact, slipped the purse into his open palm and dragged her hand up his wrist, using a single finger to draw a swirly motion on his arm. He closed his fingers around it and took half a step back, clearly uncomfortable. She laughed quietly, smirking as she stepped away. Claire shook her head.

Reaching into the pocket of his jeans, McLaren pulled out a shiny business card with his personal details on it. "Look, if you need help, just give me a call," he said firmly as he offered it to Claire. "If you're being harassed or something there are options."

The girls exchanged glances, an unspoken conversation passing between them. Claire's heart twisted, she was tired of being afraid. And how long could they run before Roxey caught up? She wanted to trust him, but it would not come as easily as he seemed to think. "We'll…think about it," she finally said, her voice wavering but resolute.

He nodded, his expression turning as he stepped back toward the door. "By the way, there's a red light flashing on the underside of the watch your friend is wearing."

As the door softly closed behind him, panic engulfed the room.

"Who's wearing a watch!" Katalyna shrieked.

"Me!" Tayla said in a shrill voice, tearing it off her wrist and dangling it away from her body like it was about to explode.

"Tayla!" Emerald whined, snatching the watch from her fingertips and holding it up to examine it. "It's probably programmed with a tracking device or something!"

"I didn't know that!" Tayla insisted, on the verge of tears.

Bonnie pushed her way into the crowd and smacked Emerald's hand, sending the watch flying onto the ground. Clearing the surrounding space, she stomped on the watch with the full force of her weight, breaking it into several pieces. The red light stopped flickering and faded out.

The shattered pieces of the watch lay scattered on the thin, dusty carpet and every woman in the room stared at the broken device as though it were a bomb about to go off, their eyes occasionally darting to one another. The anxiety pulsed in the air like a heartbeat.

"Do you think...she already knows where we are?" Tayla squeaked, her voice cracking. Emerald shot her a tiresome look, but before anyone could answer, a loud crash shattered the fragile calm.

The door to the motel room burst open, slamming against the wall, and there she stood—Roxey. Her wild red hair framed a face twisted in fury, and her eyes, dark with malice, zoned in on the group of girls huddled together in the centre of the room.

"Well, we haven't been very well behaved today, have we ladies?" she spat venomously. "You really thought you could just leave me and start doing whatever you want out here?"

Daphne, the closest to the door, yelped and backed away, but Roxey was already advancing, her hand reaching for something in her jacket pocket.

Before anyone could react, an unexpected struggle erupted. Sergeant McLaren had stormed back in, and he moved quickly, attempting to subdue Roxey from behind. Before he could get a firm hold of her, she whirled on him with cat-like speed, her elbow smashing into his jaw as she caught him off guard. The unexpected force knocked him backward, and he stumbled, crashing hard against the dresser by the wall, his chin smashing into one of the hard handles. The impact made a sickening thud, and he crumpled to the ground, momentarily dazed.

"Stay down if you know what's good for you," Roxey sneered, her lips curling into a cruel smile. She pulled out a small handgun, the black metal glinting under the dull motel light. The room seemed to shrink as she aimed the gun toward the girls, her hand steady and unyielding.

"Now," Roxey said, her voice dangerously calm, "I'm warning you. I'm giving you one chance to go home with me. We can forget all this nonsense ever happened if you come quietly. Otherwise, there will be consequences if you choose to disobey me."

Claire stood protectively in front of the others, her body trembling with adrenaline and fear. She forced herself to focus, to think past the terror clouding her mind. She couldn't let this be the end, not when freedom was so close, just a few steps away on the other side of the door.

Drawing strength from the surrounding women, she knew they would win if they stood together, no matter how hopeless it seemed. "No," she initially whispered, but her voice grew stronger. "Come with you? You're insane. We're not going back, Roxey. We're never going back."

Roxey cocked her head, almost amused, and tightened her grip on the gun. "Brave words, my darling daisy, but you know better than anyone that bravery is defiance," she warned. "And defiance is punishable." Her finger hovered over the trigger, and the girls tensed, bracing themselves for the worst.

Claire's pulse roared in her ears. She could only hope that if Roxey fired, adrenaline would surge through the others, and they'd use the boost to take off running and get away. Her eyes flicked to Sergeant McLaren, who was alert again and starting to get up, clutching his face. The tension was suffocating, like being trapped in a locked closet as the walls drifted towards the centre of the room.

"Enough games," Roxey snapped, her voice cutting through the tension. "What's it going to be?"

Following Claire's eyes, she cast a disdainful glance at Sergeant McLaren, who was pulling himself to his feet, jaw clenched in pain but eyes fierce with determination. "Oh, you think he can help you, is that it? Who is he anyway? How do you know him?"

The brave cop, now steadier and able to mask any pain coursing through him, straightened to full height. His hand rested on his holster, but he hesitated, locking eyes with Roxey's gun. "Put it down, Ma'am," he commanded, his voice gravelly but firm. "Whatever this is, it's over."

Roxey laughed, a sound so cold and brittle it felt like ice cracking underfoot. "Over?" she mocked. "It's not *over*. It can't be." She turned to face Claire, her eyes gleaming with twisted pride. "They can't leave me. We're a family."

Tayla stepped forward, surprising everyone with her eagerness to disobey the woman she once held to such a high standard. Her voice was steady, yet edged with a courage that seemed to ripple through the group. "But, we're not your family. You don't own us, Roxey. Family is supposed to be loving, not controlling." Roxey's eyes narrowed. "How can you say that? Clearly, we have some more learning to do." She adjusted her aim toward her, positioning a single finger on the trigger.

Chapter Twelve

The second Roxey's finger flexed to pull the trigger, Sergeant McLaren didn't hesitate and lunged at her. He grabbed Roxey's wrist, forcing the gun upward. The weapon discharged with a deafening bang that sent everyone scattering, but the bullet embedded harmlessly in the ceiling.

Roxey let out a furious growl, thrashing against his body but it was no use, he had a tight grip on her this time.

Claire's eyes met Emerald's, and they silently agreed: now was their chance. Guiding the others, they sprinted for the door, pulling each other along as Roxey wrestled with the cop.

Before they could make it out, Roxey broke free with a vicious manoeuvre, sending her subduer crashing against the wall beside the door, half his body blocking their path. Her fury was like a storm, unfocused and wild. As she raised the gun again, her hands shook, her composure cracking. But the cop was resilient, kicking his legs out to trip her, sending her face first into the end of the bed and tackling her onto the floor. She threw her elbow out, cracking him in the ribs, climbing on top of him as she fought to pin him to the ground.

Claire hesitated in the doorway. Should she stop to defend the man who'd just saved their lives? Guilt gnawed at her, but she knew she had to go. He was clearly doing his utmost to protect them. She couldn't turn back to help, could she? The cop's head turned involuntarily as Roxey kneed him in the face. For just a moment, his gorgeous eyes met Claire's, and she felt compelled to do something to help him.

Darting back into the room, she ripped one of the top dresser drawers out of its socket and swung it at

Roxey, collecting the back of her neck. It was enough to stun her momentarily, allowing McLaren to flip himself over and get on his feet. Claire absorbed his grateful expression for a split second, tossing the drawer onto the ground before shouting to the other girls, "Go, run!"

Adrenaline propelling them forward, no one seemed to take notice of Roxey's voice chasing the girls as they thundered down the hallway. A threat Claire was sure would come back to haunt them.

"You will never get to live your life without me!"

It felt like they'd been running for a lifetime when they finally stumbled into the field of a small, easy to miss caravan park down by Seagull Sand beach just as the sun was going down. They stopped to catch their breath.

"Well, that's just great," Katalyna moaned. "We're back to square one with less time. No money, nowhere safe to stay for the night."

Serenah took a deep breath and smiled, gesturing to the block of cabins in front of them. "It's alright, girls, we can stay here,"

"The cop took away our source of money," Tayla reminded her, clutching her side.

Serenah grinned, pulling a brown leather wallet from her jacket pocket. "Sergeant McLaren's contributions," she quipped, holding it up. "I slipped it when I gave him the woman's purse."

Tayla's eyes widened, and then laughter spilled out of her, an unrestrained, almost giddy sound. "Ree, you legend! Guess he's footing the bill tonight."

Claire, on the other hand, rolled her eyes. "Fantastic. So, the cop will be banging on our door the second you check us in."

Serenah's lips curled into a wicked smile as she gestured toward a sign by the front gates.

Claire read the bold inscription aloud. "All charges processed at checkout."

"See," Serenah said with a shrug. "He can't track us if they don't run the card until we leave."

Claire couldn't help but smile. Maybe, just maybe, they'd finally get a moment to breathe. With Tayla's tracker gone, Roxey subdued and the cop thrown off their trail, they might even be able to get a good night's sleep.

The group pooled around Serenah as she fished out a flashy looking credit card, and after a quick glance between them, she headed to the administration cabin. Minutes later, they were checked in, keys in hand, and safely holed up in two adjacent rooms across a larger sized cabin. In the dim glow of the modest beachside cabin, the women finally exhaled, releasing breaths they'd been holding all day.

The place was nothing fancy: mismatched curtains, faded wallpaper, and a buzzing neon sign outside casting a faint light through the window. There were two bedrooms per room, each with two small single beds, which was somehow comforting and made it feel like home. Positioned in the centre of the room was a lumpy grey couch, which could also be turned into a bed. Emerald and Serenah quickly made use of it, folding it out and sprawling their bodies out to watch the TV. For them, it was heaven.

"Least it's better than the last motel, I suppose." Tayla whispered, clutching her arms nervously as she slid down beside them.

The shower water was mildly hot, each of them taking turns to rinse away the grime and tension of the past few hours—or years, for that matter. Unfortunately, it was too late in the evening to duck out to a local retail store to source new clothes, so they redressed into the same clothes off their backs again.

Bonnie, hungry again and still set in her ways of providing the food, had the sense to order room service.

Not just any food, a hearty meal consisting of everything they weren't allowed to have on the ship, the kind they had only dreamed of. Plates of burgers, fries, chicken wings, and pizza were soon spread out over the lumpy fold out bed like a king's feast. They all sat together and tore into it, relishing each bite, savouring every flavour.

"This is surreal," Claire murmured between bites, her gaze drifting to the TV, where a silly comedy sitcom about six friends in New York was playing. She found herself laughing freely, something she couldn't remember doing in ages. Each laugh seemed to chip away the weight she'd carried for so long. It was an amazing feeling to be free, as scary as the outside world was.

As they all relaxed, Tayla curled up on the bed, a soft smile on her face. "You know," she said, glancing around, "for the first time...I feel like we're actually safe."

Katalyna smiled and Claire could see in her eyes how happy she was as she stroked Josie's hair, who was curled up in her lap chewing a slice of pizza.

The room went quiet, each of them taking in Tayla's words as they exchanged glances. They could hardly believe it themselves.

"Anyone else hoping that cop managed to take Roxey down?" Emerald posed.

"I reckon so," Bonnie nodded, swallowing a whole chip accidentally. She coughed, nearly choking. "You were right, Em. We should have gone to the cops as soon as we got back to the island."

Serenah scoffed. "Again, do you have any idea how stupid we would have sounded? The only reason the cop got involved was because he was still hanging around when she pulled the gun on us. He saw what she was going to do to us. Could you imagine us stumbling into the station and whining that we've been held captive for x amount of years on a boat?"

A few confused glances were exchanged, and Emerald was the only one to respond. "How does that sound stupid?"

Serenah sat forward, frowning. "Seriously?" She pulled herself onto her knees and altered her voice, mimicking an overly girlish voice as she waved her arms in a dramatic skit. "Oh, please help us, Officers. We've just escaped our deranged kidnapper. She took us, one by one and held us captive out on the ocean, locking us in a cage every time she did a supply run so we couldn't leave. You have to find her and arrest her for torturing us, and also the murders we can't prove she committed."

Emerald's face flushed and she shrank down as Serenah's act ceased, saying nothing.

"See how completely crazy that sounds, moron? Ain't no one believing a story like that." Serenah sighed, plopping back into place on the couch mattress.

"My, you're an angry little bee," Bonnie calmly pointed out to Serenah, folding her arms. She crossed the room, comforting Emerald by patting her on the shoulder.

Like a never-ending nightmare, a knock echoed through the door, jolting them all. Most of them shrank into as small of a ball as possible, but Serenah immediately sprang into action, gesturing for silence. She crept to the peephole, squinting through it. "It's him," she whispered, her voice laced in disbelief. "That Sergeant McLaren dude."

A mix of relief and wariness filled the room. Claire crossed to the door, taking a steadying breath before opening it just a crack. There he stood, his face shadowed but unmistakably concerned.

"Am I right to come in?" he asked, his tone far more harrowing than it had been during their earlier encounter.

Claire nodded, stepping out of the doorframe so he could enter the room. He took a moment to look around, observing the girls' nervous manner. "Before I get questioned over how I found you," he held his hand up to silence Serenah, "I asked the local hotels and motels to cross check all incoming check-ins for my card details. This place pinged me back when they processed your paperwork. While I'm not thrilled about you running off with my wallet," his lips curved into a faint smirk, "I'll let it slide—this time. It's clear the woman you're running from is…unhinged. Care to tell me who she is to you?"

When no one answered, he extended a hand, brows raised. "Without you touching me, I'll have my wallet back now, thanks."

Serenah bit back a snide grin, pulling his wallet out of her pocket and tossing it to him. He caught it easily, his expression shifting from mild amusement to a sobering intensity as he tucked it away, glancing once more over the girls and taking in the nervous atmosphere of the room. "Look, if it makes you feel any better, we've arrested her. She's being detained in the holding cell at the police station."

Claire lifted her chin, locking eyes with him for the first time since his arrival. "For real? That's amazing!"

Sergeant McLaren glanced at Claire thoughtfully, as if weighing what he was about to say. "Yeah," he admitted, crossing his arms. "But since I took her in, she has been completely unco-operative. Won't give us her name—aside from 'Roxey'—and won't allow her fingerprints to be taken. I've had to prepare a court request to get them. Just waiting for my boss to sign off on it before I can submit the paperwork.

"In the meantime, I pulled some footage from the hotel lobby over at the Coconut Palm. Ran her face through our databases, expecting in combination with the name 'Roxey' I'd get a hit. It's unique, and this is a smallish island, right? Figured maybe she'd escaped from a mental health facility or something with how she spoke and acted. But...nothing. Not a single match under that name with that face."

Claire looked up at him, feeling a pit form in her stomach. "No match? So...you're saying she's using a fake name?"

He gave a half nod. "Perhaps, but mostly at this stage, it just means she's not in our system for any criminal offences. I was sorta hoping you could help me, though. What's her last name?"

Claire shuddered as his question unearthed a flood of memories. *Claire Jenson.* She could see it in written form, scrawled in shaky handwriting over and over on the assignments Roxey had forced her to complete during her "schooling years." Finally, she replied. "Jenson. She always told me it was Jenson."

Sergeant McLaren reached for his phone and hit a few buttons as he murmured to himself. "Let's see if we can find any trace of you now." His voice turned professional as someone on the other end answered his call. "Yeah, Mack, I need you to run a search on a 'Roxey Jenson—"

"Roxette," Claire interrupted quickly.

"Roxette Jenson," the cop reiterated, "Yeah, that woman in holding. Attach her picture and run it through *all* databases, including missing persons. Do a general search in births, deaths and marriages too."

A moment passed as they waited, the silence deepening the pit in Claire's gut. She could feel the tension creeping into her shoulders, her fists clenched at her sides. Finally, when he received a response, the Sergeant replied, "Are you sure?"

Claire leaned in, curious.

"Definitely," the voice on the other line said. "It's a negative on that name, Henry. No records match a Roxette Jenson at all."

"Definitely," the voice on the other line said. "It's a negative on that name, Henry. No records match a Roxette Jenson at all."

Chapter Thirteen

The girls exchanged wary looks. Serenah's brow furrowed as she watched the cop, waiting for his reaction. He let out a sigh, rubbing the back of his neck as he absorbed the news.

"So, we're dealing with a smart cookie," he murmured. "She didn't even steal an identity, she's just using a fake name altogether. Bugger."

Claire's heart raced as she tried to wrap her head around the situation. "What does this mean for us?" she asked, her voice small.

The cop stared into her eyes, his expression firm. "It means you need to tell me why you're running from her in the first place. I can't really do anything unless you help me. Please fill me in on what's happened to you girls. I'd sure appreciate the insight after wrestling her like an alligator for you."

Serenah shot Claire a look, raising her eyebrows playfully before she stretched back out on the bed beside Tayla, Emerald, and Daphne, who's attention had shifted and were once again absorbed in the sitcom playing on the motel TV.

"I guess it's only fair to give you something to work with, considering you might actually be able to help," Claire replied with a grateful smile.

Like a true gentleman, the cop gestured toward the small table by the window, pulling out a seat for Claire. Once she was sitting comfortably, he took the seat opposite her and leaned forward, placing his elbow on the tabletop and resting his chin on his palm.

Claire decided to start at the very beginning, recounting her earliest memories from the moment she was kidnapped. She described the years spent under Roxey's control, the details she knew of how the other girls were taken throughout the years, and the constant fear they had lived in. By the time she'd finished, McLaren looked slightly pale, clearly shaken.

"I'm...I'm just going to send a quick message to McKenzie," he said, his voice steadying as he reached for his phone.

"McKenzie?" Claire asked, tilting her head.

"Mack. My partner," he explained. "Before the rest of the staff clock off tonight, I'll ensure the duty officer watching the holding cell knows to keep a very close eye on Roxey."

"I don't want to break up this tense little moment, but I'm going to put Josie to bed," Katalyna said, giving a gentle nod toward the little girl who was rubbing her eyes.

Claire felt as though she were purposely indicating she wanted the policeman to leave.

"Aw, do we have to, mummy?" Josie whined.

Katalyna patted her shoulder. "Yeah, baby. It's getting late and we've had a big day."

Josie pouted. "When we wake up, do we have to go back to the bad home on the boat again?"

Claire watched Katalyna's expression drop, disheartenment overwhelming her. She didn't answer, simply shaking her head instead and began to steer her little one away from the television.

"Wait up, I'm wiped," Bonnie chimed in. "I'll take the bed next to yours and Josie's, Kat."

With a chorus of "goodnight," the three of them slipped through the double doors in the centre of the room, heading into the identical cabin next door. Claire could hear Bonnie reassuring Josie that when they woke up, they'd still be in the big world.

As the door clicked shut, Sergeant McLaren turned to Claire with a sympathetic expression. "Sheesh, see, I knew there was something unusual about this...case. I guess I'm glad I did start running background checks on her. Honestly, I can't wrap my head around it—everything you've all been through. You're incredibly brave for standing up to her." He paused, leaning closer toward Claire.

"This is really your first time on land since you were six? And Josie…she was born on the boat? Has really never seen anything on land before now?"

Claire nodded, unable to prevent a girlish giggle from escaping her lips as she watched the cop's awe. "Wait, so, you believe me then? Believe us?" She quickly flicked a triumphant smile toward Serenah, smirking as though she'd won some kind of contest.

He pulled his jaw closed and nodded slowly, placing a flat hand on the table next to Claire's. "Claire, you don't have to convince me. I believe what I can see. And I saw how she treated you, saw the look in her eyes." He waited until her eyes eventually met his again, then added, "and the fear in yours. You can't fake that."

Serenah, who had been quietly listening nearby, stepped forward, her arms crossed. "Okay, great. So now that you're up to speed, Mr Law Dude, what's the plan? What happens next?"

He gave a reassuring nod, once again ignoring her attitude. "Now, we should proceed with caution. And I guess I'll try to find her real identity. Maybe she's got a record she's trying to hide." He shifted his focus back to Claire. "Don't worry, as long as we have her in custody, I'll do everything I can to make sure she stays there."

He stood up, preparing to head out. "I'll let you all get some rest. Tomorrow, I'll do everything I can to see what the next steps are for you girls. Especially sorting out some appropriate accommodation, since I've paid for tonight out of my own pocket." He glared specifically at Serenah, then smiled at Claire. "Right then. Just…stay here until I find out what your options are, okay?"

He opened the front door, hesitated, and looked back with a reassuring nod. "I'll be in touch if I have any updates for you."

Once he'd left, the rest of group settled into beds, exhaustion finally catching up with them after the whirlwind of the day's events. Claire lay awake for a while, listening to the quiet breathing of Tayla, who'd chosen the bed next to hers out of habit, the stillness of the room comforting after the turmoil of the past twenty-four hours.

Just as she started to drift off, Claire heard something topple over in the main room, sending a wave of panic through her. She sat up, swallowing nervously, and listened intently. The muffled sound of something being moved made her hold her breath. She eased out of bed, every bone in her body stiff as she crept toward the noise.

Squinting through the darkness, Claire reached for a nearby table lamp, unplugging it in one swift motion to hold it up as a weapon. Determined not to wake the others, she tiptoed into the living room area, careful not to bump the girls sleeping on the fold out bed. Moonlight shone through the gaps in the curtains, revealing Daphne's tightly curled deep brown locks as she bent over the kitchenette counter cleaning up a spilled sugar jar.

Claire sighed loudly with relief, and Daphne almost jumped out of her skin, whirling around in panic. "Just me!" Claire whispered quickly, lowering the lamp. "Are you ok?"

Daphne's shoulders relaxed, and she offered a sheepish smile, holding up the jar. "Couldn't sleep so I was gonna make some tea. Want one?"

Claire smiled and nodded. If Daphne was finally offering an olive branch, how could she refuse?

A few minutes later, the two sat quietly at the couch by the window, steaming mugs in hand. The silence between them was companionable, but tainted by unspoken thoughts. Finally, Claire broke it, her voice hesitant but curious. "Alright, what's your story, Daph? Over the years, everyone's shared snippets of their lives pre-Roxey. Their memories. But you've never said a word. How come?"

Daphne's face didn't shift much, like she'd been expecting the question. She stared into her tea for a moment before answering. "Because my life didn't really change," she said quietly. "Guess there wasn't much to tell."

The words hung in the air, and Claire thought back to Daphne's comment at the first motel they'd run to. She'd been running from someone. And a realisation struck her. "You were being controlled before, weren't you?" Claire asked softly.

Daphne's eyes welled with tears, and she nodded, her voice trembling as she spoke. "My boyfriend, Logan…ugh, he started off amazing. He was eighteen years older, a devoted single dad to a daughter who was only about five years younger than me. I believed he was the real deal, you know?" Her brows furrowed deeply as she relived her pain.

"Turns out, he was an abusive dick. The week I was meant to meet his daughter; she took off and never came back. He was furious and took all his shit out on me. Once he started, it never stopped. But he always spoilt me, showered me with gifts after he…after he hurt me. I stayed for nearly a year, but eventually I couldn't take it anymore. I was on the run from him when Roxey approached me. Stayed in that little Seawitch Motel the night before. I honestly thought I was gonna get my life back. Buy a boat and flee. But, well, you know the rest."

Claire's emotions mixed with anger and sorrow. Daphne had been so close to freedom just a few years ago, only to be trapped in an even worse way. It explained so much about her quiet despair.

"Wow, I'm so sorry," she murmured. "Thank you for confiding in me, Daph. I understand your silence now. And I promise you, this time, you'll get your freedom."

Daphne offered a faint, tearful smile, and they fell into a thoughtful silence. The weight of shared pain hung between them, but now, it felt like a bridge instead of a barrier.

When Claire finished her tea, she was beyond exhausted. She stood, placing her mug on the counter. "Night, Daph."

Daphne nodded, her expression one of quiet gratitude. "Goodnight, Claire."

The next morning, a soft knock at the door stirred most of the girls from their restless sleep. Emerald, who'd slept on the fold-out bed with Daphne and Serenah, peeked through the curtains and gave Daphne a small nod. Daphne opened it to find an administration staff member standing there, holding a small, elegant box of chocolates tied with a gold ribbon.

"With compliments for your stay here," the young lady said with a smile, placing the box on the table by the window before leaving.

Daphne gave a nonchalant shrug and moved to shut the door, but Serenah caught it just before it closed, her eyes sparkling mischievously as she glanced at a neighbouring room. She gestured, pointing out their door had been left ajar by an exiting housekeeper.

"Back in a flash," she whispered as she slipped outside. "I want to grab a fresh credit card so we can all get some new clothes."

Claire raised a brow and opened her mouth, but said nothing, too groggy to argue.

Inside their cabin, Daphne untied the ribbon on the chocolate box, the sleek bow slipping to the floor. "Hmm, fancy," she muttered, plucking a heart shaped piece from the assortment. She unwrapped it hastily and popped it into her mouth, chewing slowly as the rich, velvety flavour melted on her tongue.

But within seconds, her expression changed, confusion quickly shifting to alarm. Her body stiffened and her hands flew up to grab at her throat as she managed to gasp, "You guys…" Her voice was rasping, barely audible, as panic lit her eyes.

Before Claire had time to react, Daphne suddenly collapsed, her body vibrating uncontrollably. Foamy saliva started bubbled from her mouth as she went into a seizure, her limbs jerking violently. Panic surged through the room.

Claire rushed to Daphne's side, her heart racing. "Daphne! Oh my god, someone—call an ambulance!" she yelled, her voice shaking as she tried to steady Daphne's head to prevent her from injuring herself.

Bonnie scrambled for the phone on the end table beside the couch, dialling emergency services as Katalyna held a half-asleep Josie close, shielding her face from the frightening sight.

Serenah burst back into the room, her expression morphing from confusion to horror as she took in the scene. "What happened?" she demanded, rushing toward them.

Claire glanced at the box of chocolates, a sick realisation dawning on her. "Serenah. Daphne ate one of the chocolates. I think…I think they were filled with poison."

Chapter Fourteen

It was over in less than two minutes. Daphne's convulsions ceased as she slipped away during the vicious seizure, her body quickly becoming limp in Claire's arms. The tension in the room mounted as the girls fell into an eerie, suffocating silence. Then reality crashed down.

Claire reeled with disbelief as she stared at Daphne's still form, her unblinking eyes frozen open in terror. She pulled her arm out from beneath Daphne's body and cradled her face in her hands, sobbing uncontrollably whilst foamy saliva dripped down her wrists.

With a deep, shuddering breath, Claire forced herself to stand up. Her legs weak beneath her, she stumbled to the landline phone on the end table. Her hands trembled as she fumbled in her jeans pocket for the business card Sergeant McLaren had given her, dialling his number shakily. As the line rang, she fought to control her sobs, using her free hand to wipe her face.

When he finally picked up, she choked out the words, "Sergeant, something's happened… Daphne… she…there were these chocolates. I think they were full of poison. The ambulance is already coming, but she just…she's already gone."

For a moment, there was silence on the other end of the line. Then the cop's voice came through, sharp and urgent. "Stay where you are. I'm on my way. Don't touch anything, Claire. Do you hear me? Nothing."

Within the hour, a team of investigators flooded the room. They moved methodically, the forensic crew examining the box of chocolates and dusting for fingerprints once the medics had carefully placed Daphne's body on a stretcher. Claire recounted the details of the event to not just one, but two different cops as they assessed the scene. Neither of them as kind, open minded or accepting as McLaren had been.

The rest of the girls huddled together in shock, trying to process the horror of what had just unfolded. Josie clung to Katalyna, shaking as her mother whispered reassurances, though her own voice cracked with an element of fear.

After speaking with his colleagues outside, a uniformed Sergeant McLaren entered the room on arrival, his face grim. He motioned for Claire to step aside, lowering his voice. "Claire, I need to tell you something. Roxey…she was released first thing this morning."

Claire felt the blood drain from her face. "Released?" she hissed. "Why? How?"

He sighed, running a hand through his hair, the frustration etched into his features. "The Commander didn't exactly tell me, but from what I overheard, I think she's claiming she was arrested under false pretences. But it seems like there's more to it than that. All I know is, he acknowledged her like an old friend, interviewed her privately, then let her go." His jaw tightened as Claire's mouth hung open.

"What's even weirder is, the gun she was carrying? It's gone. Missing from the holding cell evidence locker. Like she never had a firearm at all. It vanished overnight, had already disappeared by the time the Commander got in."

Claire's mind reeled. "Vanished?" she repeated, barely able to comprehend the weight of what he was saying.

He nodded grimly. "I got curious and reviewed the footage from the caravan park beside the Seawitch Motel. Their cameras point right at the entry. Since the Seawitch doesn't have its own surveillance, I thought if I could at least show him she entered with a gun I could prove it existed, and that her intentions were certainly not false. No such luck. Their cameras went through a "technical fault" earlier in the evening and recorded nothing, so there's no proof of anything really."

Claire's fists clenched tightly, her nails biting into her palms. "So, what?" she spat, her voice cracking with anger. "You're saying you can't help us? That you think your boss is dirty or something? You just…wait until she strikes again? Until another one of us…" Her voice trailed off, the weight of the situation settling heavily over her.

Sergeant McLaren looked pained. "Claire, I understand how this sounds. Believe me, I'm as frustrated as you are. But legally, I'm boxed in. And while I admit, something doesn't seem right, I don't think the Commander is corrupt if that's what you mean. He just insists there's been no crime, so I can't hold her. According to him, she's done nothing wrong."

"Nothing wrong?" Claire's voice rose, her frustration boiling over. "She killed my parents, destroyed our lives, and now Daphne's dead because of her!"

"I understand," McLaren said, his voice softer but no less frustrated.

Claire's outburst had caused several of the police officers to look over, and Sergeant McLaren flashed them a fake smile before whispering through gritted teeth. "But where's your proof? I spoke to the reception staff here and they don't deliver chocolates, complimentary or otherwise, even if dropped off to reception and asked to. Therefore, I have no idea who she conned into bringing them to you. But again, the cameras here—the ones that might've shown the chocolates being delivered? They were shut off half an hour before you called me. Complete blackout."

Claire's anger began to shift into cold, hard fear. "So, she's free to come after us. Again. And you're telling me there's nothing you can do about it?" Her expression was biting, her fury directed at the helplessness of the situation rather than the man in front of her.

The invested cop stepped closer; his voice low but firm, like he was trying not to be overheard by the other cops. "Claire, I'm not giving up. She's not as smart as she thinks she is. I'll find a way to catch her out. Something's not right about this situation at all. But at the moment, she's got me by the balls. There isn't a shred of evidence that will tie her to Daphne's death, and I reckon she knows it. We can't pin this on her."

Claire sighed. "Okay…Daphne's incident aside, what if we go down to the cop shop ourselves? Can't *we* tell your boss all about her and how she kidnapped us?"

He grimaced. "Look, even if you girls came down to the station right now to make a claim, if she's clever enough to know how to counter there's no case. For example, there's no way to prove you and the others didn't willingly choose to live with her on the boat if that's what she throws back. See what I mean? If I were in your position, I'd be gathering solid evidence against her first. Especially since the boss seems to know something about her that we don't."

Serenah stepped forward, her voice steady but sassy. "Perfect, she's gonna keep toying with us now."

Claire felt her stomach drop. "Oh god, she really is," she said. "She knows I poisoned Rumble with chocolate. That's why she did this, it was payback. I wonder if he died."

The girls exchanged glances. "She knows she can't get us to go back to the ship, so she's gonna just kill us all off now," Bonnie remarked, making her way into the discussion.

"One by one," Tayla added, before bursting into dramatised tears.

Emerald wiped a tear from the corner of her own eye, quietly stating, "Well if we're screwed anyway, we might as well just go home then, right? Our actual one."

Sergeant McLaren's solemn expression froze on his face as he watched the girls slowly break. "Look, I suggest you get a move on. But no, I don't recommend going home. Let's just…keep other people out of the danger circle for now. Two streets over, there's a short-stay women's shelter. They offer three days free of charge with meals provided, no paperwork needed. You should be fairly safe there. In the meantime, I'm going to go back to the station and speak with my Commander again. See what I can do for you, or what I can find out."

"Thanks," Claire muttered, holding back tears.

After the police team had finally completed their work and taken Daphne away, the group made their way to the suggested women's shelter. The atmosphere was comforting, but with the weight of Daphne's loss hanging heavily over them, no one felt safe. They were given a simple breakfast, though few had much of an appetite. Claire pushed her cereal back and forth with a spoon, her mind running through the events since getting back to land. She wondered if she'd do anything differently, had she known what was going to happen.

After a long, dull day and an even longer sleepless night, Sergeant McLaren entered the shelter early the following morning, his expression a mixture of concern and relief. Gesturing for the group to follow him to a lounge area, he took a seat across from Claire and the others, pausing as if to prepare them for what he was about to say.

"Here's the thing, I spoke with my boss," he said. "I asked him to keep an open mind and relayed everything you told me this time."

"And?" Claire asked eagerly.

"I've been instructed to drop it. He says it's under control and none of my business anymore."

He paused a moment, looking around at the displeased faces of the group, a genuinely apologetic expression plastered across his features. "Naturally, his attitude only made me want to look into it more. Something about his dismissal seems off. He won't investigate her, nor allow me to. Now, it might not be useful yet, but I found some information," he continued, keeping his voice low. "I ran her picture through the newspaper archives and her face turned up a match from a 1995 article. According to this, Roxey's real name is Rose Johnson."

A murmur rippled through the group as the officer continued, pulling a printed copy of his findings from of his jacket pocket and placing the photo on the coffee table in front of him.

"Rose was married to a police officer named Chris…uh, something or other. I didn't pay much attention to him, sorry. Anyway, he was found guilty and imprisoned after he allegedly murdered their two infants—from back-to-back pregnancies—and blamed it on SIDS both times." He took a breath, as if to process the awfulness of it himself. "The case caused a major scandal, and Rose disappeared from the public eye not long after her husband was convicted. No one's seen or heard from her since."

The room fell silent, each of the girls absorbing this dark piece of Roxey's past. Claire exchanged glances with the others, a shared look of concern forming between them.

Emerald sat quietly, her eyes downcast as she whispered, "I don't understand, does finding this article somehow help you stop her from coming for us? I'm done with this limbo, I wanna go home now. I just want to see my parents and start getting on with my life."

The girls went silent, everyone in full agreement with her words. For those who had family out there waiting, the longing to see them again and get back to their old lives was something they all shared, but had been pushed down in the chaos.

Serenah stood abruptly, shooting Emerald a look that was both fierce and sympathetic. "We all want that, Emerald," she said, her voice full of attitude. "But we knew before we left that we'd have to stay together until Roxey was off our back. Splitting up now would be a huge mistake."

Sergeant McLaren nodded, reinforcing Serenah's words. "She's right. Look, I can't tell you what to do, but if it were me…well, Roxey has made it clear that she'll do anything to stay in control. If you go home, it's likely she'll follow you. She'd know that's your end goal."

Tayla's face paled as she processed his words. "Wait… are you saying that if we go back home *ever*, we'd be putting our families in danger too?"

McLaren studied her face, his expression sombre. "That's pretty much the gist at the moment, unfortunately. I have no doubt she'd hurt your families if it meant staying in the driver seat. But it won't be forever. I just need a bit more time to find something damning on her. Figure out what's going on, what the Commander won't tell me. In the meantime, if you'll each give me your full name, I think it's best if I make contact for you. I'll check in and call your families to explain what's happened. At least keeping them informed will help keep them safe. And I'm sure they'd want to know that you're alive and what really happened to you all these years."

Serenah shrugged as McLaren pulled out a notepad and looked up, ready to write. "Serenah Leif," she sighed. "Doubt my parents even noticed I was missing, considering how they threw me out. But let me know how they react, I guess."

He nodded, staying professional as he jotted it down. He turned to the next person.

"Emerald Locke. Could you tell my parents… I've missed them?" Her voice wavered.

McLaren gave a comforting nod and turned to Katalyna.

"Katalyna Belford. To save yourself some time, you can skip my call, hon—no one will be looking for me. My parents won't give a damn where I've been." Her casual nonchalance didn't mask the resignation beneath it.

Josie glanced at her, a hint of sadness in her eyes. "What about your brother, Mummy," she asked inquisitively.

Katalyna raised her eyebrows, confusion creeping across her face.

"Brother?" Claire asked, surprised. She had always been under the impression Katalyna was an only child, as she had said so herself many times.

"How did you know I had a brother, baby?" Katalyna asked Josie.

"You've talked about him before, in your sleep," she replied with a shrug.

Katalyna looked around at the curious faces staring at her, waiting for her to explain. "My brother's a loser, I just pretend he doesn't exist," she said firmly. "I wouldn't have wanted him to know Josie even if I did get to raise her on the island. He's been charged with domestic violence more than once." She nodded at the cop, reiterating firmly, "I don't want him contacted, thanks."

The information about Katalyna's family washed over the group like an uncomfortable tidal wave, no one wanting to say anything on the matter.

Claire felt a chill wash over her. Family trauma could cause some serious damage. "You guys…," she found herself speaking out loud without realising, "this life Roxey built with us, this 'family' as she always called it… do you reckon it was, like, trauma related because she'd lost her own?"

The cop nodded slowly, flicking a glance at each of the girls. There were a few nods, but no one answered.

Venturing a comforting response, McLaren said, "Huh. I didn't even think of it like that, but yeah. Makes sense I suppose. Sounds like she's been harbouring a lot of anger and resentment toward the world."

Moving past the tension, Bonnie chimed in next, her gesture full of angst. "Bonnie Acklind. I hadn't spoken to my family for months before I 'took the job' last year." She made air quotes with her fingers, her sarcasm intended to hide her resentment. "I was too busy to go see them…"

Tayla didn't wait for Bonnie to finish speaking, nor to be asked and launched into a long story about her father, the renowned dentist, along with three pages worth of notes for McLaren to pass on, making him chuckle as he jotted everything down.

Finally, he turned to Claire. "I… I don't know my real last name," she murmured.

He paused, surprised. "You don't remember it?"

Claire frowned, searching her brain for the thousandth time over the years. "No, I really don't. I guess she made sure I'd forget it. I'm sorry, I know that doesn't help, does it? But, I mean, my parents are dead anyway. I'm not sure who you'd be calling."

McLaren looked into her eyes, a deeply sympathetic stare. "You never know, you might have an aunt or a grandparent out there who's missed you terribly."

Claire nodded, eyes glistening with the tears she refused to let fall. "Maybe. But honestly, you'd be better off putting the extra time into finding out which of their parents sent that note to Roxey. It'd be nice to know who gave us the inspiration to escape her, you know."

Sergeant McLaren stood up and flicked his notebook closed, tucking it away along with the printed article. "Will do. But please, let me know if you remember your last name. It'll make it easier to find your parents' murder case. I'd like to have a look at those files. Could be something useful in there that didn't mean anything back then but does now." He nodded, more to himself than anyone else and turned to leave. "I'll be in touch."

Like someone had stuck a knife in her suddenly, Bonnie blurted, "Hang on a sec! You said she was married to a cop named Chris, right?"

He thought about it for a second, then said curiously, "Yeah. Why's that?"

Bonnie's eyes widened, piecing things together in her own mind as everyone waited, intrigued. "Was his name Christopher Isaac by any chance?"

McLaren's eyebrows shot up as he pulled the article back out of his pocket, scanning the printed information carefully. "Ah yes, that was it. How did you know that?" he asked.

Bonnie explained, hesitation in her voice. "When I was a kid, my parents talked a lot about Chris going to jail. They swore he was innocent. We even went to visit him once in there, when I was about twelve. He's…he's my cousin."

Chapter Fifteen

As Bonnie's revelation hung in the air, the room plunged into an uneasy silence. The group's shock was almost palpable, with each of them trying to piece together what this connection meant, not just for Bonnie, but for all of them.

Finally, Sergeant McLaren cleared his throat, cutting through the stillness. "Alright then," he said, "Er, I'll get in touch with your families. I'm sorry there's not much else I can do for you at this point. I can only recommend laying low and only going out in pairs at minimum, if you have to at all." He paused, lazily pointing a finger and adding, "and one more thing, don't eat anything you didn't order."

As he made to leave again, Katalyna stopped him. "Wait a sec," she remarked. "I'm still not sure what we're supposed to do in the meantime, hon. You're warning our families to be careful, fine. And I think we all agree that we're grateful you're trying to help us, despite being told to butt out," she gestured to the group with an open palm, only continuing once everyone else had nodded in agreement. "But what's the plan for stopping Roxey from coming after us?"

The cop turned, seemingly anxious about the question. "I don't know what to tell you. There's no way I can, really. All I can do is dig into Rox—Rose Johnson's past. I have to figure out where she's been in the twenty-three years since this article. The trail doesn't end there. We know a few of those years include her kidnapping you girls, but I need evidence. Someone out there knows something I can use to build a case against her to take this further. At the moment, that's all I've got. You're on your own for now, I'm sorry."

Once the door closed behind him, Serenah turned to Bonnie. "Don't you think it's strange that your cousin was *married* to Roxey? Sorry, *Rose?*"

Bonnie nodded slowly, her expression haunted. "To be honest, what's stranger is thinking of her being human enough to marry. Let alone have had babies."

"It's weird, isn't it?" Tayla added. "To imagine her having a life before all… this."

"I kind of feel sorry for her," Katalyna admitted, immediately drawing stunned looks from the others. "No, not like *actually* sorry," she clarified, raising her hands defensively. "I just mean…losing her children like that? Having the one person you trust—your husband—take your little babies' lives? That would destroy anyone. No wonder she turned into a monster."

Serenah shot to her feet, shaking her head. "No. Sorry, but no. Whatever she went through doesn't excuse what she's done to us. I don't care about her past. There's no justification for the hell she's put us through."

Katalyna shrugged, her voice quieter now. "I'm not saying it excuses her. I'm just saying I get how family betrayal can ruin someone. As the little sister who idolised him, it destroyed my mental health for a while when I found out Logan was convicted for abusing his girlfriends…" Her voice trailed off.

"Logan?" Claire asked, her head snapping up.

"Yeah. My brother," Katalyna said slowly, giving a small nod.

Claire exhaled slowly. "Oh my god." Memories swirled as she mulled it over—Daphne's confession, the details in Roxey's journal. Her hands trembled as the pieces began to fall into place. "Logan's girlfriend, Daphne," she whispered, almost to herself, getting louder the more times she rephrased her revelation. "Daphne's boyfriend, Logan. Logan's sister Katalyna."

Katalyna frowned. "Huh?"

Claire stood up, reeling. "Katalyna! Last night," she said, her voice growing more urgent, "Daphne told me about the man she was dating before Roxey took her. How he used to…hurt her. That's why she never opened up to us. She went from one nightmare to another trying to escape him. Look, I never told you guys, but Roxey kept a journal—" Claire's voice broke for a moment before she pressed on. "It had notes about us. About our lives, our pasts. Daphne's boyfriend…his name was Logan. I think it's the same guy, your brother. She said he was way older. There's no way it can be that much of a coincidence."

Katalyna's eyes widened in shock, her mouth opening to respond, but no words came. "Another connection between us…" Katalyna finally murmured. "Does anyone else here know Logan Belford?"

The girls shook their heads, looking between each other curiously.

"What about Christopher Isacc? Anyone else related to him?" Bonnie asked.

Again, everyone shook their heads.

"I don't know," Katalyna said slowly. "It's weird, but maybe it is just one of those things. We were all taken from the island, after all."

Claire nodded, but felt uneasy. Something about the connections just felt like an unsolved puzzle.

Serenah looked annoyed. "Claire, why didn't you tell us about Roxey's journal? Better yet, why didn't you tell the cop? You realise that's basically a written confession, right?"

Claire was taken aback, realising her mistake. "I'm sorry, you're right. Honestly, since we left the ship, I pretty much forgot about it until now. It didn't even occur to me to bring it up!"

Emerald leaned in, ready to defend Claire. "It's a great concept and all, to use it against her, but there's one problem. You'd have to go get it. Who knows where she's moved the boat to, for starters. And I don't know about you, but I'm not going out of my way to find her or her ship. We go back to get that journal, we won't be getting off again."

"Ugh, she's right," Bonnie said. "And we can't send the cops, they would need a warrant to search her things, which they won't get unless McLaren can prove to his boss she's dirty first."

"So…what now?" Serenah asked with a shrug. "I sure can't just sit here and wait for the naïve cop to tell us what to do next. You heard him, we're on our own. 'Specially since it sounds like Roxey is paying off the big boss or something. We've only got one more night's accommodation in this place, and it's not like we've got backup cash. We need to survive while McLaren digs up something on Roxey. If he can. That means finding actual work and getting paid."

Bonnie leaned back, tucking a strand of her pink fringe behind her ear. "Okay, so we split up, leave in pairs and grab whatever cash jobs we can find. It could take ages for the cop to get back to us. I agree, we have to live in the meantime."

Tayla nodded thoughtfully. "Hey, do you reckon I should try the beachside café I used to work at? If I can get them to take me on, it's a start."

Serenah perked up. "Yep, and I'm going to see if the strip club will take me back. Now that I'm an adult, maybe they won't toss me out this time. Even without ID." She smirked. "Besides, I know the ropes there, and it's quick, easy money."

One by one, the women exchanged ideas and hopes, realising this was the first time they were free to make choices of their own.

Until Katalyna's voice draped over them like a wet blanket, dampening their fire. "Hang on, girls. You can't just go back to your old jobs. Don't you think Roxey will be expecting that? If she's hot on our tail, she'll start looking for us at places she knows we'd go. It's no different to staying away from family for now."

A murmur of agreement rippled through the room. Serenah frowned, but conceded. "I suppose you've got a point. Maybe we rethink that plan. Oooh, okay, what if a group of us go down to the strip club? I reckon we'd be safe. They don't care about real names, and disguises are part of the gig anyway."

Katalyna's irritation flared. "Can we not discuss *that* job further? Little ears," she said, nodding toward Josie, who was sitting nearby drawing on a piece of newspaper with crayons. "Honestly, honey, you and your bloody strip club. I just don't think it's a good idea."

Before the conversation could spiral into an argument, Claire raised her voice. "Alright, new plan. We go looking for simple cash jobs, no business's that require names or identification of any kind *and* we don't go to anywhere familiar. Think pamphlet delivery or meal runner. Agreed?"

The group exchanged glances and nodded. For now, it was a plan. An imperfect strategy, but better than nothing.

They left the shelter together as one large group, but quickly split up in pairs, heading in different directions. Claire and Emerald wandered along the closest boardwalk, the salty breeze of the ocean tangling their hair. Though her mind churned with the day's events, Claire battled herself to stay focused. Her goal was simple: find a newspaper stand or one of the vendors she'd seen so often from afar. There were always people giving away samples or handing out flyers near the sand, and she hoped one might pay her a few dollars to lend a hand. Back when Roxey occasionally brought the ship close enough to shore, Claire had observed them at a distance and yearned to see what all the beachgoers were so excited about at the market.

As Claire and Emerald strolled along, Claire felt a strange pull, like she was being drawn to a memory just out of reach. She embraced it, slipping off her shoes and carrying them as the warm breeze whipped around her. The sensation of the wind in her hair was familiar, but the act of freely walking along a beautiful beachside with her toes in the sand was entirely new, almost surreal. The girls passed a row of vendor stands, where bargain hunters haggled over trinkets at a bustling weekend market.

Gradually, the noise faded as they moved toward a quieter stretch of the beach, flanked by houses. That's when Claire saw it. The house stood out immediately—a weathered beach cottage, its aged charm mismatched against the sleek modern beachfront homes on either side.

The sight of it stopped Claire in her tracks. Something about its weatherworn facade stirred a memory, elusive and incomplete, like a dream she couldn't quite remember. "Do you… recognise that house?" she asked, grabbing Emerald's shoulder to halt her.

Emerald squinted, shaking her head. "Not really," she said, mild confusion clouding her voice. "Why? Does it mean something to you?"

Claire didn't answer. She was already moving, her curiosity too strong to resist.

They approached cautiously, and Claire immediately observed the way the backyard sloped, leading to an eerily familiar garden at the bottom. Her memories stirred, knitting together fragments of her past, and suddenly, she was sure. This was it. This was where she'd lived with her parents the night Roxey had come for her.

The house appeared abandoned, its windows dark and lifeless, but Claire didn't care if someone lived there now. She ran an open palm along the back fence, remembering ducking under it as she ran away, all those years ago. Looking up, her eyes locked onto the neighbouring house. She couldn't remember anything about the people who lived there, but if anyone had witnessed what happened that night, they were the only ones with a chance. Perhaps they could give her some information, useful or not. Maybe they had seen something in the lead up to her kidnapping that could tie Roxey to the scene, no matter what she called herself at the time.

Swallowing her nerves, she moseyed over to the house on the left and knocked on the door. When the door creaked open, an older woman appeared with a smile, but her expression shifted quickly. Eyes widening as they settled on Claire, she brought a hand to her mouth in surprise.

"Hello there," the woman whispered, "goodness, you look so much like her."

"Like… who?" Claire's voice was barely audible, caught between fear and a fragile thread of hope.

The woman seemed lost in thought for a moment, her gaze distant. "The little girl who used to live next door, years ago. Sweetest child."

Claire's pulse quickened. "Little girl? Sorry to bother you, but do you remember anything about her or her parents? Did they have relatives that visited? Anything at all you can tell me about that family?" The questions tumbled out in a rush, her desperation overriding her manners.

The woman furrowed her brows thoughtfully, then shook her head. "Not really. They kept to themselves, especially in those last months before… well, before the murders." She sighed, her eyes shadowed. "It was all over the news. Terrible thing."

Claire was amazed. Itching for confirmation, she asked softly. "Yes, horrible. The little girl's name, do you remember it?"

The woman smiled softly, a fondness in her eyes. "Yes. Claire. I believe it was Claire."

A tear escaped the corner of Claire's eye and she wiped it away quickly. She struggled to steady her voice. "Do you remember anything else about them? Their last name, maybe?"

The woman nodded, her eyes lighting up with recognition. "Of course. Gordan. David and Amara Gordan."

David and Amara. The names lit up in Claire's mind like a lightbulb, and it felt right. Like a puzzle piece slotting into place.

"They were kind, quiet folks. I used to go to the same church they did. Well, I still go there. The church is where their daughter was found, you know."

Claire snapped back into focus like a rubber band. "Found?" The word felt heavy, as though it carried the weight of her entire past.

"Yes," the old lady nodded, "Oh, the Gordan couple adopted her without hesitation when the pastor discovered her."

Claire's mouth hung open. "Discovered her? You're talking about Claire? *Claire* was adopted by the Gordan's?"

"That's right," the woman said gently.

A second tear escaped the corner of Claire's eye, but this time she let it fall. She held onto the moment, letting herself imagine—just for a second—a world where she'd grown up with her adoptive parents, surrounded by love, not fear. In a weird way, knowing that she had been adopted made her love her parents more. They'd chosen her. And loved her so much that they'd died trying to protect her.

"What about the murderer?" Claire asked, burning for more answers now. "Were there ever any leads on her?"

The woman frowned.

"Sorry, dear, I don't understand?"

Claire paused, observing the woman's genuine confusion. "The woman who killed David and Amara Gordan," she asked, her voice tightening as her throat constricted. "Did the police ever have a suspect?"

The old lady blinked, her expression shifting. "No, no. There wasn't any murderer, dear. It was a family tragedy."

Claire tilted her head. "What do you mean?"

"It was Amara Gordan who turned on them," the woman said softly, her voice laden with sorrow. "She killed her husband and their sweet daughter before taking her own life. The police never even found Claire's body."

Chapter Sixteen

"No! What? You're…you must be wrong!" Claire spat, the words leaving her mouth harsher than she intended.

The old lady recoiled, her eyes widening as she leaned back, acting as though Claire had struck her. Emerald's hand rested on Claire's shoulder, the gentle pressure both grounding and guiding her. Emerald subtly nodded toward the woman, as though silently urging Claire to apologise.

Claire swallowed hard, guilt tangling with her simmering anger. "I'm sorry," she murmured, her voice strained. The apology felt hollow, tainted by the hopelessness roiling within her. How could Roxey have orchestrated such a web of lies? Not only managing to frame her mother for her father's murder, but Claire's too. It seemed Roxey had created the perfect way to ensure Claire disappeared off the face of the earth so no one would have known to come looking for her.

"Thank you for everything," Claire managed, extending a trembling hand to the woman before turning abruptly back down the path. Her heart pounded as she strode away, her head reeling. The name rang in her ears—*Claire Gordan*. It was the first time she had a last name that felt like it belonged to her, yet it still wasn't the name she'd been born with. Even so, it felt like a thread connecting her to a life Roxey couldn't erase.

Emerald caught up with her, panting. "Wow, so how do you feel knowing you were adopted," she asked with a cheeky smile. "And, why exactly are we rushing off?"

"It doesn't feel real," Claire admitted, stopping abruptly to face Emerald. "But I think it's a bigger deal than you realise, Emmy. For starters, I actually have a name. My family's name, not hers. Now I have something to give to the cop. I'm sure he can open up their murder investigation again with new evidence. Maybe he might be able to find something—*anything*—on Roxey. We might even be able to tie her to their murder now. Who knows, maybe the Gordan's knew her before she did what she did to them. There's gotta be some reason she went after them; no way it was a random attack. Think about it, she didn't kill anyone else's parents."

"I'm so happy for you, Claire. Really." Emerald hesitated, her voice laced with scepticism. "But let's be real for a second. What new evidence? The cop can use your name to look up their murder like he wanted to, sure, but we know Roxey's smart. We know she obviously wasn't caught for your parents' murders, so her name isn't going to magically pop up in their case file now. Us learning your history surely wouldn't give us a shortcut to convicting her, would it?" She folded her arms. "Though I must admit, I never thought about how weird it was until now that she only murdered your parents and took you so much younger than everyone else."

"Exactly," Claire muttered, swallowing the knot of frustration in her throat. "Somehow, I feel like there's a new strand of hope to cling to or something. I mean, we just found out she had my mother framed for killing me. It has to mean something, to change the whole case if I prove I'm alive, right? *I'm* the evidence."

Emerald nodded. "Yeah, alright. You may have a point. It could at least give us a backing to throw kidnapping claims at her. I still don't think it will mean much if they don't have a clue she was involved though."

Claire smiled weakly. "Mmm. Is it weird that suddenly I don't even care what happens now? I mean, I want her to pay for what she's done of course, but right now, it's not as high up on the importance scale as it used to be. Everything just changed for me, Em.

"Whether we can have Roxey charged or not, you have no idea what it means to me knowing I have a biological family out there somewhere. Maybe I can be reunited with them when this is over, like the rest of you guys. Even if…"

She took a shaky breath. "Even if my birth mother did give me up. Don't you think any mother would want to know their child didn't get to grow up in the loving home she envisioned? I don't know what I want more, to see Roxey in prison or meet my parents."

Emerald gave her a sidelong glance, as if she were unsure what to say, but Claire didn't need her sympathy, or her negativity as her face more clearly projected.

A shiver crept up Claire's spine. She turned slightly, her eyes narrowing as she scanned their surroundings. Someone was watching them. Over Emerald's shoulder, she spotted a man standing at a distance, partially hidden behind a palm tree. A sense of déjà vu overwhelmed her, and she squinted trying to prove to herself that it wasn't the same person who'd been staring at her in front of the bakery. But it was.

The man stood tall and broad-shouldered, his crisp navy shirt and black slacks suggesting a professional disposition. This time, he approached with cautious steps, his face unreadable under the brim of his fedora. Claire's instincts screamed at her to turn and bolt, but her feet remained rooted to the ground. Emerald shifted, grabbing onto Claire's arm, her posture defensive as the man stopped a few feet away, raising flat hands in a gesture of peace.

"Hi," he began, his deep voice calm but impersonal. "Sorry, I hope I didn't startle you. Please allow me to officially introduce myself. I'm McKenzie Adams. Er, from the police station. I work with Sergeant McLaren. He asked me to keep an eye on you. I just…wanted to see you…see that you're alright."

Claire blinked, momentarily thrown off by the name and the deep voice that came with it. She could have sworn McKenzie was a woman, perhaps someone warmer and chirpier from the snippet of the voice she'd heard coming through the phone. Narrowing her eyes as she tried to reconcile his towering figure with the person she had pictured in her head, she crossed her arms, her body taut with suspicion.

"I…uh. I saw you across the street at the bakery," she said. "Before we met your partner. How do we know you're not just a hired hand of Roxey's, sent to bring us more poison?"

Emerald shot Claire a surprised glance but remained silent. The man frowned and, mindful of their unease, reached slowly into his back pocket to produce a badge. He held it out for them to inspect, the polished silver glinting in the sunlight. There was no photo attached, but the name was accurate to his introduction. As he lowered his arm again, Claire caught a strong whiff of cigarette smoke and sandalwood, a combination that oddly enough, she felt like she knew.

"I understand your hesitation," he said calmly, his attempt at portraying a professional attitude fluctuating the more he spoke. "But this is the *first* time you've seen me. I know you've been through a lot. But I think we can work together to get this bitch, yeah? McLaren seems to know what he's doing."

The girls exchanged a glance, and he rushed to continue. "Er, I mean, we're all on the same team but he's good at his job. I want to see Roxey pay for what she's done to you. Where are you girls staying at the moment? McLaren's busy for the rest of the day, but I'd like to stop in and gain some insight of my own so I can help put this case together."

Claire's eyes narrowed further. Something about his demeanour felt uneasy—a little too eager, a little too convenient. She studied him, unable to figure out why he looked so familiar. She was sure he was the same person who'd been staring at her outside the bakery. But even then, there was something else about him she couldn't quite place. His eyes…they were so dark, a rich brown so deep they almost appeared black. She knew those eyes from somewhere. But where else would she have seen him?

Shaking herself free from the trance she was being sucked into, she decided it was time to leave. "Look, uh, thanks for checking in, but I reckon we should probably get back to the others. I'm sure if you go back to the station, Sergeant McLaren would be able to give you the information he's already compiled. Including where we're staying."

As she turned to leave, Claire found herself surprised he didn't try to stop them. Instead, he nodded and stepped back, reinforcing the idea that he may have been genuine about being one of the good guys. But as they walked away, his voice rang out, asking them to wait. He caught up quickly, handing Claire a similar business card to McLaren's.

"Claire, one way or another, I'm going to hunt Roxey down and make her pay for what she's done to you. If you run into trouble and McLaren isn't available, call me."

Without another word, they watched him walk off, his steps almost mechanical as he disappeared down the boardwalk. It almost seemed as though he was heading toward Claire's old neighbour's house.

Claire studied the card, trying not to question his strange behaviour. An additional phone number was scrawled beneath the crossed-out printed one.

"Yeah, was it just me, or did he give off an extra suspicious vibe?" Emerald breathed as the girls began to head back toward the road.

"Oh, thank God. I thought I was the only one who felt that way." Claire exhaled, her pulse still racing. "I don't know about you, but I'm thinking screw getting a cashy today, I just wanna go back to the shelter where we're safe and not out in the open anymore. We still have tomorrow."

Emerald nodded, and the two quickened their pace, weaving through the streets until they reached the safety of the women's shelter.

They slipped back inside the dining hall, realising they'd just missed lunch, as there were staff clearing the tables. Claire groaned quietly, as did her stomach. Serenah was waiting near the back, her posture tense but hopeful. Claire didn't recognise her initially, seeing the others first, as she wore a long, straight black wig that fell over her shoulders and halfway down her back, framing her face in a way that altered her appearance altogether. She caught their eyes and managed a small smile, beckoning them over.

"I know it was against the rules or whatever, but you can't be mad cause I got us a pretty penny," Serenah said in a low voice as they approached, pulling a crumpled stack of bills from her bra. "Did a trial shift. Cash in hand from all the nightshift workers who come in for the breakfast buffet after work. We're set for a couple of days at least, can get out of this shelter and get a hotel room again. Paid for without stolen cards to trace. Bossman said I can come back tonight if I like. You can make a week's worth of income doing a full night shift, so we'll be sweet."

She reached up and tugged off the wig, fluffing out her natural beachy waves. "Oh, and don't worry, managements changed again so new owners and no one I knew on staff."

Following a surge of initial irritation, relief washed over Claire. "Serenah, that's amazing. Thank you." She hadn't realised how anxious she'd been over needing money until she saw it laid out on the table in front of her.

"Yeah, isn't it fricking fabulous, huh," Katalyna cut in, rolling her eyes. She was clearly not happy Serenah had gone against the group's agreement not to return anywhere familiar. "Sure, we'll be able to pay cash at a hotel tonight with your sweaty boob money."

She stepped closer to Serenah, narrowing her eyes into a threatening glare. "But honey, I sure hope Roxey isn't staking out our old jobs, expecting exactly what you've just done. You'd wanna hope you weren't followed."

They stared at each other for a minute, until Claire interrupted. "Sooo, I found out my folks, the ones Roxey murdered were actually my adoptive parents. That's interesting, huh?"

The room fell into an attentive silence as Claire recounted everything she and Emerald had learned about her pre-Roxey life whilst out, including retelling their unsettling encounter with McKenzie Adams.

Bonnie's expression turned grim when Claire passed her the business card he'd provided. "Claire, you need to call McLaren. Tell him everything. I'm sure he'd be able to do something with that information, but more importantly—" Her eyes narrowed as she flipped the card between her fingers. "I don't think Adams was a real cop. McLaren didn't mention anything about sending someone to check up on you today."

Serenah's hand shot out like a snapping turtle, yanking the card from between Bonnie's fingers. "Yeah, look at this. Why is the printed number scribbled out?" She held it up, her eyes scanning the alteration like it was going to move. "That's a redirected call if I've ever seen one."

Claire knew they were right, but as she pulled out McLaren's business card once more, she hesitated.

"What's the matter?" Katalyna asked gently, watching her pause.

Claire bit her lip. "I don't know. Don't you think he'll get annoyed if I call him again? He's already helping us under the radar…I just don't want to push our luck."

Emerald shook her head with certainty. "Nah, he'd definitely want to be in the loop with this. Besides, she's dragging his name through the mud. Seems to me like he'd want more ammunition."

"Absolutely," Bonnie agreed. "If this shady stranger works for Roxey, maybe *he* knows something about her that we can use to incriminate her ass."

Claire smiled, her friends' reassurances giving her courage. Nodding, she asked the hostel staff if she could borrow the phone at the front desk. With a deep breath, she punched in the numbers. A simple action that was still so foreign to her. She wasn't sure what she was expecting Sergeant McLaren to say, but still managed to be taken by surprise.

"Er, Claire, McKenzie Adams *is* a woman. I don't know who approached you at the beach, but they sure aren't who they said they were. Mack reported her badge as stolen this morning."

Claire felt as though she might throw up, and signalled for Emerald to come over to the phone. She jogged over and put her ear up to the receiver beside Claire's.

"Look, I think we need to address this as a threat," McLaren continued. "My instinct tells me he's someone Roxey knows who's trying to gain information on your whereabouts."

Claire's heart sank as she listened to him let out a frustrated sigh.

"Just, wait there, okay?" he said. "I'll sort something out and be there soon. I have a solution."

Claire nodded, then realised he couldn't see her. "Sure. I'm sorry if I'm being a pain."

"It's not you," he said simply, and the line went silent.

Something about Sergeant McLaren's arrival made Claire feel safer. Like a suit of armour had suddenly been slipped over the walls of the shelter. "Sorry it took me a little longer than expected to get here," he said as she led him in. "I, er, had to have a meeting with the boss."

She nodded and gestured toward the complimentary coffee cart in the lounge. "Coffee?"

"Love one," he replied, walking with her.

Claire noticed his eyes darting between his watch and beeper like they were about to go off. As she prepared the coffee with the provided pod machine, Claire watched him check the devices at least four times. "Look, if we're causing trouble for you, please don't go out of your way to help us."

He waved her off. "Nah, please, this is one of the reasons I love what I do. It's just, this whole case is unique, too big city crazy for such a small island. That's why my Commander thinks it's farfetched or something, I guess. He doesn't want it leaked to the press, that's for sure." Not wanting to meet his eyes, Claire looked down. "Look, are you sure he's not being paid off by Roxey or something?" she mumbled.

He shook his head without hesitation. "No way. There has to be something else going on…probably none of my business." He glared at the wall in silence, as though he were deep in thought. "Nah, I'm more inclined to believe he already has an open investigation on her, thus the hush surrounding the subject. I mean, he did ask me to file a report on what you girls had told me. But when I told him I had a lead on the person who nabbed Mack's badge, he had to let me come pursue that first."

Claire handed him a full paper cup with a hesitant smile. "Well…thanks for your help in the process. It's nice to know there's at least one person outside our little circle who's willing to believe in the crazy and follow this thing through."

He took a long, savouring sip of coffee, like he'd been parched for hours. "You're not crazy, Claire. But she might be. That's why I want to keep looking into it for you." Claire smiled and started mixing a cup for herself when Josie came flying over.

"Aunty Claire!" she bellowed, throwing her arms around Claire's waist and almost sending her toppling. "Mummy said to ask, can you please make me a hot chocolate?"

Claire chuckled and hugged the little girl back. "Aw, of course I can, sweetie."

Once she'd fulfilled Josie's request, sending her back to the group with extra marshmallows, she turned back to a smiling McLaren. "So, what's this solution for finding out if Roxey has a hire trying to find our location?"

He lowered the cup, his eyes twinkling. "Easy. You give him a call and tell him to meet you here. I'll wait behind the door with a pair of handcuffs at the ready. After we deal with him, I have a few things to tell you ladies, too."

It didn't take long after Claire called the shady guy for him to show up, leaving Claire to wonder if he'd been far away from their location at all. When the knock came, Claire opened the door, her pulse roaring in her ears as she invited him in. He looked over Claire's shoulder, observing the concern on the other girls' faces before carefully stepping over the threshold.

Before McLaren could step out from behind the door and surprise him, Serenah's sharp intake of breath broke the tension. Cocking her head in a mixture of shock and confusion, she wandered forward like she'd just seen a ghost.

"Is that you, Uncle Michael?"

Chapter Seventeen

The man who'd initially claimed to be McKenzie Adams blinked, his expression shifting to pure joy as his eyes locked with Serenah's. "Serenah... wow kiddo, is that really you? I..." He hesitated, his brows pulling together, as though struggling to reconcile his emotions. "I mean, of course it's you. Last time I saw you, you were practically a kid. And look at you now, a young woman. What's it been? Six years?"

Serenah nodded and surged forward, her body moving before she had fully processed the moment. Michael opened his arms, catching her in a warm, genuine embrace. When she pulled back, she blinked rapidly, swatting her hair out of her face to wipe away a stray tear. "Wait, is that why you were impersonating a cop? Were you...trying to find me?"

Michael's brows furrowed, his lips pressing into a thin line before he sighed. "I, well—yeah. Of course, I was trying to find you. I wanted to make sure you were safe." His voice was laced with a mixture of surprise and something else Claire couldn't quite place, making her feel a tad uneasy about his genuineness.

Near the door, Sergeant McLaren stood with arms crossed, exchanging a wary glance with Claire before stepping forward. "Michael, is it? Impersonating a police officer is a serious offense, Michael. I should arrest you right now."

Michael's posture stiffened, his jaw clicking as his expression hardened. "Serenah's my little sister's only daughter. She's been worried sick about her since she went missing. I had to make sure she was alright."

McLaren's eyes narrowed. "Uh huh...so why follow Claire and Emerald as a cop then? I'm failing to see how that was necessary."

Michael hesitated, shifting on his feet nervously. "Look, after repeatedly hearing the cops telling me there was nothing more they could do…well, a person can grow pretty tired of 'leaving it to them.' I kept looking for her obviously and it was like a miracle when I spotted her eating lunch at my favourite bakery. I saw this pair there with her. I didn't know if she'd remember me, so I knew I had to find a way to get close, help from the inside. I want to bring Roxey down."

McLaren's suspicion deepened. "Right. That's why you were so surprised to see her just now, huh? Given that you already saw her at the bakery and all? And how do you know who Roxey is?"

Michael pressed his lips together but didn't respond.

Serenah swallowed hard and stepped in front of her uncle before the rivalry between them escalated further. "Time out. There's no need for the third degree, he's telling the truth…I'm sure it's just—it's been so long. I know he means well."

McLaren exhaled through his nose, his stance relaxing slightly but still firm. "Fine. Hand over Mack's badge. I'm letting you off with a warning. But if you try anything like this again, there won't be leniency. Understood?"

Michael nodded stiffly, passing over the stolen ID badge to the cop whilst he spoke to Serenah. "You know your mother has missed you like crazy."

Sergeant McLaren moved forward. "Now that I can believe, considering she told me the same thing." Stepping around Michael to address the whole room, he announced, "Ladies, now that it's been brought up, you should know I've spoken to your families, like I said I would. Had each of them come down to the station actually. They were extremely grateful for the update.

Serenah, your parents were under the assumption that you'd run away to start your own life."

Michael nodded. Emerald inhaled sharply as McLaren turned to her. "Emerald, your parents were under the same impression. They presumed you buckled under pressure and skipped town. Your dad wanted me to tell you—"

Tayla cut in impatiently. "Me first. My dad, what did my dad say?"

McLaren hesitated before responding, his expression tinged with irritation. "Actually, your parents were the only ones who knew you were missing. But your father denied having sent that note to Roxey. They put out all the feelers they could at the time you disappeared, but the longer it went, the colder their leads became.

There was a missing person's case opened on you, but apparently it was dismissed after your aunt spotted you at a motel over the bridge. I'm guessing your parents just accepted that you'd moved to the city to start your own life."

Tayla frowned. "I don't have an aunt. My mother is an only child, and my father has two unmarried brothers."

McLaren pulled a strange expression and cleared his throat. "I wondered. Ah, and here's the thing. I showed Roxey's photo to all of your families. No one recognised her name, but when your father saw her photo, he did remember who she was. He knew her when she was Rose Isaac. His best friend's wife. He didn't suspect her involvement in your disappearance at all."

Tayla's face turned pale. "Wait, Chris Isacc…was my dad's best friend Chris?" she blurted as she turned to look at Bonnie. "Bon's cousin Chris?"

Bonnie's lips parted, shock flashing across her face. "I thought you said you didn't know him, Tayla?"

At first it seemed Tayla was too busy processing to speak, but then she remarked defensively, "I didn't know his last name, but I grew up knowing him as Uncle Chris. My mum's a nurse and she worked a lot of overnight shifts, so he'd stay over. Kept my dad company."

Bonnie shook her head, biting down on her lip as she exchanged a sly glance with Katalyna. "Anyway...," she said casually after a few moments, "anyone else getting the feeling that Roxey knew about the connections between us? Knew who we were before taking us? Seems too much of a coincidence now..."

Katalyna nodded slowly. "Usually I'd say no, but it feels... intentional. Like she chose each of us for a reason."

Claire watched the exchange, her pulse pounding as the conversation swirled around her. She edged closer to McLaren, beginning her own discussion. "Sergeant McLaren, I need to tell you something."

He met her eyes with a warm glow. "Henry," he corrected gently.

Claire blinked. "Sorry?" she asked, puzzled.

"Well, we'll be dealing with each other a lot, so a first name basis is in order now, yes? Call me Henry." He smiled.

A flicker of warmth spread through Claire's chest, and despite everything, she returned his smile. "Right. Henry. Anyway, I hope it's not too much to ask now, but you know how I couldn't remember my last name? Well, I know it now. I just learned I'm Claire Gordan." She recounted her earlier encounter with her childhood home's neighbour whilst Henry listened intently.

When she finished, she inhaled deeply. "I know it's not a lot to go on," she finished, "but I'm hoping you might be able to turn up some more information from my parents' murder. Maybe we'll get lucky and find something new or useful about Roxey's past, especially if she's slipped up by faking my death." He smiled. "That's brilliant, Claire. I'm sure we can do something useful with that information."

Out of the corner of her eye, Claire observed Michael standing and conversing with Serenah and the others. Even so, he was watching her. A pit formed in her gut, and she turned her back to Henry.

Henry considered her rigid behaviour change and frowned, his gaze shifting past her and landing on Michael. "Do you want me to run a background check on him too?" He asked, raising an eyebrow. "I mean, I get he's Serenah's uncle but I get the feeling he's hiding something."

Claire exhaled slowly. "Good idea," she nodded.

"You'll be alright now then?" he added.

She nodded again, offering a small smile. "Um, yeah, Serenah got a cash job and made some money, so we have a little bit of genuine cash now. We're going to leave the shelter and get a proper hotel room again."

He nodded slowly. "Good. That's good. When you're settled, give me a call from a nearby payphone to let me know where you're staying. I'm going to head back to the station. Gotta get back to work." He gave Claire a cheeky wink. "But don't worry, I'll also start the next round of digging up dirt. I just have to speak with Emerald first."

He glanced over Claire's shoulder, locating Emerald and sidestepped Claire to approach her. "Sorry to interrupt, but could I talk to you for a moment, Emerald."

She didn't move and indicated with her hands that he was free to speak.

He glanced at the others, but obeyed her request. "When I told him it may still be a while before he could see you, your father asked me to pass on a message."

She appeared apprehensive, but intrigued.

"Ah, there's no easy way to say this, and I'm sorry to have to tell you, but Elena, your mother… she passed away."

Claire watched as Emerald practically crumbled. "What? No. That's impossible. It's only been two years… I've only been gone two years! She wasn't even sick."

Claire could see Henry's genuine heartbreak as he observed Emerald's pain. His expression filled with genuine sorrow. "Apparently, she was. Brain cancer. Because of the tumour's location, well, it was inoperable. I'm so sorry."

Emerald's hands shot to her face, pressing her cheeks with her palms. When Katalyna offered a hug, Emerald collapsed into her arms, sobbing uncontrollably. Claire and Bonnie joined, enveloping her in a protective embrace as her grief echoed through the room.

"I'll leave you to grieve. Call me if you find out any new information." Henry tipped his head, gave Emerald a fleeting look of sympathy, and exited the shelter.

"I think I should get going too," Michael said awkwardly. "Now that I know you're being taken care of and all. The number on the bottom of the card I gave you is obviously *my* phone number. Let me know if you girls need help, a place to stay, anything at all."

The group remained silent, but Serenah asked, "You sure you won't stay a while? We've got loads of catching up to do."

He shook his head. "In light of your friend's news, I think it's best if I leave you to it for now, at least. But I'm still here for you if you'd prefer an unpaid roof over your head."

Serenah hugged him briefly. "It's best we keep away from family at the moment, less collateral and all that."

Before he left, he cast one last pining look at Claire, then shut the door behind him with a friendly nod.

"Come on girls, we've got to get a move on now," Tayla urged, not seeming to care too much about Emerald's loss. "Ugh, shouldn't we be checking into a new hotel by now. Maybe somewhere with a pool or at least a TV. There's nothing to do here, I'm bored."

Katalyna shot her the dirtiest look and Tayla scrunched up her nose in return.

Emerald looked up, scowling, but it was Josie who spoke before she did, pointing out a very firm index finger. "That's very rude Tayla. You have to be nice when someone dies." Then Josie patted Emerald on the arm and wrapped her arms around her waist.

Teary eyed, Emerald still managed a smile as she played with Josie's ginger locks. "Too right, Jojo. Look, you guys can leave if you want, but I'm not going."

Claire rubbed her shoulder. "It's okay, no rush. We don't have to leave here just yet."

But Emerald shook her head. "No, you don't understand. I'm not going with you at all. I want to go home. My dad...I need to see him."

Bonnie stepped forward, her voice gentle. "Emerald, it's not safe yet. The only thing we have going for us at the moment is the safety of a hidden location. She'd definitely know where you used to live."

Emerald's eyes filled with tears again. "It doesn't matter. I can't keep running, I need to go home, I have to see my dad. Even if it's just once."

Serenah pursed her lips, folding her arms in disapproval. "I literally just told my uncle we weren't staying with family, for the sake of all involved, and now that's exactly what you wanna go and do?"

Katalyna spoke softly with a supportive backbone to her words. "Em, she's probably been waiting for one of us to go home. Roxey—"

"Ugh, I don't care!" Emerald screamed, throwing her hands up. "I'm so sick of Roxey this, Roxey that. Roxey can go and jump off a frickin' bridge! I'm not playing this game anymore. We got off the damn boat so we could go home, right? So we could take *back* our lives? Even if she does come to dad's, tracks us down, she can't take us all on, right? Strength in numbers. It has to be different out here or we may as well have just stayed put."

Katalyna exchanged a glance with Claire, who exchanged a glance with Serenah, who briefly sought non-verbal opinions from Tayla and Bonnie before shrugging. "I actually agree with her. It could take months, or even years to build a case on the bitch. We gotta get back to normal eventually."

Claire nodded reluctantly. "Here we go. Come on, we'll take you home together, Em. Together. Safety in numbers."

Once Emerald was feeling more settled, the group thanked the shelter staff for their hospitality and, after using an island directory to locate the house, made the tense trip to Emerald's family home. It was nestled on a quiet, picture-perfect suburban street on the outskirts of the city on the other side of the island. Far away from the tourist hustle and bustle of the beaches, thankfully.

Emerald lingered on the porch, her hand hovering over the doorbell. The others hung back, exchanging nervous glances, each one feeling the weight of the moment. Claire was anxious to see how Emerald's father would react to her sudden arrival, after being told he couldn't see her. As Emerald pressed down on the doorbell, Claire felt a deep ache in her heart, a bittersweet longing swelling in her chest. She couldn't help but wish she was the one in Emerald's position, standing on the brink of reunion with her long-lost parent.

Footsteps echoed from inside the house and Claire could see Emerald's body tense up, bracing for the moment. The door swung open, and the good-looking man in his mid-forties who answered blinked, momentarily bewildered as he scanned the group before his eyes finally settled on the young woman before him.

His face transformed from confusion to disbelief, his voice cracking as he whispered, "Emmie?"

Emerald nodded, her lips quivering, and before she could speak, he lunged forward, sweeping her into a powerful embrace. She broke down, sobbing into his shoulder as he clung to her, his own eyes welling with tears.

A few moments later, once the initial shock began to subside, Emerald's father gently pulled back, his eyes studying her face with a mixture of wonder and grief. "It's uncanny," he murmured, "you've hardly changed, yet you look so much more like your mother now that you're older."

Emerald smiled, her cheeks filling in with a pinkish glow.

Turning to the rest of the group, he offered a welcoming gesture toward the house. "You must be the rest of this woman's 'victims.' Joshua Locke, pleased to meet you." He held out his palm, warmly shaking each of the women's hands politely. "Please, come in. I'm sure I've got some juice in the fridge or cookies somewhere in the cupboard." He looked down at Josie, smiling.

"Oh, that's alright, sir," Claire said, shaking her head. "We don't want to impose. Just wanted to make sure Emerald got home safely."

He smiled. "Nonsense, you're perfectly welcome." He turned around with a pip in his step, but the moment he stepped over the threshold, was met with a frying pan to the face. A sharp, sickening crack rang out as Joshua staggered, crumpling to his knees with a heavy thud. Clutching his head, he looked up at his attacker in a daze. "Sarah?" he asked, his voice strangled and heavy with confusion as he collapsed entirely, passing out on the floor.

The group gasped, frozen in place as Roxey emerged from the shadows just inside the house, her face twisted in a cruel snarl. She dropped the pan with a clatter and pulled out a grey handgun, her knuckles white around the grip as she pointed it at Emerald's father.
"I think you had all better come inside now," she hissed as she kicked the door open wider, gesturing for them to enter.

Chapter Eighteen

It seemed an eternity had passed before anyone moved, every second stretching unbearably as Roxey's hand hovered firmly in place. Finally, with a sharp gesture, she motioned them forward, her finger curling over the trigger. As they carefully slid past Roxey, one by one, Emerald's face reflected her mounting fear, her eyes darting to her father's slumped heap on the floor. The door slammed shut behind them, and Roxey leaned back against it, the sound reverberating like a death knell sealing their fate.

"How the hell did you know we came here?" Emerald squeaked, attempting to kneel to check on Joshua.

Roxey cleared her throat, tapping the nail of her index finger on the side of the gun as a non-verbal threat, forcing Emerald to rise.

"What are you going to do, Roxey?" Claire asked, sidestepping in front of Emerald protectively.

"That depends on what happens next, my girl," Roxey sneered through clenched teeth. "And Em, not that I have to explain myself to you, but since you asked…well, not so nicely, simple. I stuck a bug on one of daddy's beloved catalogue deliveries. Did it to all your families, in fact. He brought it inside, I listened and waited. When the cop called here, the second I heard ol' Joshy here say his wife was dead, I knew you'd be the first to end up back 'home.'" She smirked. "Even though mama made you feel like you weren't good enough, you still come running back for her memory. Isn't that oh so sweet?"

Emerald twitched, rage flickering in her eyes. "How dare you," she hissed, her voice fluctuating. Standing beside her, Bonnie's hand gripped Emerald's arm tightly, keeping her from lunging. But not from speaking. "You don't get to criticise my parents. You don't know the first thing about what home or family means, Roxey."

Roxey's smirk deepened. "Oh, sweet girl, I know *exactly* what it means. Home is a place where everyone knows their role, where no one dares step out of line. Where loyalty is everything and no one leaves." Her narrowed eyes flicked toward Joshua's unconscious form, and a shadow crossed her face. "Home is something your father here failed to provide. You don't need him."

Serenah's voice rose, defiant despite the tremor beneath it. "No, I'm pretty sure we don't need you."

Roxey's irritation flickered across her face. "Aw, now that's a bit harsh. You lot have absolutely no idea the pain you've caused me, do you?" She paused and her eyes swept over them, daring someone to answer.

Serenah braved a jab. "The pain *we've* caused *you*? Are you kidding? You kept us locked up like animals in the zoo of Roxey for years!"

Roxey's returned glare could have cut glass. "But were you not cared for?" she demanded, dangerously flexing her trigger finger. "We had a proper family system going. You don't just up and abandon family the way you girls left me."

Serenah let out a frustrated cry. "Ugh, again with the family line. It's bullshit, Roxey. Don't you get it yet? We don't want to live in isolation anymore or exist in a world ruled by your threats."

Roxey's face flushed a light shade of pink. Claire couldn't tell if she was embarrassed or annoyed. Until she spoke in a tone so harsh it made Claire's skin tighten. "I had to threaten you. Otherwise, none of you would have stayed with me, would you?"

"I don't get it, though. Why? Why did you need us to stay with you?" Tayla asked, her words coming out soft and shaky. "Is this some kind of game to you?"

Roxey said nothing, staring at Tayla with a heavily disappointed expression.

She lowered the gun ever so slightly, giving Claire a boost of courage. Maybe they could talk her down, defuse the bomb. "Why did you choose us to be your family, Roxey? To replace your lost babies?"

Roxey's head dipped. Not by much, but enough to soften her face into an expression resembling empathy. "I have my reasons," she said quietly. "One day you'll understand my darling daisy. Revenge is best when it's drawn out as long as possible. But now you've gone and thrown a spanner in the works, and I've had to make some adjustments. Nothing I can't work around, though."

"So…it is a game," Katalyna snapped, crossing her arms tightly as she shielded her daughter with her body. Her voice cracked with fury, and fear. "Is that why you murdered Daph with poison?" The accusation landed like a slap.

Roxey paused, studying each of the girls carefully. "Funny you mention murder," she said slowly, her lips twisting into a bitter smile. "You didn't seem to mind the idea when you poisoned my dog." She paused, glaring between every face in the group, each looking as remorseful as the next. "Yeah, I decided to go home to see if I could figure out how you lot managed to get off the ship undetected in the first place. Imagine my surprise when I discovered a very sick Rumble, barely clinging to life. Thankfully, I was able to get him to a vet in time. He's been hospitalised for monitoring, no thanks to you."

Claire felt a pang of guilt, sharp and bitter. She'd known it had to be done, but the weight of that choice still pressed on her. Gesturing as a sense of power came over her, she said, "I'm sorry about Rumble, I really am." Her voice remained firm despite the lump in her throat. "But enough was enough. You brought that on yourself by using him as a barrier." She studied the weapon in Roxey's hand, observing how it continued to move lower the longer the conversation flowed.

For a fleeting moment, Roxey's expression faultered, but it quickly hardened again. She reached into the pocket of her jeans, sliding out a pair of white gloves. "No matter," Roxey said perkily as she slipped them on. "Like I said, the plot has changed. I have a new plan now." She tensed her gun wielding hand, aiming it directly at Joshua's head.

"That's enough," Bonnie snapped, stepping forward. Her voice was calm but unyielding. "Roxey, you've lost the plot. Seriously, let's talk this through before you do something you can't take back."

Roxey's eyes narrowed, the gun twitching slightly in her grip. "Ha. Don't play peacemaker, Bonnie. We're long past that. You lot destroyed everything."

"Okay, sure, you're right," Bonnie admitted, swallowing a hint of sarcasm as she tried to help defuse Roxey. "But no matter what you do now, you need to understand we're never going to come back to that ship. We're done playing family with you. Hurt us, hurt our loved ones—it doesn't matter. It's over, Roxey. It's time to let us go."

"Foolish girl, I'm quite aware of that," Roxey murmured, retracting the weapon to talk with her hands. Claire watched her calculated movements and took a deep breath, preparing herself to leap forward and knock the gun from her hand.

"But guess what, it's never going to be over!" Roxey hissed. "I warned you there would be consequences for choosing to go down this path."

With a sudden, jerking motion, she lined the gun up with Joshua's head, her finger motioning to pull down on the trigger. But Emerald was already moving.

"No!" she lunged forward. The room exploded into chaos as Emerald and Roxey collided, the gun twisting wildly in Roxey's hand as Emerald tried to remove it from her grasp.

Claire rushed at the entwined battling women, hoping to aid in retrieving the gun. Her decision proved to be ill-timed. Just as she grabbed onto Roxey's arm, the wrestling pair thrashed sideways, throwing her into the floor lamp beside them. Unable to break her fall, Claire and the lamp toppled into the glass coffee table nearby, smashing the top surface on impact and driving her arm elbow first into the wreckage.

Claire winced in pain, pulling herself up and flicking the loose shards of glass from her forearms and wrists. She wiped the streams of blood across her pants, looking up just in time to see the other girls split up as they ran forward. Katalyna shoved Josie down behind a bulbous pot plant beside the front door and jogged over to help Claire up, whilst Bonnie headed the rest of the group, dashing toward Roxey and Emerald's brawl. Before anyone could do much more, a deafening shot rang out, echoing through the house like a thunderclap. Everything stopped.

Bonnie staggered back, her hands clutching her torso. Blood seeped through her fingers, staining her floral shirt crimson. Her legs buckled, and she collapsed, her face pale and her eyes glassed over.

Emerald screamed, frozen in place, her hand wrapped on top of the arm Roxey had used to pull the trigger. "Oh, no. Bonnie!"

Claire leapt over the broken table and dropped to her knees, pressing her hands against the wound in

Bonnie's stomach. "Shit. Stay with us! Please, stay with us!"

A soft moan from the corner broke through the mounting tension. The sound of the gunshot had stirred Joshua to consciousness; he weakly lifted his head and blinked in confusion.

Roxey, breathing heavily, flicked a glance between the injured Bonnie and the awakening Joshua. She looked down at the gun in her hand, and then, with a sneer, she tossed it onto the floor, sliding it right up to Joshua's feet. "Well, well," she snarled, "look who's finally awake. Let's see if daddy can figure out what not to do next." Roxey grabbed onto Emerald's arm, pulling her in front of her body like a hostage.

Joshua rubbed his face and groaned, his hand reaching instinctively for the gun.

"Dad, no!" Emerald shouted, but it was too late. His bare fingers closed around the handle.

Roxey forced a laugh. "Well done. Now, gunshots attract attention, don't they? I suspect the police will be here shortly." She slowly peeled off the pair of gloves she'd put on earlier, holding them up mockingly before shoving them in her pocket. "Pity your father just shot your friend in a tragic accident, hey Em?" Her voice dripped with malice as she backed toward the door, clutching Emerald tightly. "See, I had intended to shoot *him* and place the blame on you, Emerald, you know, destroying your life and forcing you to flee to avoid the law…but I suppose this will have to do for now."

"Get her," Bonnie whispered through gritted teeth, her hand weakly grasping Claire's arm. "Don't let her out of here."

Before anyone could move, the front door burst open with a thunderous crash, and Sergeant McLaren stormed in, his gun drawn and steady, aimed directly at

Roxey. His expression a mixture of determination and fury. "Roxey," he barked. "Stay where you are."

Roxey froze for a split second, her eyes narrowing as she sized him up. A slow, venomous smile spread across her face. "Well, if it isn't the *lawman*. Took you long enough," she sneered.

"Don't test me," Henry growled, his grip on the gun unwavering. "You aren't getting away this time."

"Is that so?" Roxey said girlishly, a bitter laugh escaping her lips. "And who's going to stop me? This mob of sheep and their lapdog cop? You have no idea what you've gotten yourself into." Her hand darted to her side, reaching for a blade concealed in her jacket. Without hesitation, McLaren fired, the crack of the gunshot splitting the air.

Chapter Nineteen

Roxey stumbled but didn't fall, the bullet only grazing her arm. With a snarl of pain, she spun on her heel, tossed the knife at a nearby glass window and bolted through the opening seconds after the glass shattered.

"Dammit!" McLaren hissed, lowering his weapon as he jogged toward the doorway.

"Wait, Henry, please don't leave!" Claire cried. "Bonnie's hurt. It's bad!"

McLaren hesitated, torn between his duty to pursue Roxey and the desperate plea in Claire's voice. His attention shifted to Bonnie, who was sprawled on the floor, her breathing shallow.

"No," Bonnie wheezed, her voice faint but steady, "don't let her get away. I'll be fine."

"Not without help, you won't," Claire said with exasperation, grabbing onto the nearest hand she could find. "Emerald, keep the pressure on her wound."

"Already doing it," Emerald said through clenched teeth, her hands slick with blood as she pressed firmly against Bonnie's skin. "But she needs a hospital. *Now.*"

McLaren pressed a few buttons on his phone and crouched beside Bonnie, his expression reflecting genuine concern. "Backup's coming. Don't worry, she'll get a ride to the hospital as quickly as physically possible." He glanced at Claire, placing a calming hand on her shoulder. "Can you handle it from here if I go after Roxey?"

Claire's jaw tightened, and she nodded as she looked around at the rest of the group. "We'll take care of Bonnie. You have to catch her."

McLaren turned to Bonnie, his expression softening. "Hang in there. You're a tough nut." Bonnie smiled faintly, and McLaren rose, bolting out the door whilst shouting into his radio. The room fell into a tense silence, broken only by Bonnie's laboured breaths and the muffled sound of sirens approaching in the distance.

"Claire," Emerald whispered, her voice barely holding together. "What if she doesn't make it?"

"She will," Claire replied despite the tremor in her hands as she adjusted the pressure on Bonnie's wound. "Bonnie's a fighter. She'll pull through."

Moments later, flashing red and blue lights illuminated the windows as the wail of sirens pierced the tense air. An ambulance screeched to a halt outside, and within seconds, paramedics rushed in, their faces calm but focused as they assessed Bonnie's condition.

Behind them, a woman entered wearing the same uniform McLaren did, yet hers was crisp & pristinely pressed. Claire didn't recognise her until she spoke to one of the paramedics, her voice revealing her to be the real McKenzie Adams. She was younger than Claire expected, maybe around Katalyna's age, and carried herself with rigid confidence as her pale green eyes zoned in on the chaos like a drill sergeant inspecting the barracks. She looked like the kind of woman who corrected grammar during a hostage situation.

"Your friend's lost a lot of blood," one of the medics informed the group as they carefully transferred Bonnie onto the stretcher. "We'll do everything we can."

"Ma'am," the formal female cop said, tapping Claire's shoulder with clipped formality. "I'm Constable Adams. I'll need you to give me a statement on what happened here, if you think you're up to it."

Claire nodded. "Just… give me a second. Please."

As Bonnie was wheeled past, her eyelids fluttered open briefly. "Be careful," she rasped, her hazy, pale blue eyes locking on Claire.

"We will," Claire promised, her voice cracking as she walked alongside her.

"Aunty Bonnie!" Josie's cry cut through the air like glass, her tiny legs pumping as she chased after the stretcher, tears streaming down her face. Turning to Katalyna, she pleaded frantically, "Can we go with her mummy? Please? You have to make sure she gets better!"

Katalyna stroked Josie's head, blinked back a tear and smiled. "Hang on a moment."

She waved the ambulance staff down before scooping Josie up and plopping her into the back of the van. She turned to the rest of the group, who'd gathered on the driveway to see Bonnie off, and said softly, "Jo's right. We'll go with her. Roxey won't risk showing up there. Too many people. We'll be safe."

Claire flashed her a half-smile and Katalyna climbed into the back of the van, taking a seat beside the bed. Claire caught a glimpse of her clutching Bonnie's hand before the medics slammed the doors shut. The van's flashing lights receded into the night, taking Katalyna, Josie and Bonnie away and the rest of the group lingered momentarily in a huddle, their faces pale and strained.

Inside, silence settled like dust. Joshua sank into a chair, wincing as he pressed a hand to the growing bruise on his temple where the frying pan had struck. Emerald sat beside him briefly, but, unable to contain her emotion, she began to rock back and forth and ultimately decided to get up.

"She needs to make it," Emerald muttered as she paced tight circles, her arms wrapped around herself like armour. "Bonnie can't—she just can't—"

"She'll be okay," Claire cut in, her voice steady but quiet. "Katalyna won't leave her side. If anyone can give her the strength to fight, it's her."

The stern constable reappeared beside Claire, with arched brows that barely concealed her impatience. She said nothing, but Claire knew what she wanted to ask.

"Yes, ok," Claire said. "What do you want to know?"

"Just start from the top, please. What happened here that led to a shot being fired? Who pulled the trigger? Give me your version."

Claire swallowed the lump in her throat and began to describe the entire event as she remembered it. Her words came slow at first, like dragging herself through molasses, but Emerald and Serenah stepped in, filling in the blanks when Claire struggled to recount the events leading up to the moment Bonnie was shot.

With a joint effort, they pieced together the chaos. Once she'd finished scribbling notes, Adams pulled out her phone and, without so much as a nod of thanks, called McLaren to ask his whereabouts.

A short exchange later, she turned and exited through the front door, footsteps sharp and purposeful, heading off to wherever he was waiting. Joshua, who had been listening but remained silent since the paramedics left, finally lifted his head. His face was pale, etched not only with disbelief but something far heavier. The grief clung to him like a second skin. Or was it guilt?

"Roxey," he said quietly, more to himself than anyone else, his voice hollow as he shook his head slowly and sat on the edge of the couch. "Sarah. I can't believe this."

Emerald froze mid-step, spinning to face him. "Dad. What are you talking about?"

"She used to be so…kind," Joshua murmured as he stared into the distance. "I never thought she'd be capable of, well, of this."

Claire stepped forward cautiously, sensing something unravelling beneath his words. "I'm sorry, what? You knew her? Before…all of this?"

Joshua let out a long, weighted sigh, dragging both hands down his face like he was trying to scrub the years away.

Emerald stepped up beside him, placing a hand on his shoulder. "Yep. We went to the same high school. Grew up in the same neighbourhood." He looked up, his eyes momentarily lit by a fragile memory. "Her name is Roxey now?" he asked, more to confirm than to question. "Interesting. Back then, she was Sarah Twidale. Cute. Charming. Ambitious. A little intense, maybe, but not violent. Not twisted...not when we were first together, anyway."

His voice softened to a near-whisper. "We, uh, dated for a couple years toward the end of high school. But then she disappeared for a few months and when she came back...well, now that I think about it, something about her was different. She apologised for leaving and insisted we had to pick up where we left off. I was just happy to see her and agreed to get engaged. That was right after graduation."

He paused, his voice dipping.

"She was my first real love."

The weight of his confession settled like a lead blanket. No one spoke. No one moved.

"First love?" Serenah finally echoed, her voice cutting through the silence like a shard of glass. "Charming? How does someone go from a sweet young girl to..." She gestured broadly at the room, where the blood, chaos, and fear Roxey had left behind still lingered in the air.

"I don't know," Joshua admitted, his voice cracking slightly. "We might have an inkling," Katalyna murmured. Claire's mouth twitched as she remembered Roxey had lost two infants in her early twenties, just a few years after her high school journey had ended. Joshua's expression twisted with something dark and self-blaming. "Oh god...is this all my fault?" He looked down, closing his eyes tightly as though he were in pain. Emerald shook her head, but he didn't notice and kept talking. "I can't believe I didn't recognise her photo when the cop showed it to me. Probably because her hair used to be so blonde that it looked bleached. But her voice…" He paused, haunted. "I'd know her voice anywhere. The last time I heard her speak…it was the day she called me after our wedding—well, what was supposed to be our wedding—crying. She was completely shattered."

"Wedding?" Emerald blinked, her confusion clear. "You two actually made it to the wedding? Wait—what happened between you?"

Joshua looked away, guilt spreading across his features. "Em, just remember I was a kid, okay?" He sighed. "I didn't show up. She did."

Emerald's posture visibly dropped, her shoulders sagging with disbelief.

"I was barely eighteen. The morning of, I just panicked. Realised I wasn't ready, that I was too young to get married. I knew she'd be hurt, sure, but I hoped she'd realise I was right and move on with her life. Now I'm starting to think maybe…maybe that's when something inside her cracked."

"Or maybe," Emerald snapped, her voice ice-cold, "she was already unhinged, and you just instinctively knew it."

Joshua looked up, meeting her piercing gaze. For a moment, he didn't speak, but when he did, his voice was tinged with regret. "You might be right. Maybe I just saw the warning signs. She was never the warm, nurturing type, like Elena. She was the opposite of your mother, Emmie. But I do regret leaving her the way I did. You hear these stories of people who experience a traumatic event and end up going crazy."

Serenah rolled her eyes. "Being left at the altar isn't an excuse for kidnapping and murder. I don't think that's quite enough trauma to flip that switch."

"It's really not," Tayla agreed, folding her arms.

Joshua nodded, staring at the floor.

Pulling a face as she constructed a timeline in her mind, Claire murmured, "Maybe not, but think about it." As their heads snapped up, she said loudly, "Anyone else reckon that the combo of being left at the altar by your first love and then having your second destroy your family might be enough to drive you to psycho town?"

She looked around the room, gauging the faces of the group. Most shared a similar look, and Claire could tell they agreed with her, but were confused by her defence. "I'm not saying I agree with how she's behaved, but the more we find out about her, the better off we are. Like McLaren said, it's evidence we need. Proof she's got a history of mental trauma may be enough to make the cops believe she's a capable killer and start investigating her if they aren't already."

Tayla groaned, sharing her opinion for the first time since their arrival. "Yeah, okay, she sucks. But she's smarter than we are and we don't have that kind of time. You heard her, she's gonna blame one of us for shooting Bonnie. And, like, she's gone now, but she'll come after us again. So, who's next?"

Claire exchanged a glance with the others. "Calm down, Tayla. Just think, every time she finds us, we get stronger at fighting back."

"Yeah, or someone gets killed!" Tayla argued.

The front door creaked, and Sergeant McLaren stepped inside, his face pale and drawn. The atmosphere shifted instantly. He walked over to the group, sliding his phone back into his pocket.

"I'm sorry."

He stopped beside Claire, who'd practically stopped breathing as she waited silently for him to continue. "The ambulance staff just called me."

He looked directly into Claire's eyes, his voice

almost breaking. "Bonnie passed away as they pulled into the hospital car park."

Chapter Twenty

Emerald gasped, her hand flying to her mouth as her eyes filled with tears that quickly spilled down her cheeks. The shock hit her like a wave. Serenah stumbled back, collapsing onto the couch with a vacant stare, her skin ghostly pale. Claire clenched her jaw, every muscle in her body taut as she fought to hold back the tears threatening to fall. Her mind spiralled—grief, guilt, and rage tangled in her chest.

"Bonnie…" Emerald whispered, her voice thin and quaking.

Tayla stood frozen, pale as a sheet, as if her body had suddenly forgotten how to function. Her expression was pinched, stricken, like she might be sick right there on the floor.

Unable to fight her emotions, Emerald broke down into a dramatic mess. Sobbing, she collapsed into Joshua's arms, the sound raw and childlike. He wrapped her in a strong, steady embrace, the kind a father gives when words simply aren't enough.

Claire watched them with a strange ache in her chest, she could see in that moment just how much he'd missed holding her. Several, emotional minutes passed, each person processing the news as best they could without crumbling completely.

"I—look, I don't even know what to say right now," Joshua said softly, still holding Emerald close. "But I do know you girls have been through hell. You shouldn't have to go through any more of it alone."

He looked up and toward the group, compassion weaved into his voice. "Please, stay here. As guests. I've got more than enough space. Em still has her own room set up and there's two spares upstairs. Plus, the couches are free if we need them. It'll eliminate the element of surprise if she already knows where you are."

Claire nodded, her throat burning. "Thank you, Joshua. That's…really kind of you."

Serenah hesitated, cradling herself protectively as she shot Claire a look. "We'll try not to overstay. We don't want to be a burden."

"Don't even worry about it," Joshua assured her. "I don't mind the company. Honestly." He rested a hand on the back of Emerald's head. "You've no idea how grateful I am that you helped get Emmie home, but you all need a safe place to rest too. I'm not about to send you back to the streets. I know Em has a whole wardrobe upstairs bursting with clothes too, I'm sure you'd all appreciate a change."

He briefly glanced between them, as though measuring their size with his brain, and nodded to himself. "If any of you don't quite fit Em's tiny outfits, my wife had quite the collection too."

The group murmured a quiet thanks as they began to let their guard down and settle in, exhaustion and grief hanging over them like a storm cloud in the air.

Joshua motioned to the adjacent family room. "There's a TV in there if you like, or a computer in the study. Make yourselves comfortable." He let Emerald go and left the room fleetingly.

Despite the pain they were in, there were a few wide-eyed glances of joy exchanged between the group. Joshua returned with a mop, bucket of soapy water, and some sponges. As he began to clean the bloody smears trailed across his floor, Claire watched as Tayla and Serenah branched off, heading for the family room.

Silent tears ran down her face, but she made no effort to stop them, dropping into an armchair with a defeated slump. She sat rigidly at the edge of the couch, her face tight and aching, not just from her earlier fall.

Sergeant McLaren grabbed a few tissues from the

box knocked off the coffee table onto the floor. He bent down in front of Claire, offering them to her without saying a word. She graciously took them and dabbed her face.

Across from her, Emerald perched uneasily on the edge of the couch, her face drawn. Joshua kept looking between her and the floor, occasionally meeting her eyes. After the third time, he finally spoke, putting down the cleaning supplies.

"There's something I need to say, Em. I should've said it sooner, but I didn't know how. And with all the chaos..."

"What's up, Dad?"

Joshua's throat bobbed as he swallowed hard. He rubbed his hands together, gathering his thoughts.

Emerald's brows furrowed. "What? Just say it, you may as well now."

He exhaled slowly, casting a side glance at Claire and the cop.

Sensing that they needed some time together, Claire rose, accepting the hand up that Henry offered her.

"Nuh uh, don't leave," Emerald demanded. "Dad, Claire's pretty much the only person who kept me going while Roxey had us trapped on that boat. She's my moral support. Whatever you've got to tell me, you can say it in front of her."

The shrill ring of Sergeant McLaren's phone interrupted like a crack of thunder. He gave a nod to the three of them before stepping outside to take the call, the front door creaking shut behind him.

Joshua nodded to Claire and took Emerald by the hands as Claire sunk back into her seat. "Firstly, I'm so sorry, sweetie. For everything your mum and I put you through. I know you hated us, hated the way she pushed you to do better. To be better. Your mother...when you disappeared...we thought you took off because of all the pressure."

Tears welled in Emerald's eyes, but she blinked them back defiantly as she became increasingly annoyed. "So, what, you want to tell me now that you finally get it? Get how hard it was to be perfect at everything." Her voice wavered with disbelief and the edges of a long-buried fury. "Did you guys even *look* for me? Or just not bother because you thought I ran away?"

Joshua flinched, the pain in his eyes unmistakable. "Of course we looked. We reported you missing right away, spent months checking everywhere we thought you'd go. We even monitored the barges and bus stations, and headed back to the main city across the bridge a few times. But eventually, Mum got so sick we just couldn't put the effort in anymore. And I had to focus all I had on her. Taking care of her, watching her fade…"

He barely managed to choke out the last sentence, closing his eyes in an effort to stay strong. "Emmie, before she passed, she made me promise that if you ever came back, I had to tell you how sorry she was for not letting you live your own life. When the doctors told her they couldn't operate, that it was only a matter of time, she lost herself a little. She pushed you so hard because she wanted to make sure you'd succeed in life before she passed."

Emerald stood up abruptly, pacing. "What are you talking about? I thought she got sick after I was kidnapped?"

Joshua froze, his eyes grew wide. "N…No. She was diagnosed not long after you started high school. She didn't want you to know because she didn't want it to be a burden on your grades." He paused, his voice growing quiet. "She was going to tell you after graduation."

Emerald stopped pacing, her breath shaky. "That's not fair," she snapped. "I should've been with her. I should've known."

Joshua stood up and stepped forward, his voice softer now, filled with quiet regret. "She didn't want you to carry that weight. She just wanted you to get through high school unscathed, paving the path to a successful future. Not be the kid with the dying mother everyone felt sorry for."

Tears brimmed in Emerald's eyes again, and she blinked them away, shaking her head. "This is bullshit."

Joshua was taken aback. "Em, I can never apologise enough for not finding you… for not knowing it was a kidnapping. It didn't even occur to me that Sarah would be involved, especially to come for you all these years later."

Emerald put her hand up to stop him from speaking. "Roxey—" she bit down on the name, her voice cracking, "Roxey stole everything. She robbed me of saying goodbye to my mother. But maybe if you'd been honest with me, told me Mum was sick, I may not have even been at school that day. I may never have been taken."

Joshua's brow furrowed. He opened his mouth to speak, but no words came. Emerald was silent for a moment, her eyes rimmed red, her breathing shaky. Then finally, her composure broke. The tears came fast and full, and this time, she didn't fight them.

Joshua stepped forward without hesitation, pulling her into a fierce, steady hug. "I know this doesn't make it any better, but you're home and I'm here now. And I'm going to help however I can. You're trying to put her away now, right? Make her pay for the stolen years?"

Emerald pulled back, wiping her face. "Yeah. We hope. But she's slippery, always one step ahead."

He gave her a reassuring smile. "She just murdered your friend with a room full of witnesses. I don't care if she tries to blame me, there's no way she'll get away with that."

Emerald took a deep breath, her eyes puffy but her posture composed. Claire patted her on the shoulder and flashed her a peaceful smile. There was something different about her now—fragile, yes, but anchored. She'd gotten the closure she'd been missing. Claire glanced at Joshua, his face projecting an essence of calm, and Claire could tell the weight was off both their shoulders.

In the family room, the other pair sat quietly, grief and exhaustion the main theme of the atmosphere surrounding them. Serenah curled up on the armchair, her knees hugged tightly to her chest, eyes red and swollen from crying. Tayla stood quietly at the window, her silhouette outlined by the streetlights. She didn't speak, didn't move—just stared out at the street as if searching for a piece of herself out there. Her arms were crossed, not out of defiance, out of fear. Joshua led Claire and Emerald to join them, merging the group together again.

"Right then," Joshua said, clearing his throat gently. "Why don't I cook us a nice dinner?"

Claire looked at him, surprised by the offer. "You don't have to do that," she said quietly.

"I'd love to," Joshua insisted. "Everyone could use a home-cooked, *family* meal, I should think."

The girls exchanged weary glances. Grateful as they were for the offer, the words "home-cooked" and "family" carried their own ghosts, their own bittersweet meanings. Meals around Roxey's table had been anything but comforting. And now, with Bonnie gone, those words cut deep.

"I'll help you cook, Dad," Emerald offered, her voice fragile but with a flicker of light behind it. There was a childlike eagerness spreading across her face that hadn't been there before. Joshua smiled at her, something proud and wounded in his expression, and gestured toward the kitchen. Serenah stood after a moment, brushing her sleeves and trailing after them silently, like she needed something—*anything*—to do with her hands.

Joshua turned back to Claire and Tayla. "You two be alright out here?"

Claire nodded.

"Oh, Mr…Emerald's dad," Tayla chimed, stepping away from the window with a hopeful look. "Do you have a bath?"

Joshua blinked, then laughed, a warm, genuine sound that seemed to lift the air slightly. "Yes, I do."

Tayla's eyes lit up like it was Christmas. "No way! Can I use it? I haven't seen a real bathtub in, like, forever. Let alone used one!"

Joshua chuckled, nodding toward the stairs. "Sure, kiddo. Second door on the right as you come off the landing."

Tayla squealed softly and did a little dance of joy before practically skipping toward the staircase, her energy briefly infectious.

Claire smiled faintly at the display, then moved toward the dining table, her legs heavy beneath her. As she pulled out a chair and sat down, the front door clicked.

Sergeant McLaren stepped inside, his expression unreadable, phone in hand. From behind the breakfast bench, Joshua caught sight of him.

"You still on duty, McLaren?"

Henry sighed, rubbing the back of his neck. "Not really. Just tying up loose ends before morning."

"Well, then," Joshua said firmly, "I imagine this case is unlike anything you've ever dealt with. Must be hard work. Why don't you take a breather and join us for dinner?"

McLaren hesitated, glancing around the room as if assessing whether he belonged here. "I wouldn't want to intrude."

"You wouldn't be," Claire interjected, surprising herself as a sudden urge to keep him around a little longer overcame her. "Please stay."

McLaren's stoic demeanour softened. "Alright then. Just for a bit."

Joshua nodded in approval, but his smiling face morphed into a concerned expression as he watched Claire screw up her nose and gag.

Before he could ask, Claire whined, "Oh, god, what's that smell? It's assaulting my nose."

Joshua raised his nose to the air and took in a whiff. "Burnt…how? What are they already burning? 'Scuse me, better make sure these girls don't burn down my kitchen, hey." He disappeared around the corner toward the stove.

For some reason, Claire found it awkward, suddenly being left alone with Sergeant McLaren. They sat stiffly at opposite ends of the table, making eye contact every so often. She offered a soft, uncertain smile, and he reciprocated, but neither of them spoke for several long minutes. The silence wasn't uncomfortable exactly— just *heavy*, as if something unspoken hovered in the air between them. When Claire raised her hand to tuck her hair behind her ear, Henry gasped.

"Claire, your arm. I didn't realise you were hurt. What happened?"

She frowned, glancing down at her shredded skin like she'd only just remembered it was there. "Oh, that was before. I was trying to help… well, anyway, it's all good. Doesn't even hurt."

He kicked his chair out and stepped toward her slowly, his voice lowering. "Maybe not now. I'm sure the adrenaline's still taking care of that. You'll feel it soon." He reached out and carefully took her left arm in his hands, his palm gliding lightly along the surface.

Claire half-expected herself to jerk away out of habit, but she didn't. She didn't even flinch.

"Almost looks like road rash, doesn't it?" He gently pulled her other arm away from her body, flexing both her wrists close to his body. "Yep, there's still a heap of tiny shards in there," he murmured, inspecting the cuts closely. "We'll have to pull them all out so your skin can heal."

She nodded, her mouth dry. He took her hand without hesitation and guided her back toward the living room, muttering under his breath, "I know I saw a bathroom over here somewhere."

They stumbled into the cramped downstairs bathroom, a room barely big enough for a toilet and vanity. Henry released her hand and began rifling through the drawers with a sudden urgency, retrieving a packet of cotton balls, tweezers, bandages and a bottle of disinfectant. He gestured for her to extend her arm.

She did, slowly, as she stared directly into his eyes. Taking hold of it again, he brushed his fingers over the wounds in a gesture that was more comfort than inspection, then began using the tweezers to pluck the thick, glinting shards from her skin. Each time she winced, he paused, looking into her eyes as though trying to steady her with his body language alone. And somehow it worked. Though the pain had definitely kicked in now, Claire felt as though his soothing stare was nulling the ache somehow. His eyes were calm. Warm. She found herself getting lost in them, drifting away from the sting.

When he'd removed the last of the glass, he soaked a few cotton balls with disinfectant and gently positioned her arms out, parallel to her chest.

"This is going to sting a little," he warned quietly. She nodded, jaw clenched, and braced for the burn. The moment the cotton swabbed her skin, it came—but she didn't look away. It was nothing compared to some of the pain she'd been through over the years. Once the cuts were clean, Henry wrapped her arms with the bandages in a firm but careful swaddle. As he let her arms go, his gaze didn't follow. It stayed fixed on hers, and slowly, the space between them seemed to shrink. Especially the space between their faces. Even more so the space between their lips

Chapter Twenty-One

Claire's breath caught in her chest, and she exhaled, just loud enough to slice through the dead silence of the air. Reacting instantly, Henry suddenly pulled back, as if remembering himself. Her mind playing catch up, it suddenly dawned on her that he'd nearly kissed her.

"Anyway, uh, Mack called me before," he said quickly, his voice flustered, eyes darting away as he fumbled to pack up the medical supplies. "We've been trying to come up with a way to prove you're the same Claire Gordan who was supposedly murdered as a child. You know, without DNA to compare to. It's going to be a more difficult task than expected, given you have zero history since you were six. Oh, and I got those background check results on Michael too. He's clean. Is who he says. Serenah's uncle and all that. Pretty good mechanic too, from what his customer's reviews say."

Claire was dazed, her brain still playing his reaction on a loop. "Uh, right. Cool. Well, that's good, I guess. About Michael, I mean. Not so much for me, but I really appreciate you trying. Oh, I uh, have another Roxey identity for you to chase too. If you're interested, that is. When she was eighteen…maybe even younger, apparently her name used to be Sarah Twidale."

Henry nodded a little too fast, seizing the shift in topic. "Excellent," he nervously chuckled. "I'm sure that'll give us a new lead."

"Yep," Claire agreed, lifting herself up onto the vanity bench beside the sink. "There's gotta be a reason she changed her name, right?"

He nodded, and Claire continued, speaking faster. "Henry, there's something else you should know. She said she had a plan. That we destroyed it or messed it up or whatever. Mentioned something about revenge being best when it's drawn out…what do you think that means?"

Their eyes met, each as deep in thought as the other. Then he answered. "I wish I knew. But to me, it means she's revealed a weakness. Her revenge plan is what's going to help bring her down."

Silence settled over them again. This time, heavier. Neither of them seemed to know what to say, or do, next.

Almost an hour later, the comforting aroma of heated roast chicken and garlic potatoes filled the room, wrapping around them like a fuzzy blanket. Joshua entered with full platters in both hands, setting them down gently at the centre of the table. A simple salad and warm bread rounded out the spread, the combination of colours lighting up the table. They all took their seats, the soft clinking of silverware the only sound for a moment. Joshua served each plate generously, piling on more than anyone needed, like he was trying to nourish something far deeper than just their hunger.

Katalyna and Josie had rejoined the group not long before dinner was served. Henry had generously paid for a cab to bring them home from the hospital, since there wasn't much point in being by Bonnie's side now.

"Thank you," Claire murmured as Joshua passed her a full plate, and she meant it with her whole heart. It was the strangest feeling, something as simple as being served food along with everyone else.

Though they'd had family dinners every night on Roxey's ship, ritualistic, tight-lipped, sometimes strained, this one was something else entirely. There was a softness in the Locke's home, an ease. She looked around at the others and felt something unfamiliar settle in her chest. Wholesome. That's what it was. Even with grief still etched across their features, there was a quiet shine behind their eyes, like the beginning of something healing.

Once the plates were empty and the room had fallen into a satisfied hush, Joshua rose and began clearing dishes, waving off Claire's attempt to help. "You are a guest. I'll handle this."

McLaren stacked a few of the serving trays, his expression shifting, returning to something more formal. "I should get going. Thanks again for having me."

Claire walked him to the door, Joshua following a few steps behind. "Thanks again for everything you're doing to help these girls," Joshua said, offering a firm handshake.

"Just doing my job," McLaren replied, though his eyes lingered on Claire for a moment longer than necessary. "Er…take care of yourself, Claire. And keep an eye on those grazes, alright? Wouldn't want you, er, getting an infection or anything."

She smiled nervously. "I will," she promised, her voice squeakier than intended. "Please let us know if you find anything about why Sarah Twidale changed her name. Or a way to bring me back from the dead."

He smiled and nodded, placing his hat on and tipping it in a gesture that felt more personal than professional, before stepping out into the night.

The door clicked shut behind him. Claire turned to find herself face-to-face with Joshua, who wore a barely concealed, playful smirk.

"He's pretty young for a cop, huh," he said coyly.

Claire's cheeks flushed. "Is he…? I wouldn't really know, to be honest."

Joshua raised his eyebrows, gave a knowing nod, and turned back toward the group. "Alright, I'm getting these dishes done and heading straight for bed I think."

Emerald let out a stifled yawn, rubbing her eyes. "Yeah, I'm wiped. I could say goodnight. Dad, thanks for dinner." She giggled lightly, a genuinely joyful sound, and added, "I'm gonna go up to my bedroom now."

"Enjoy, kiddo," Joshua said affectionately.

"Glad to have you home."

Like ducks in a row, the girls headed upstairs. Emerald laid out a spare mattress for Serenah on her bedroom floor so they could share the space, similar to how they used to on the ship. Katalyna and Josie claimed the first guest room, leaving the second to Tayla and Claire. Claire couldn't help but notice how fluid and natural it all felt, how easily they slipped into their room-sharing habits, despite the fact that they could change it up if they wanted to.

Tayla lingered on the landing, her expression flat and distant.

"You not ready for bed yet?" Claire asked curiously from the doorway.

"No. I mean, yeah, I'm tired," Tayla said quietly. "But I was just thinking. It's, uh, weird to be in an actual house again, isn't it?"

Claire stared at her, then let her eyes drift along the walls beside her. "I guess. I don't really remember what it was like to live in a house."

Tayla pivoted on the spot, running her hand along the railing. "Hm. No, you wouldn't, would you? You were practically a baby when she got you."

Claire tipped her head, gesturing as she turned away. "Yep. Night then."

Tayla spoke quickly, causing Claire to halt in the doorframe. "I haven't actually told you how she stole me, have I?"

Claire shook her head a few times, though her mind drifted to Roxey's journal. She remembered reading about Tayla's capture but struggled to recall the details. Possibly because she didn't care about her at the time.

"I was fourteen," Tayla murmured. "One

morning at work, this frail old woman shuffled into the café. She was cloaked in tattered rags and looked as though a gust of wind might knock her over. Like a humble idiot, I took pity on her and insisted she accept a free meal. She agreed and I seated her outside on the patio. When the food was ready, I carried it out, but she wasn't there. I spotted her across the street, slumped against a building, clutching her chest. It looked like she was having a heart attack. I didn't think, I just dashed over to her. That's when she straightened up with that sinister smirk of hers and grabbed me, covering my face with this chemically smelling rag."

A tear rolled down Tayla's cheek, and she wiped it away hastily. "Everything went black."

For the first time in a long time, Claire genuinely felt sorry for her. "She used the same stuff on me. I feel your pain. And no, you've never really told me the whole story before. But I'm glad you did now." Her feet moved on their own, and suddenly she found herself beside Tayla, staring off into the distance, as deep in thought as she appeared to be.

The next morning, sunlight filtered through the windows in soft golden streams, casting lazy patterns on the floor. The smell of fresh coffee floated through the house as Joshua moved about the kitchen.

Claire sat at the table, her hands wrapped around a warm cappuccino, brewed fresh from Joshua's bench top espresso machine. Tayla appeared moments later, her hair wild from an uneven sleep. It was the least groomed Claire had ever seen her look. She dropped into the seat beside Claire and blinked groggily at the mug Joshua placed in front of her, still half asleep. After a few sips, her eyes wandered to Emerald, who stood near the counter chatting with her father. Her voice was light—brighter than it had been in years—as she recounted her happiest childhood memories with a soft, nostalgic grin.

Watching their interaction, Tayla's jaw tensed.

"You okay?" Claire asked.

Tayla hesitated, then bitterly murmured quietly, "Emerald gets to see her dad."

Claire frowned. "Yeah…"

Tayla looked down at her coffee, her voice flat. "Yeah. Even though McLaren was all 'don't go home, you can't see your families yet.' But she went anyway. And she got what she wanted. Even after Roxey came for us, Emerald gets to stay here. Her home. And we're fine, aren't we?"

Claire's brow furrowed. "Tayla…we're not all fine, are we? Bonnie died because Emerald came home. I mean, I get what you're saying, but if we lose someone every time one of us makes a decision like that…well Roxey wins, doesn't she?"

Tayla's lips parted as she pondered what Claire had just said. "Right," she said finally.

Claire rubbed her arm absently. "Still…I do think you should be able to call him. Your dad. Why don't you ask Joshua if you can use his landline? Roxey already knows where we are. What harm is there in a phone call?"

Tayla's expression lit up. "You know what, you're actually smart!"

Emerald turned toward them from the counter, sensing the shift. "Everything alright?"

Tayla straightened up, setting her coffee down with a thump. "Yeah, actually. If it's alright with your dad…I think I'm gonna call mine. Hope my parents have the same number."

Emerald grinned. "That's awesome, Tayla. You totally should."

Joshua smiled from near the stove. "There's a phone in the family room."

Tayla stood up, determination settling on her features. "Thanks, man."

Serenah watched her leave, then sighed, rubbing at her temple. She gave a sarcastic chuckle and slid into Tayla's chair. "What do you think, Claire? Should I give mine a call too?" Taking a swig of her coffee, she continued to fake laugh into her mug.

Claire shrugged with a small smile. "I don't see why not."

Serenah rolled her eyes.

While Tayla made her call, Joshua set down plates of bacon, scrambled eggs, and toast. The others trickled in happily, a bounce to their step that Claire had never seen. As Josie and Katalyna settled at the table, Claire found herself watching them in silent admiration. Josie in particular looked so alive. Playful. Like a normal kid. She was playing with one of Emerald's childhood dolls and grinning from ear to ear. Her energy reverberated through Katalyna, who looked ten years younger.

When Tayla returned to the group, she was even more mopey than before. Her eyes glistened with tears as she slumped into the room.

"What happened?" Claire asked.

"No answer," Tayla said, snatching a slice of toast. "Guess they're not home."

"Your turn," Claire said, turning to Serenah.

Serenah, seemingly lost in her own head, swallowed her mouthful of food hard and smiled sheepishly. "Uh. You know I was joking, right?" she admitted. "You realise my parents probably won't even *want* to talk to me."

"I reckon they will," Claire said with a hint of certainty. Serenah hesitated, then shrugged and got to her feet. "Come with me?" she asked, half-joking. "You know, moral support and all that. Or in case they piss me off and I hurl the phone across the room."

Claire let out a dry laugh. "Righto." Claire perched on the arm of the couch as Serenah dialled.

For a few minutes, everything seemed to be going fine—Serenah's voice was quiet, a little shaky, but getting steadier. Claire decided to give her some space and stood to leave, when suddenly Serenah dropped the phone like it had burned her, her mouth hanging open in stunned silence.

"Serenah? What happened?" Claire said, hurrying over. She picked up the cordless receiver and tried to hand it back to her. Serenah just shook her head, her eyes wide.

Claire put the phone up to her ear instead, listening to Serenah's mother's panicked voice. "Hello? Yeah, it's ok Mrs. Leif," Claire said. "Uh, Serenah just...dropped the phone. It's her friend Claire."

On the other end, a woman's voice came through, startled. "Claire! Oh gosh, is it really you?"

Claire frowned, nodding slowly, then realised she couldn't see her. "...Yes? It's, I mean, I'm really Claire. Did I... miss something?" She turned her head toward Serenah, as though searching for a clue, but she didn't engage.

A long sigh pushed its way through Claire's ear. "Oh. I see now. He didn't tell either of you. I freaked Serenah out, didn't I? I just...told her that Michael stopped by after seeing you girls yesterday."

Claire narrowed her eyes, thinking it over. "Sorry, I don't mean to be nosy, but he's your brother, right? Why would that freak her out?

"Well, not that part," she replied, a catch in her voice. "Look, Claire, this really isn't my place. I think you should just wait to talk to him..."

Claire's heart sped up. She looked up at Serenah, who'd barely moved other than to close her mouth. "Look, I don't mean to be rude, but if there's something to say, I think you should just say it."

There was silence on the other end, followed by a

deep sigh. "I just mentioned how amazed Michael was to find you two girls together, part of the same kidnapping. Ugh, I thought he would have just blurted it all out the second he saw you. He was so happy."

Claire's stomach dropped. "About what?"
The voice on the other end paused, then said gently, "Claire, Michael didn't know Serenah was with you. He was looking for someone else. He's been trying to track down his daughter, the baby he gave up for adoption." Her voice grew softer, but firmer. "He…was trying to find *you*."

Chapter Twenty-Two

Claire couldn't find the words she wanted to say. Her fingers trembled as she set the receiver down on the end table gently, like it might explode if she moved too fast. She stepped back, her world spinning off its axis. She had a father. A living, biological parent. And she'd already met him—without knowing. Worse still, he had been searching for her, possibly for years and she'd given him a hard time. The weight of it made her knees weak.

Serenah, composed now after having time to process the same information, picked the phone back up and resumed the conversation with a calmness that Claire couldn't begin to access.

Claire could hear Serenah's voice, but couldn't make out any of the words. The sound simply floated around her like static, muffled and meaningless. When Serenah finally hung up, the sharp click of the phone being set down brought Claire back into focus.

"Claire, did you hear me?"

"Huh?"

Serenah rolled her eyes. "You know you have to talk to him now, right?"

"We do?" Claire asked, disorientated. "I mean, I do?"

"Yeah. Bet you anything he knows more than he's let on. Maybe even something about her past."

Claire shook her head slowly, still grasping at the frayed edges of reality. "Roxey? Why…why exactly do you think he knows anything about her?"

Serenah stepped forward and grabbed Claire by the shoulders, shaking her just enough to snap the daze. "Claire, come on. Wake up. Seems like we all have a connection, right? And now it's really starting to look like none of this was random. It's like bringing down a serial killer, we gotta follow her train of thought to catch her in a slip up."

Claire tilted her head, trying to keep up as Serenah continued, her words gaining speed.

"I mean, think about it. She went on about some big plan for revenge, right? Look at it this way, we all mean something to someone who betrayed her. She was left at the altar by Mr Locke, humiliated and rejected. Years later, she kidnaps his kid. Then there's that Chris Isaac dude. She married the guy, and he wrecked their family. Murdered her kids. So, what does she do? She goes after *his cousin* and *his best friend's daughter*."

Serenah tilted her head, muttering to herself for a moment, "Probably his lover's daughter, from what Tayla said, but, ya know." She nodded, then started pacing, throwing her hands around. "And we know Katalyna and Daphne share a connection, right? Logan's sister and partner. Makes you wonder, doesn't it? Logan must have pissed Roxey off somehow, too. It's like…like we're the trophies of her scars or something."

Claire nodded, her eyes widening as she caught on. "Now you and me…we turn out to be cousins…" she muttered.

"Exactly!" Serenah threw her hands up. "And Michael is our shared relative. So, ask yourself Claire. What did *he* do to her?"

Claire stared into the abyss, her heart pounding like a drum in her chest. Then finally, she let out a sharp breath. "Alright, I'll call him."

With trembling fingers, she reached into her pocket and pulled out the card with Michael's number scrawled on it. She lifted the phone—then slammed it back down just as quickly, startled by her own hesitation.

"What the hell, Claire?" Serenah blurted, waving her hand.

Claire winced. "Well, should I call Henry first?

Just to keep him in the loop?"

Serenah smirked. "Sure. Your choice."

Claire hesitated, then shook her head, deciding against it. Henry had enough on his plate. She'd talk to Michael first. Alone. See if knew something useful.

"You like him, don't you," Serenah teased, watching Claire argue incoherently with herself.

"Huh?" Claire looked up.

Serenah stared down her nose, giving Claire her classic, "I know better than you" look.

"Oh, stop it Serenah," Claire huffed. She could feel her face getting warm. "He's just been so receptive to our mess, that's all. Is he good looking? Yeah. But I like that he genuinely cares. I'd feel the same way if he were a woman."

Serenah smirked and raised her eyebrows ever so slightly. "Hey, whatever floats your boat. I'm just saying, he's got a thing for you too. There was an instant connection between you, we all saw it."

Claire crossed her arms defensively. "Okay, can we just drop it now? I can't even begin to think about that at the moment." She picked up the receiver again and tossed it to Serenah. "Call Michael. I don't even know what to say."

After a brief argument over who should make the call, Serenah gave in, muttering something about Claire being a mess under her breath. Michael agreed to come by, under the impression he was taking Serenah out for a late breakfast to catch up. "Come on," Serenah gestured, already leaving the room. "We should go let the others know."

Claire nodded, though her throat felt dry as dust and her legs didn't appear to want to move. The pair made their way back to the kitchen, Serenah practically bouncing off the walls as she announced their newfound family connection. Though Claire couldn't help but notice the way she laughed about it, almost as though it was something of a joke to her.

Michael arrived not long after the girls had brought everyone up to speed on their theory about Roxey's revenge. Claire had spent the last fifteen minutes pacing the dining room, her stomach twisted in knots. Every creak in the floorboards, every tick of the clock seemed amplified. Then came the sound of a car pulling into the driveway. And footsteps on the porch. Yet Claire still jumped when the knock came. Her eyes met Serenah's, who gave a tense, almost imperceptible nod.

Taking a steadying breath, Claire crossed the room and yanked open the door. Michael stood there on the porch with his hands buried deep in his coat pockets. The moment he saw Claire, his eyes shadowed over with something unreadable. A tinge of fear, perhaps? Concern? Regret?

"Er, hey, Claire," he said quietly, softer than she'd ever heard a person speak. He scoped past her, his eyes landing on Serenah's firm stance before coming back to her. "Oh, uh…are you coming too?"

Claire shook her head and gestured with her palm, stepping aside wordlessly. Michael walked in as though Claire was a bomb seconds away from going off, his eyes nervously flickering between her and Serenah. He must have sensed the still tension in the room because he didn't sit down, even after Serenah gestured for him to.

Claire closed the door and leant her back against it, searching her brain for an opening line, but couldn't find the right words. Luckily for her, Serenah wasn't about to waste time.

"You lied to me," she snapped, crossing her arms. "You said you were looking for me all this time, but that's not quite true, is it?"

Michael exhaled heavily, dragging a hand across

his jaw. "I didn't lie, Serenah. You asked and I just—"

Claire cut in, the words landing in her mouth and pouring out faster than she could control the flow. "Henry was right, wasn't he? It wasn't Serenah you spotted at the bakery, was it? It was me. You've been looking for *me*, haven't you? Because you're my biological father."

Michael looked at her. Really looked. There was no denial, no scramble for words. Just a slow nod. "Yeah, I am," he admitted. "And I was. From the second I found out you were still alive."

Claire felt as though her heart might burst out of her chest. She turned her head away from him, catching herself in a mirror hanging on the wall beside the door. The sight of her own eyes scared her, jolting a flicker of recognition. And she suddenly realised why Michael had looked so familiar to her when he'd approached her on the beach. Claire had inherited her father's eyes, there was no doubt about that. They were replicated, the same eerily deep brown colour that almost looked black. It was like she'd found a piece of herself somehow. Losing her composure, Claire's knees wobbled beneath her.

Serenah surged forward, grabbing her hand to steady Claire's weight. "And you didn't think to mention any of this before?" she snapped. "You let her go on believing she had no one who cared, while pretending you gave a shit about me instead?"

Michael's voice rose in frustration. "Now hold on just a second, young lady. Don't you *dare* think for one second I don't care about you. I didn't know you were missing, and neither did your mother. We all assumed you took off to the city after you had that huge fight with your dad. You know, since he told you to pack your bags and get your head sorted. It's not like you gave them a choice. You weren't exactly a prodigy teenager, and your disappearance fit the mould for how you acted. I mean, come on kiddo, smoking and partying by twelve? Drinking by fifteen? No punishment or warning seemed to make a dent in correcting your behaviour. They were at their wits end, had given up. We all thought you'd just pop up again when you were ready."

He paused, lowering his voice and speaking directly to Claire. "For a long time, I was under the impression you were dead. I thought…I thought I'd lost you forever, Claire. But when I found out you were alive, I had to be careful. Roxey, well you should know she's not someone you just confront."

Claire clenched her fists. "You still should have told me who you were instead of impersonating a cop to get close to me."

"I know," Michael said. "I'm sorry. But honestly, would you have believed me? You needed more time to figure out for yourself who you were, where you came from." He took a step toward her, but Claire stepped back. She wasn't ready—not yet.

"Tell me now," she said aggressively, "Where do I come from? Why did you give me up…why didn't *you* raise me?"

Michael blinked rapidly. Then, with a quiet exhale, he slumped onto the end of the couch, dropping his elbows on his knees, anxiously clasping his hands together tightly. It was like he was trying to compose himself. "There's not really much to tell you," he muttered. "I wasn't in a position to bring you up."

"What about my birth mother?"

He looked up. "What?"

Claire didn't move. "What happened to my biological mother?"

"Your mother was…well, let's just say she had her own struggles."

The muscles in Claire's cheeks twitched. "What does that mean, she had struggles? Was she depressed?

Did she die?"

Michael didn't answer at first, hanging his head like he was thinking too hard to hold the weight of his skull. "Let's just say…she's no longer with us, and there was nothing I could have done to save her. Anyway, I didn't want to, but I left you at the church when I realised I couldn't raise a three-month-old by myself."

"But *why?*" Claire asked, her irritation flaring.

Michael's tone turned blunt, almost defensive. "It doesn't matter why, it was the best thing for you. I made sure you were safe, that someone from the church adopted you, and I kept tabs on your family through the community, from a distance."

He scrubbed a hand down his face. "When I read in the paper about what happened to them, to you, it nearly killed me. I felt like I'd failed you all over again. And I believed what everyone else did—that your adoptive mother killed you after murdering your father." He paused, the weight of the years heavy in his eyes. "Then, a couple months ago, I just so happened to be in the grocery store when…*Roxey*…came in. She was talking to that young blonde, going on about her plans for her daughter, Claire. She didn't say much I could hear, but it was enough to make my skin crawl."

Claire felt as though she might hyperventilate, her lungs doubling their speed as she listened.

"Didn't take too long to figure out she went weekly," Michael continued. "She showed up every Friday, always the same time. I listened when I could. Three weeks ago, she spotted me. I tried to confront her. She told me to back off—warned me, actually. Naturally, the next week, I slipped a note into her basket."

Claire gasped loudly as her hands flew to her mouth. "It was *you!* You wrote that note?"

Michael looked surprised.

"You knew about my note?"

"Yes," Claire breathed. "That note…that torn up letter was the reason I decided it was worth dying if need be to come back to the land. *You saved me.*"

For a moment, no one moved. Claire felt a pull, an instinctive ache to do something. She just wasn't sure what it was. All at the same time, she wanted to run into his arms, to yell at him, to cry, to hide. But she just stood there, frozen. Michael on the other hand, didn't hesitate. He stood slowly and carefully offering her a hug. This time, she let him. She felt like a little girl again, memories of being hugged by her adoptive father flooding her brain as he wrapped her into a tight embrace. As his arms closed around her, the tears came freely, tracing down her cheeks and soaking into the material on his chest.

The sudden ringtone from Michael's phone cut their hug short. He pulled back reluctantly, giving Claire an apologetic look as he checked the screen with a concerned frown. "I'm so sorry, I have to take this…" Without waiting for a response, he made a beeline for the family room, answering the call once out of earshot.

The room was suddenly too quiet. Claire's skin prickled with unease.

Serenah gave Claire a knowing look and put her hands on her hips as she nodded her head in Michael's direction. "He knows Roxey for sure," she said definitively, "Did you hear the way he hesitated when he said her name? He recognised her when she walked into that store."

Claire didn't disagree. Wiping her cheeks free from tears, she sighed. "I'll press him when he gets back. Make him tell me what he knows."

A knock sounded at the front door, stirring the sudden silence of the room. Claire flinched. Serenah instinctively grabbed her arm, a flicker of concern shadowing her eyes as they darted toward the entrance.

Before either of them had time to decide what to

do, Joshua came flying out of the kitchen, placing himself squarely between them and the door. He motioned for them to step back, then cautiously opened it, peering through a small crack before allowing it to freely open. Relief washed over his face, his shoulders visibly dropping as he recognised the man standing outside.

"Henry," Claire said, initially happy to see him. But the moment she saw the firm lines etched into Sergeant McLaren's face, her stomach twisted. "What's wrong?"

Henry shifted his footing, glancing between Joshua, Serenah, and Claire like he would do anything at that moment not to be there. His hesitation sent a ripple of dread through the room. "A couple things, really."

Joshua stepped aside, gesturing him in. He nodded and stepping into the living area, slipping his hands into his pants pockets.
After a few moments of silence, he finally spoke.

"Well, first of all, thanks for the heads up about Roxey having been Sarah Twidale. Turns out, that identity is the only one attached to a birth record. Sarah Rose Twidale is the name her parents gave her. Unfortunately though, Sarah has no criminal history either. However, I did find something else."

Claire bit down on her lip.

"When Sarah was nineteen, she got married. To a man named Logan Belford."

Serenah's eyebrows shot up and she blurted, "As in, Kat's brother?" Shaking her head as she chuckled nervously, she shouted across the room, "Katalyna! McLaren's here. You should hear this!"

Joshua face morphed into a weird scowl. "I guess she *really* wanted to get married," he chuckled in a semi joking manner. "That would have happened mere months after we broke up."

Katalyna came in fast, with Josie, Tayla, and

Emerald trailing behind, all of them wide-eyed with curiosity. Seeing McLaren, Emerald quickly crossed to her father's side like a scared child hiding from a stranger.

"What's going on?" Katalyna asked, scanning the room as though she was performing a health check.

"Say that again," Serenah prompted Henry.

He exhaled, clearly not thrilled to repeat it. "Roxey was born as Sarah Twidale. At nineteen, she got married to a Mr Logan Belford. He's your older brother, right?"

Katalyna's face drained of all colour. "No friggin' way," she breathed, her voice barely an octave higher than the sound of her breath.

Looking up at her shaken mother, Josie wrapped her arms around Katalyna's legs. Claire took a few steps toward the pair to pat Kat on the shoulder, a comfort she did not even seem to notice.

Serenah glared at Katalyna and threw out an accusation. "Why would you hide that? How could you not know your brother married Roxey?"

"I would have been *seven* at the time," Katalyna snapped. "He was twelve years older than me, always doing his own thing. Besides, he left home when he was seventeen. My parents tried to control him, but he pushed back against their expectations and cut them off. If he got married at nineteen, he wouldn't have told us."

She paused, then asked McLaren with a hesitant edge, "What happened between them? Why'd they split?"

Claire knew the answer before Henry replied. She had a feeling Katalyna did too but was searching for confirmation.

"He abused her. In less than a year there were multiple reports of domestic violence filed, mostly by their neighbours. That's when police got involved. The assigned cop, Chris Isaac."

Katalyna nodded, her face no less pale than

before.

"He was the one who managed to put Logan away for long enough to scrub her identity and gave her a new one. Rose Johnson. And you know the rest." He paused to push a button on the little radio that was attached to his belt, silencing the static laden voices that suddenly projected through the room.

"Look, I still don't know when or why she ditched that name to become Roxette Jenson, but something tells me there's another identity missing in between. Since Rose Johnson vanished in ninety-six..." his voice faded out quickly, like he wanted to ramble but had to force himself to stop.

Claire watched Henry closely. He was holding something back, she could see it in his eyes. She could feel it.

Before she could press him, he cleared his throat to speak again, shifting his body into a rigid stance. "Anyway, I'll leave you with that. I can't help you look into this anymore, I'm in enough trouble as it is. Now, the reason I officially came...I'm here for you, Joshua."

Everyone looked at him.

"I have to place you under arrest. For the death of Bonnie Acklind. I'm sorry."

Chapter Twenty-Three

The room exploded in noise and motion. Except for Joshua, who clamoured up, stunned.

"You're kidding," he breathed.

Henry shook his head and pulled a pair of handcuffs from his back pocket.

Emerald's hand shot dramatically to her cheek. "No, you can't do this. You *know* it was Roxey who shot Bonnie."

Henry kept his voice level, but firm as he moved behind Joshua. "Actually, I don't. The gun…it was registered to him. It has his fingerprints on it. From the perspective of every other cop, it's just a home invasion gone bad. And I don't have a choice, my boss is calling the shots on this incident." The handcuffs clicked as they were secured in place. "You girls can come down to the station at some point to make a statement if you think it will help," he added. "For now, I have to take him into custody and get his version of what happened here last night."

Claire quickly grew defensive. "Statement? But I already gave a statement. I spoke with your partner. Ask her. We *all* saw what happened. How does that not count?"

Joshua didn't resist as Henry recited his rights, adjusting the shackles around his wrists to ensure they'd locked in place. He looked to Emerald, concern swimming in his eyes. "Stay here, Emmie. She's gonna be waiting for you to leave the house. I've never even owned a gun, this won't go further."

Claire stepped forward. "Don't do this Henry, you know he didn't shoot her."

Henry avoided her eyes. "Sorry, Miss. I'll check out Adam's notes. Someone will be in touch."

"*Miss?*" Claire repeated, insulted. "What did they *say* to you? Who's gotten into your head?"

He looked irritable and began to mutter under his breath as though reciting a loop. "Just doing my job. Just gotta do the job." With that, he turned and led Joshua out the door in silence. Everyone stood as though glued in place, unsure what to do or say.

When the landline phone rang seconds after the door clicked shut, Claire jumped. Katalyna darted to grab the ringing phone as the rest of the group shuffled into the family room, a quiet tension building. "Hello?" she said, a suspicious edge in her voice. Her expression darkened the longer she listened to the caller speak, the little lines on her forehead furrowing deeper with each passing second. After a brief, mostly one-sided conversation, she hung up the receiver. "That was a Commander Morris from the cop station. He wants us to come down…as soon as we can."

Claire narrowed her eyes, folding her arms across her chest. "Really? They can't have Joshua down there yet, can they?"

Katalyna shook her head slowly. "No, don't think so. Seemed more to me like he wanted to talk to us about Roxey. He mentioned her name."

"Well, that's a good thing, right?" Emerald gleamed, her eyes lighting up with tentative hope. "I reckon we might be safe. Maybe they've found something incriminating on her."

"Maybe…" Claire murmured. She wasn't sure why, but she felt uneasy. Something about Emerald's hopefulness triggered a sense of deep concern. And for some reason, all she could do was think about Henry and his new cold demeanour. He'd said his boss was calling the shots now. And now Commander Morris was summoning them to the station, after insisting previously there was nothing they could do.

Katalyna nodded with a shrug. "I say we go. It's time to stop the nonsense."

Claire glanced around. The air had shifted, like something silent and invisible passed between the girls. Their eyes nervously shifted between each other. Until Tayla finally broke the quiet.

"Let's just do it, you guys. They're cops, it's not like they're going to hurt us."

As they prepared to leave, Claire paused as the earlier incomplete conversation with Michael came creeping into her mind. She'd forgotten all about him in the commotion. He'd come down that way to take a phone call earlier and hadn't popped back up yet. She felt it in her gut. Something was off.

"Hang on you guys, I'll be right back," she said, already turning back. "Michael?" She moved quickly, checking the kitchen in case he'd changed the course of his path whilst talking. "Michael?" But he wasn't there. She searched the entire downstairs floor, her voice rising each time she called out. "Michael?" Panic crept up her spine as she climbed the stairs. "...Dad?" He wasn't to be seen on the second floor either.

She ran back to the group, who's now gathered in the living room, her heart thudding harder than before. "You guys, Michael is gone."

Katalyna frowned in response, and Serenah asked, "What do you mean, gone?"

"I don't know. Remember he took a call? Then he left the room...and now he's not here," Claire said breathlessly, her frustration brimming to the surface.

Emerald shrugged with forced nonchalance. "I'm sure he just had something to take care of...maybe something came up."

"Without saying goodbye?" Claire snapped. Emerald didn't answer. No one did. But Tayla tugged the front door open.

"Right. Let's go. We're wasting time now. He's a grown man, right? I'm sure he just had something to do. He's not exactly used to having to check in with a family."

As the others hovered by the open doorway, Katalyna stepped back, her hand pressed on Josie's shoulder. "We're going to stay here, if you don't mind," she said. "I don't think Josie needs to be involved in whatever's going to happen down at the cop shop."

Claire nodded. "Fair enough."

The walk to the station was short, but it may as well have been a marathon. Each minute dragged, and Claire's nerves tangled tighter with each step. As much as she hoped Henry would be back at the station by the time she got there, she also thought about how strangely he'd acted earlier, and the anxiety bloomed deeper. This would be her first time seeing Henry in his environment, not theirs and she sensed his shift toward them would only worsen, especially since he'd insinuated they had gotten him in trouble.

By the time they stepped through the doors, Claire felt like her heart was pounding in her throat. Something felt wrong, like they were walking into a trap, not safety. She spotted McKenzie Adams at the front desk and offered a small, polite smile. McKenzie didn't return it, instead, she dipped her head, avoiding eye contact entirely. The coldness of it sent a shiver down Claire's spine. Even so, Claire walked right up to the desk, instilled with false confidence, and said, "Good morning, we're here to speak with a Commander Morris. We, er, got a call a little earlier."

McKenzie's response was clipped, her returned smile more like a grimace when she finally looked up. She picked up the desk phone and pushed a button by the screen. "Sir? Yeah, they're here."

Claire felt an uncomfortable mass form in her

throat. Something about her tone didn't sit right.

"Please take a seat," McKenzie gestured, again without making eye contact.

Claire narrowed her eyes, staring at the top of the Constable's tightly-wound brunette bun, but said nothing. The girls sat down to wait in a fancy looking holding area. There was even a well-kept coffee station with a pod machine which, given her background in café skills, Tayla appeared fascinated with.

Several long, stretching minutes later, a man emerged from a glass door behind the main desk. He was tall, broad, and confident, wearing a fancier version of Henry's uniform. His deeply darkened skin complimented the colour of the embroidered jacket in an eerily authoritarian way.

"Good day ladies," he greeted, tilting his head. "I'm Commander Morris. You probably hadn't heard of me until today, but I'm quite familiar with your…case. Sergeant McLaren has been asked to, shall we say, pass the baton."

Claire frowned. Despite her clearly disheartened expression, the man continued smoothly. "There're some things we need to discuss. If you'll please follow me, I have a room waiting for you."

The girls exchanged uneasy glances, but Claire stood first, leading the way. They were ushered into a cold interrogation room, the kind with the large glass mirrors Claire knew were harbouring an abundance of recording devices.

Commander Morris sat at the head of the table. His presence was calculated, every movement precise. As the girls each slid into a chair, he dropped a folder of paperwork onto the desk.

"First of all, thank you for coming in so quickly. I understand the last few days have been…complicated. In any case, I'd like to hear your thoughts on how your treatment is going so far."

Claire blinked rapidly. "Our thoughts on our, uh, treatment…so far?"

Serenah scoffed. "Sorry? What exactly is that supposed to mean?"

Claire turned her head and widened her eyes slightly, a silent plea for her to show an ounce of respect for once, but Serenah didn't budge.

The senior cop ignored the tension and opened the folder, spreading papers across the desk. "Your doctor came down to the station when you got out. She told me everything that happened. Said you escaped from her care, her facility. She's very worried about your safety and has asked for our help to get you back home, since you're refusing to co-operate."

Claire's stomach dropped like a stone in water. "Doctor?" she echoed, her voice a mere whisper.

"Oh no," Tayla muttered loudly.

Commander Morris nodded, expressing genuine concern. "Yes…your doctor. Doctor Johnson?"

Emerald dropped her head into her hands with a groan. Claire covered her mouth with one hand, propping her elbow on the table to steady herself.

"Uh, would that be a Doctor Roxey, or maybe Rose Johnson?" she asked.

He frowned, turning a page around so she could see it. "No. Regina Johnson." He pointed to a photocopy of a medical badge. Identifying her as a psychological health professional, Roxey's photo appeared in the identification window. "Are you alright, Miss?"

After a sideways glance at the others, Claire cleared her throat. "Could you…um, maybe fill us in on what you've been told? We're just a little…confused."

A meek knock on the door cut through the tension. McKenzie's head peeked in. "Sir, I'm so sorry to interrupt, but you have an urgent phone call."

He sighed, visibly annoyed as he closed the folder and excused himself. In passing, he directed McKenzie to "get McLaren to take over for a moment."

She called Henry from the wall-mounted phone by the door, then stood sentry in the hallway with folded arms.

Claire's fingers curled into her sleeves. The second the door closed behind McKenzie, Serenah shot up like a bullet, snatching the folder.

"Serenah!" Emerald scolded.

Serenah ignored her, flipping rapidly through the pages. Her eyes widened, and she gasped. "Oh my god, you guys. This is bad."

"What is it?" Tayla squeaked, kicking her chair out of the way as she leaned forward.

Serenah looked up, her face pale. "Roxey—she's full psychotic. This isn't just some revenge plan. This is a full-blown cover up. There's paperwork and everything...oh, so much paperwork. She's thought of everything."

"What? Show me that!" Claire choked, yanking the folder from her. As she read, her stomach twisted tighter with every line. The others leaned in, eyes scanning the pages over her shoulder, the silence broken only by the occasional sharp breath or muffled curse.

According to the documents, Roxey was known as "Dr Regina Johnson," a mental health specialist for troubled young women. There were detailed files with supporting documentation in which she claimed to operate a "sea therapy rehabilitation program," complete with contracts signed by each of their families, giving consent for their "psychiatric treatment" out on the water.

Each of the girls had a file outlining convincing descriptions of their fabricated disorders—"dangerous bouts of defiance," "emotional instability," "violent behaviour"—paired with vague treatment timelines. Claire's hands went cold as she flipped through them trying to find hers. But it didn't exist.

"Ugh, look what's in my file!" Tayla cried, disgruntled, as she stopped Claire's hand on her page. Claire scanned the words, shaking her head.

"Multiple arson attempts on family," Tayla groaned.

Without warning, the door clicked and she dropped the folder as though she'd been scalded, scrambling to plop back into her seat in unison with the others. They composed their faces as the door swung open.

"It's alright, Adams, I got this," came McLaren's voice. He nodded to McKenzie, who backed out without a glance. He shut the door behind him and took the seat at the head of the table.

Claire let out a breath she didn't know she was holding. "Oh, thank God. Henry, what's going on?"

He grimaced, correcting her. "It's Sergeant McLaren, Miss."

Claire swallowed. The formality in his request felt like a slap. His eyes softened for the briefest moment, but he quickly looked down at the folder on the table. Trying not to let it get to her, she brushed it off. "Ok, er, sorry. *Sir*. But seriously, what is happening?"

Henry sighed heavily, picking up one of the pages from the folder. He scanned it, then looked up, his teeth clenched. "Why don't you tell me? I'm the one who just found out what's really happened. You can stop pretending. You know, you almost had me fooled, Claire. I really thought you were in trouble. But you forgot to mention you were on the run from your doctor. From treatment."

The words hit her like bricks. "Sergeant," she said, trying to keep her voice steady, "everything I've told you was the truth. She's the liar. Everything in that folder...she made it all up. It's fake."

He shook his head. "The Commander called me into his office when I got back here with Mr Locke. He explained everything," he said, avoiding her eyes. "How all the years of trauma pushed her to become a psychiatrist...he already knew about Dr Johnson's program, that's why he told me to leave it alone. I knew there was something else going on behind the scenes. Guess he was hoping she could just get you girls to go back to the facility without a fuss or police involvement. It makes sense now..." He trailed off, as though he were convincing himself of what he was saying.

Serenah slammed her hand on the table. "After everything you've seen and heard? After she attacked you, you believe this crap? She gave you a fake name when you arrested her!"

"She admitted she made up the name Roxey because she was trying to protect her identity," he replied, almost mechanically. "Her program isn't technically government-approved. She confessed to that when she told the Commander what she had been doing with you girls. He made her pay the fine for not registering, but agreed to give the program a chance since she had permission from the patient families."

Claire's mind reeled. "And Bonnie? Daphne? You know what she did to them."

Henry looked uncomfortable. "No, actually I don't. The evidence suggests Joshua Locke shot Bonnie as a reaction when you lot burst into his home unannounced. And as of about half an hour ago, Daphne's murderer has been arrested too."

"Wait, what?" Tayla said, her face scrunching in disbelief. "Who's been arrested?"

"Logan Belford. Daphne's ex-partner. There was an outstanding domestic dispute, and I suppose he caught up with her," Henry said with a forced certainty. "He's Katalyna's brother, right? Seems to me she may have been protecting him, that's why she didn't want to talk about him, huh? Speaking of which, where is she, by the way?"

Serenah glared at him. "She stayed back with Josie. She didn't want her kid to be exposed to this crap and stayed back."

Henry raised an eyebrow. "Figures."

Claire bit her lip, hard. "Please tell me you're kidding. Tell me you're just covering because we're in the cop station and you know there's people listening. You saw Joshua's genuine relief to having his daughter home. His kindness and hospitality when we showed up and *knocked* on the front door. You don't think he would have mentioned signing her away to a psychiatric facility?"

"His wife signed the papers," Henry interrupted coldly. "Maybe he didn't know."

Claire could see underneath his icy exterior, he was hurting. He didn't really believe what he'd been told, and was acting more as though he was under threat. It was in his eyes. She powered on.

"Trust your gut, what does it tell you? You saw it in her eyes, heard it in her voice the first time she came after us. She's not what she's telling you all she is; she's a murderer. Look at these files, Henry, just look at them. I don't even have one, what do you make of that? I'm dead, remember? This is a game to her. And she's winning." Claire lent back and folded her arms.

Henry looked away. "Commander Morris reiterated why we don't get too close to our cases. Why we don't get personal. I should've known better and just listened when he said it was under control."

A sharp knock interrupted the silence. The door opened just a crack, and Commander Morris peeked in, motioning for Henry to step outside. Henry swept a glance over the girls and stepped out.

Serenah waited until the door clicked shut and rushed to it, pressing her ear up against the frame. She listened intently and after a moment, she turned around, worry plain on her face. "She's coming, you guys. He just said they're getting the paperwork sorted so she can take us back to the 'facility.' In straightjackets if they have to."

Her statement ignited a fear in the room like an invisible explosion. Tayla and Emerald jumped to their feet, breathing quick and shallow. Instead of panicking, Claire concentrated, scanning the room. Searching the walls for another exit. Her eyes locked on the ceiling vent above the table. Serenah followed her stare, and they looked at each other, exchanging a silent agreement.

"Girls, we're not waiting around," Claire announced, pointing out the vent. "We're going up."

Tayla looked at her like she'd grown a second head. "Gross," she said, screwing up her nose.

"Yeah, because that's what matters right now, Tay," Serenah said, rolling her eyes as she hoisted herself onto the table. She rocked it, gaging its sturdiness. "It's solid. Let's do this."

Claire joined her. Together, they reached up, their fingers fumbling to open the vent clasp. Claire gripped it and with minor effort, the grate came loose with a clang. Claire grimaced as the sound echoed off the walls, far too loudly. She glanced over, but the door remained shut.

Working in unison, she and Serenah lowered the grate, setting it down on the table gently. Claire boosted Serenah up first. She disappeared into the vent with surprising agility, checking first if the vent was clear enough to crawl through. After a brief test, she stuck out her thumb and nodded.

Emerald climbed onto the table and with minimal assistance from Claire, hoisted her body into the hole. Tayla followed reluctantly, muttering a series of complaints under her breath. Finally, it was Claire's turn, the other three pulling her up from above.

The air in the vent was thick and warm, the metal groaning faintly beneath their weight as they crawled. Every breath sounded like a roll of thunder. After a short stretch, the vent curved and ended at a panel in the wall. Serenah kicked it open and dropped down onto a skip bin, offering a hand to pull the others through. The alley behind the station greeted them—narrow, shadowed, and gloriously free of police.

Claire barely had time to savour the moment when a shriek sliced through the air. She whipped around to see McKenzie standing before them, one of her hands clasped around Emerald's wrist. The other tucked in her jacket pocket. Her expression wasn't surprised. It was smug.

"What? How did you—?" Claire's voice spluttered as she tried to spit out the words she wanted to say.

"Sweetie," McKenzie teased in a sickly-sweet voice, very unlike her usual stick in the mud tone, "there's cameras everywhere in a cop shop. Surely you knew that?"

Claire couldn't help but notice how much she suddenly reminded her of Roxey.

Serenah let out a fake laugh, but it died the second McKenzie drew a silenced gun from her jacket, simultaneously clamping down tighter on Emerald's wrist.

"I suggest you young ladies come back inside, so Sarah can take you back to the facility," she said smoothly. "I wouldn't want anyone to get hurt trying to escape."

Claire froze. "Sarah? Why did you call her Sarah?"

After a brief flicker of concern crossed her face, McKenzie's lips curled into a smirk. A very familiar looking smirk. "Right. I forgot she hadn't told you. I'm her daughter."

Chapter Twenty-Four

Claire felt as though she might vomit. Planted in place, she swallowed hard, attempting to fight the lump that was making its way up her throat. Around her, the others looked just as shell-shocked—eyes wide, hearts visibly racing in their chests. The alley felt colder now, tighter somehow, the surrounding building walls closing in.

Before anyone could get a word out, McKenzie gave a small, firm nod. "Yeah," she said calmly. "See, like you, I know she only goes by Roxette Jenson in public to protect her identity. She told me the government didn't approve of her treatment method, so she had to keep it on the down low."

Emerald turned her head slightly, a tremble of fear in her voice. "So, you're…what? A dirty cop helping a criminal?"

McKenzie's expression dropped, a pained look in her eyes. "Absolutely not. When McLaren pinned her for trying to detain you, she asked me to get rid of the gun so the cops wouldn't get the wrong idea about her. I said I would, but only if she talked to my boss so we could sort everything out the legal way. I mean, she might be up for legal implications anyway because you girls had to go and escape in the first place. But at least this way she's not going to get herself into more trouble by going about things the wrong way."

Her voice was steady, but Claire could hear something else under it—resentment? "Don't you understand how lucky you are to have been with her and not in a traditional facility?" McKenzie continued. Why are you doing this? You know she's trying to help you. I want to understand."

"Oh, *please*," Serenah snapped, rolling her eyes with unfiltered disdain. "You clearly don't understand anything, least of all what kind of monster your mother is. If she is, in fact, your mother. You may know her real name, or any other one she's gone by, but her doctor cover up is a load of crap. She's a kidnapper and a murderer. Clearly, she's lying to you too."

McKenzie's face tightened and her sly smile morphed into a glare. "You do have a mouth on you, don't you?" she said coolly, with a false calm that only made the tension worse. Her fingers flexed as she took a threatening step forward. "She hasn't lied to me at all, I'm quite aware who she was born as and who she was before she became a doctor."

Claire could feel a burst of anger bubbling to the surface, but she managed to soothe it before she spoke, not wanting to escalate the situation. "She's not a doctor, Constable. She faked all of that to cover her own ass and avoid arrest for kidnapping us all."

The cop glared, and for a moment, Claire thought she might have gotten to her, made her see sense. But then she chuckled. "Yeah, sure. Now that's a heck of an elaborate cover up. Nice one, by the way, convincing McLaren to help you try to incriminate her without telling him the truth. But your tricks won't work on me. Now let's stop the nonsense and go back inside. They'll be here soon. Don't make me call for backup."

Claire and Serenah exchanged a glance. "Um, *they'll* be here?" Claire said, calmly, yet fearful of the answer.

McKenzie nodded. "The other doctors. She's decided to have you transferred to the hospital's traditional mental ward. Feels it for everyone's best interests now."

Emerald met Claire's eyes with a silent, urgent, desperate plea. Claire's brain was on overdrive. There was no version of reality where going back inside meant anything but the end of hope. With Roxey's forged documents, fake credentials, and her twisted psychiatric cover story she'd woven law enforcement into, there'd be no more explaining. No more escaping.

Suddenly, a pained cry sliced through the air. Tayla clutched her stomach and doubled over, howling. "Oh, you guys," she wailed in anguish. "I think I stabbed myself crawling out of that vent. It hurts so much! There was something sharp. Rusted metal or something…" She pulled her hand back, revealing a nasty looking wound. Blood, thick and brownish-red, smeared across her shirt and coated her palm.

McKenzie seemed thrown off. Suspicion flickered across her face, but so did something else. Concern. Hesitantly, she released Emerald's arm and stepped toward Tayla.

"It's okay," McKenzie said softly. "I'll get you some medical help. Not a worry."

Claire watched as Tayla bent over again, this time dropping low into a crouching position and whimpering dramatically like a wounded dog. McKenzie knelt beside her, extending an arm to help Tayla up as she glanced behind her at the vent in the wall as though trying to find the dangerous object.

It appeared that was all Tayla was waiting for. Quick as lightning, she fell forward onto her knees in an unexpected attack. First scooping up a fistful of dirt, Tayla sprung up and, with a sudden, fierce motion, flung it vigorously into McKenzie's eyes. The constable shrieked, blinded and caught off guard. Claire's mouth dropped open, but there was no time to revel in the marvel of Tayla's plan.

McKenzie's hand spasmed as she desperately tried to clean her eyes, and a gunshot echoed through the alley like thunder as her weapon discharged wildly.

"Leg it!" Tayla screamed.

But they were already moving. The group fled, wasting no time as they sprinted from the alley out onto the street. It wasn't until they were several blocks from the police station that they slowed to a fast walk, gasping for air. Coming to a sudden halt, Claire dropped and caught her hands on her knees, her heart still galloping. The sound of a shared giggle breaking out between the girls forced her to look up.

"Holy crap, Tay, that was brilliant!" Emerald burst out, clapping her on the back. "Seriously, I can't believe you thought of that!"

Claire nodded, grinning through the shock. "Yeah. I mean, you even *touched* dirt to do it."

Tayla crossed her arms with mock offense. "Hey, I can be smart. I'm not *completely* useless."

"Could've fooled me," Serenah teased, folding her arms and shrugging.

Her breathing regulating again, Claire stood up and unclenched. "Where'd you get the fake blood though?"

With a flourish, Tayla opened her palm and reached into her pocket with the other hand, pulling out a crushed capsule and placing it down like a display. "Coffee pod. I started to make myself a coffee in the waiting room, but then that Commander dude came out. For some reason, I panicked and jammed it in my pocket."

"Well, I'm glad you did," Serenah said, frowning as she bent to grab her thigh. "Huh," she muttered casually, glancing down. "That'd be why my leg is killing me."

Investigating her skin through a hole in her jeans, she pulled her hand back, a red and glistening smear drawing attention.

Tayla clamped a hand over her mouth. "Oh my god, you're actually bleeding, Ree," she gasped.

Claire leaned in, alarmed. There was a deep wound in Serenah's leg, bleeding rapidly. Puzzled, Claire looked up. "Serenah, did that wild shot hit you?"

Serenah's brow furrowed with a genuine confusion. "Maybe? I did feel something scratch me as we took off, but I didn't think much of it. Didn't start to hurt until just now."

Emerald examined the wound with narrowed eyes. "Yeah, cause you were too busy worrying about getting away. Does it need treatment?"

Serenah shrugged it off, wiping it with a wince. "Nah, it's just a graze. I'll live."

Tayla wiped a few tears from her eyes. Claire couldn't tell if she was laughing or crying. Maybe both.

Claire turned away slightly, rubbing some of the gunk from the vent off her arms. The high of their escape was already dissolving into dread. "Well, what now?" she asked, her voice edged with weariness. "Seriously, guys, what do we do now?"

Serenah let a light scoff leave her lips. "Roxey has the law eating out of her hands. She's turned everything against us. We're screwed."

Claire's heart plummeted. She hated how much truth was in those words. But she wasn't ready to give up fighting. She'd stay on the run forever if she had to. "We have to prove somehow that those papers are false," Claire suggested. "Catch her out in the lie."

Emerald groaned. "Haha. Sure. That'll happen."

The pain in her leg obviously getting to her, Serenah turned and sat on the nearest curb. "I have to agree at this point. If she's been feeding the cops lies, maybe for years, about us, about her 'credentials,' no way we're getting them to believe otherwise. We'd literally need a confession."

Tayla nodded. "Ree's right. Hey, do you think McKenzie is really her daughter? She seems like a stickler for rules. If we can prove to her that Roxey's lying to her too, maybe she'll help us?"

Claire sighed, her shoulders sagging under the weight of everything crashing down around her. Every instinct screamed at her to run, to disappear into the crowds, hitch a ride off the island and never look back. But she knew she couldn't. And she wouldn't go without them. "I don't think it's worth trying to prove anything anymore. It won't work. I just want to run," she said quietly, then firmer, "but we have to prepare and do this all together. We need to go back to your place, Em. Katalyna and Josie—they have no idea what's happening. What if the cops show up there to take them away or something?"

Finally, after a few glances and half-hearted shrugs, they unanimously decided to head back to the Locke residence. Even if briefly, it was the only place they had to regroup.

Bursting in, Claire called down the hall. "Kat! Katalyna?"

Thudding footsteps echoed from the landing before Katalyna appeared. Jogging down the stairs, her eyes wide and panicked, she swept a glance over the girls. Fixing on Serenah's bloodied jeans and the large mud brown stain on Tayla's shirt, she gulped, "Claire? Girls? Oh my gosh what's happened?"

Claire didn't answer right away. She crossed the room in three quick strides and wrapped her arms around Katalyna, holding her like a lifeline. "Kat…they tried to keep us. Roxey…she's twisted everything. She's made it look like we're all psychiatric patients so she can drag us back with her, legally. The cops are on her side."

Katalyna's expression dropped, her shoulders stiffening. "What are you talking about?" Her voice was high, a mix of disbelief and fear.

Claire crossed the room and plopped down onto the couch, her knees giving out. The words poured from her, breathless, rushed, barely making sense as she detailed the escape, the station, the lies, the gunshot—everything. When she finally paused to breathe, Katalyna didn't waste a second.

"I have to get Josie. Now. We're getting out of this mess once and for all."

"I agree," Claire said, a tinge of desperation overtaking her frustration. "But where are we supposed to go now? Roxey's got the cops wrapped around her little finger. We'll never get away now. They'll find us. No matter where we hide."

Katalyna hesitated. Claire could almost see the cogs ticking in her brain. The war going on inside her. The fear.

Serenah groaned as she lowered herself beside Claire, her face pale. "I hate to be the buzzkill here, but I'm not going anywhere until I get this leg sorted out." She lifted her hand from her thigh. Blood bloomed like ink across her jeans and started running freely down her leg.

"Shit, Serenah." Claire jumped up in a flash. I thought you said it was just a graze!"

"I *thought* it was!" Serenah snapped, wincing. "Then I realised it was getting worse the longer I've been sitting. Stupid adrenaline wearing off."

"I'll go…find a first aid kit," Katalyna said monotoned, already halfway out of the room, moving like a ghost toward the kitchen.

"It's in the bathroom, Kat!" Emerald called after her. "Not the kitchen!"

But Katalyna didn't stop, trudging forward like she was being pulled along an invisible track.

Serenah leaned closer to Claire. Her voice dropped to a whisper, laced with pain. "Look, first aid supplies aren't going to cut it. I have to go to a hospital or something and get this stitched up. The bullet is probably still in there or something. Just take the others and get going."

Claire shook her head fiercely. "Nah, we're not leaving you behind. You think you can limp to the ER by yourself? No way."

Serenah grimaced as she adjusted her posture. "You really don't have to. You know they'll be coming soon. Probably on their way now, so there's no time to argue about it. There's a wad of cash in the kitchen, the money I earned from stripping. It's in an envelope under the fruit bowl. I can get a cab to the emergency room and you can take the rest."

Claire closed her eyes slowly, then reopened them as she ran her fingers down her cheek. "The cash is in the kitchen?" Her eyes met Emerald's and she could tell her mind was hit with the same conclusion. Claire jogged to the kitchen.

Her stomach sank the moment she saw the overturned fruit bowl and a single fifty-dollar bill lying beside a torn envelope. A bowl of abandoned snacks sat knocked over on the floor beside a small pile of dolls and their accessories. Claire lifted her head, her eyes zoning in on the open side door.

Chapter Twenty-Five

"I can't believe she'd do that," Claire whispered aloud, picking up the lonely yellow note. She walked back to the living room, holding the fifty in the air like a flag.

Serenah pursed her lips. "She took the rest of the money and fled with her kid, didn't she?"

Claire nodded. "She left us just enough, I suppose." Turning to the others, she shrugged. "Well, Em, Tay. You have a choice now, too. Whether it's Roxey, the cops, or a team of doctors with padded vans, someone's coming. Roxey's going to win this game after all. They think we're the crazy ones, not her."

She swallowed hard. "Even McLaren. If you want to make a break for it too, I suggest you get going."

Emerald glanced at Tayla, like she was hoping she'd speak first. But Tayla stayed quiet. Emerald cleared her throat. "No. I'm coming with you guys. With my dad…since Roxey framed my dad, I've got no family left. I stay here, and I'm getting hauled back kicking and screaming for sure."

Tayla rubbed her arm nervously. "I think I'm out," she said at last. "I'm done. I'm gonna go call my dad. I want to go home."

"Just be careful, Tay," Serenah said. "You'll either be putting them in danger or trapping yourself. Roxey won't call off the pigs just because you're back in your parents' arms."

Tayla frowned. "My parents didn't sign those papers. They'll tell the cops or looney doctors the truth if they try to come and get me."

Claire reached out, gently touching Tayla's arm. "If that's what you want, then do what you think is right. Just let me get Serenah a cab first." She stepped away into the family room, her fingers shaking as she called a taxi.

Even after they'd confirmed the address and hung up, Claire hesitated to put the receiver down. She reached into her pocket and pulled out the edited business card Michael had given her.

Making a quick decision, she dialled the number, hoping he'd answer and come to her rescue. But no such luck.

Back in the living room, Serenah called out, more strained this time. "Claire! It's really starting to bleed again! How long will they be?"

"They didn't say," Claire replied, heading back to the main area. "But I don't think it will be long."

Tayla took a shaky breath and stood. "Right. I'm gonna call my parents now. Have them come get me."

Claire managed a half-smile. "Good on you."

Fifteen minutes later, a horn echoed from the front of the house. "Finally," Serenah muttered, wincing as she stretched her leg out. Her skin had gone pale, and there was barely a patch of her leg left untouched by the deep crimson soaking through her pants. Her breaths were short and unsteady now, her strength clearly overtaken by the pain.

Claire and Emerald helped her to her feet, looping their arms beneath hers to support her weight. "Your parents will be here soon, Tayla?" Claire asked, glancing toward the front door, bracing herself for the next step.

Tayla's eyes brimmed with tears. Seemingly oblivious to the dire state Serenah was in, she mumbled. "I've tried five times, Claire. No one will answer."

Claire's nod was curt, restrained. "You can still come with us instead of waiting to get hold of them."

Tayla hesitated, but shook her head. "No. I'm going to try Dad's office. He'll be there."

"See ya later, Tay," Serenah managed weakly, encouraging Claire to keep moving. The phone began to ring just as Claire helped Serenah cross the threshold.

Tayla jumped as though she'd been prodded with a taser. "Oh, that'll be them!"

"Good luck with seeing your folks again," Claire called as she bolted across the room.

The taxi driver took one look at Serenah's blood-stained jeans and ghost-pale face and silently opened the back door. Claire lowered Serenah into the taxi, whilst Emerald supported her torso weight.

"Hospital, please," Claire instructed once they had all buckled in. She held the headrest of the seat in front of her tightly, unsure how she'd feel when the vehicle began to move.

He didn't say a word, but his eyes flickered constantly to the rearview mirror the whole time he drove, and the speed of the vehicle indicated his stress. The sensation of being in a moving car was intense, and the consistent weaving through traffic was making Claire extremely nauseous. Still, she gripped Serenah's hand and tried to pretend she was on a ride. If she ever wanted to go on a theme park rollercoaster, she imagined it would have to feel similar.

A short while later, inside the hospital, everything blurred together. The brightness of the fluorescent lights, the sterile tang in the air, the hurried voices of nurses—it all swept over Claire like static.

Emerald huddled in a ball as they waited in a curtain walled room just behind the swinging doors that separated the treatment areas from the rest of the ER. With Serenah's condition, it hadn't taken long to be seen by a small team of doctors and nurses. They had taken her straight for an x-ray, worried about internal fragments leftover from the bullet's entry.

Claire couldn't sit still. Her legs moved on their own, pacing in small, sharp turns. Her mind churned, every thought a dead end. Had the cops notified anyone to keep a look out for them? If McKenzie had realised the stray bullet had hit Serenah, hospitals would be the first place they'd check. What if the nurses realised who they were and kept them in some kind of lockdown ward, waiting for Roxey to pick them up? She felt like a fugitive.

Claire halted when a conversation from outside the curtain caught her attention. A desk nurse was talking to someone about them. And that someone's voice was very familiar. Sergeant Mclaren?

"I think they're in assessment room four? Yeah, just past the curtain, second on the right."

She crept closer to the curtain just as it was yanked aside. Her feet planted on the spot as Henry stepped into the area. Almost nose to nose with him, Claire's entire body tensed.

"What…what are you doing here?" she asked, swallowing nervously.

McLaren sidestepped her and closed the curtain behind him, his expression sombre, but relieved. "I stopped by Emerald's place. Tayla said you'd come here." He looked her up and down, as though checking for injury. "Is everyone alright?"

Claire's eyes narrowed. "Well, Serenah got shot trying to escape *your* partner. Who, by the way, Roxey's manipulated into helping her this whole time. Just like the rest of you. So, no—not exactly."

"I know," he said quietly.

Emerald arced up from the corner, suddenly attentive. "What do you mean, *you know?*"

Henry looked up, as though he hadn't noticed her before. Claire spotted a slim folder in his hands, something she hadn't seen initially. "After we spoke at the station, I had this…feeling I couldn't shake," he said. "Something wasn't sitting right. I went through and actually read the documents. You were right, by the way, there's no file on you. But I don't know what's stranger, that, or the fact that Tayla is supposedly an arsonist."

He laughed dryly, shaking his head. "No way she's the type, she's too much of a princess. And in the nicest way I can say so, doesn't seem smart enough to pull it off. Then I started picking apart the notes Mack gave me. That's when I noticed on the bottom of the background check I had her complete on Michael, it was marked, 'Page 1 of 2.' But she only gave me the first page."

He looked at Claire. "Made me wonder why she was hiding paperwork from me. So, I went digging through her desk."

Claire arched an eyebrow. "And?"

"For starters, I found the gun. Not a department-issued one, I crosschecked its serial number. Turned out to be the firearm that went missing from the evidence locker after I booked Roxey. The one she pulled on me in that hotel the first time I…met you."

His jaw tensed as he swallowed nervously. He pulled a photo from the folder he was holding and passed it to Claire. "Found this too."

Claire's eyes scanned the faded beach backdrop, zoning in on the pair of women centred in the frame. There was Roxey, perhaps a few years younger than she was now, posed with her arm around a blonde woman. "Is that McKenzie?" she muttered, squinting.

"Yep," McLaren said, pointing. "That's Mack alright. She dyed over the bleach blonde about three years ago, not long after I met her. Looks like they've known each other for a long time, but she's never mentioned her to me. Not even when I arrested her. See the caption?" He turned the picture over.

Claire scoffed, almost bitter. "Me and Sarah. Thanks for finally finding me." Thrusting the photo back at him, she remarked, "Yeah, you could say that. Like I said, she's been helping Roxey. She's known about her real background all along."

Henry tucked the photo back into the folder. Claire was relieved. She smiled weakly, meeting his eyes.

"I'm sorry, Claire," he said. "I should have believed you. The second I started to really think about it, look into it, the more things didn't add up. And I just…*knew*. I knew you were telling the truth. Do you know why Mack's covering for her?"

Claire sighed. "Thank you for looking into it. I appreciate you taking a moment to see the other side, I really do. As for McKenzie, I don't really know any of the details, and I don't know if it's true, or some big scandal or whatever, but Mack told us she's Roxey's biological daughter."

He cocked his head, processing the information. "Oh."

Claire nodded. "I got the impression, however, that Roxey has fooled her with the mental doctor story, too. But, well, Roxey asked her to make the gun disappear. So, she did. She would've done it just to protect her mother, without really thinking why our supposed doctor would have pulled a gun on us in the first place. Look, I'm glad you're finally catching up. But unless you can *do* something with this information—"

"I want to help get this lie cleared up, Claire," McLaren interrupted, stepping closer. His voice dropped low. "I became a cop to make people exactly like Roxey pay for their actions. But unless we can get a confession from her, I have no idea what I'm supposed to do. With these medical files…and the license is extremely well done. They won't run checks on its forgery without cause. Only the Commander has access to that database."

He threw a hand into his hair and tugged, frustration taking over his usual calm. "It's only gonna be an easy fix if I can present some sort of proof that she's made it all up."

Claire's mind sparked. She turned her head slowly. "What if we can? What if she kept a diary? Wrote down all the details about us, how she kidnapped us, everything she planned?"

He chuckled and pushed his hair back. "Well, that would be very stupid on her part, and I don't think she could worm her way out of that." His expression turned serious. "Wait, why do you ask?"

"Because it just so happens that she did. On her ship, in her room, usually under her pillow…there's a handwritten diary with every little detail. She wrote about every abduction, every lie. It's all there. That would certainly counter her little doctor notes, right?"

A grin broke across his face. He dropped the folder onto the nearest chair in his excitement and pulled her into a spontaneous hug.

Claire was too stunned to react and stood stiffly, her arms pinned to her side.

A stray paper flew out of the folder as it hit the surface and flitted onto the ground. Emerald bent to pick it up and went utterly still, letting out an audible gasp.

"What's that?" Claire asked, her eyes darting to Emerald's shocked expression as McLaren released her.

Henry scratched his neck sheepishly. "Oh—yeah, that. Forgot to mention that."

"What's *that*?" Claire repeated, curious.

Emerald handed Claire the paper without a word, a coy smile etched on her face. Claire took it cautiously, reading the words as McLaren spoke them. "I found that second page from Michael's background check in Mack's desk. He's your biological father. And it seems he and his wife had two babies, not just one." Claire looked up slowly, numb.

"Apparently you're a twin, Claire.

Chapter Twenty-Six

"I'm sorry, what?" Claire reeled, her voice cracking in disbelief. "And you didn't think to tell me this first up?"

Henry's shoulders sagged, an apologetic look washing across his face. "Yeah, I'm sorry," he said, scratching the back of his neck. "I sorta got too focused on Roxey and Mack. But, just to be clear, before you get too excited about it…you don't have a sister anymore. She's passed away. So, to be fair, the sibling part is no longer relevant."

Claire stared at him, stunned, her breath caught somewhere between her ribs like an icepick. "Oh. Well, *I* still think it's pretty important," she snapped. "What happened to her? When? Oh—were we identical?" The questions tumbled from her lips like a dam had burst and almost mashed together as one.

Henry held up a hand to steady her, and waited for her to take a breath before answering. "I have no idea if you were identical," he said gently. "I suppose that's something you'd have to ask your father." He paused. "I get the feeling you already knew about Michael being your father. You don't seem surprised."

Claire shrugged half-heartedly. "I only just found out this morning. We called Serenah's mother, and she told me."

Henry nodded.

"Do you know what happened to my sister?"

"She was only an infant when she passed. Just three months old. The report said to SIDS."

Claire's face twisted as the word sunk in, unease prickling her spine like icy rain. "Three months old… SIDS, huh?" she repeated slowly, narrowing her eyes. The words didn't make sense, like puzzle pieces jammed into the wrong places. She felt like there was something oddly familiar or coincidental about that information, but couldn't quite put her finger on what it was.

Before the thought could settle, the room dividing curtain snapped back with a metallic *shrrip*, making everyone flinch. A plump nurse poked her head in first, then pushed Serenah through in a wheelchair. Her injured leg was propped up awkwardly on a cushion, and she screwed up her face in pain as they came to a sudden halt at the bed.

"Serenah!" Emerald gasped, sounding relieved to have the tension in the room broken by anything at all. "How are you feeling?"

Serenah flopped her head to the side and shot Emerald a sarcastic "are you kidding" look.

Claire turned to the nurse. "Is she going to be okay?" she asked.

"I'm fine, thanks," Serenah grumbled, standing with a grimace and hobbling a few steps to pull herself onto the hospital bed. The motions looked painful, like every joint in her lower half had been replaced with splinters.

The nurse smiled kindly, helping Serenah lie back and adjusting the pillows behind her with practiced ease. "Oh, she'll be just fine. The bullet must have ricocheted off a nearby wall and shot a piece of brick back into her leg. That's all we found in there. It was quite deep, but don't worry, the doctor removed it. She'll have to stay in for the night, but we can release her tomorrow morning."

She nodded politely to Henry, gave the rest of them a quick once-over, and disappeared without another word.

"Overnight?" Serenah repeated, her expression falling. "By the way, what's *he* doing here?" She gave a curt nod in Henry's direction, her steely glare evident that she wasn't in the mood to deal with him.

"Don't worry, he came to apologise," Claire mumbled. "He knows what's really going on." Her mind still buzzed from what she'd just learned about her twin. She turned back to Henry. "Is she going to be safe here overnight? Do you know if anyone's looking for us?"

Henry checked his pager, the screen lighting up faintly in his hand. "No updates about trying to track your location yet. Last I heard, Mack was filling out the paperwork for her gun misfire and giving them an incident report on your escape."

He glanced at his watch. "It's already five in the afternoon. There's a tiny chance they'll run a whereabout check tonight, but honestly? I doubt it. You're not considered dangerous, per say. It'll probably be tomorrow morning."

Emerald climbed carefully onto the bed beside Serenah just as a cheerful voice outside the curtain announced, "Knock, knock!" Pushed by an aproned server, a metal trolley creaked as it rolled in, the clatter of cutlery and plastic tray lids echoing in the room.

Behind her, another nurse appeared and pushed her way through, this one older, holding a clipboard and an air of breezy authority. "Just need to run some checks before dinner, Serenah," she said, squeezing in between Claire and the trolley. "My, my—it's busy in here."

She scribbled something and glanced up. "After you have a bite to eat, we'll get you transferred to a proper ward upstairs." She looked between the group. "My apologies, but I'm afraid only one visitor will be able to stay with her overnight."

Claire and Emerald exchanged a glance, their worry unspoken but loud.

Serenah waved a hand. "It's all good. Go home, both of you. I don't need anyone sleeping in a bloody chair beside me."

Ignoring her, Emerald turned away, her voice barely above a whisper. "One of us should stay here with Serenah. And I really don't want to go home tonight, Claire. With or without you there, I can't sleep in my room at Dad's. Not knowing…where Dad is."

Claire's stomach clenched. She didn't want to argue, but there was no way she could stay at Emerald's house alone. She'd be a sitting duck. "Em, what are we gonna do? I don't think either of us should be going back to yours at all. First thing tomorrow, someone's gonna be on that doorstep. If not tonight."

Henry cleared his throat awkwardly. "I can put one of you up for the night. Or both if you prefer. My couch folds out into a double bed. No one would look for you there."

Serenah gave a coy smirk. "It's settled, then. Emmie stays with me. Claire can sleep with the cop." She paused just long enough for the joke to register, observing the reddening of Henry's face and the horror on Claire's. "Gosh, gutter minds. I meant, *at* the cop's place, of course."

Claire gave her a withering glare and glanced sideways to gauge Henry's reaction. His face had flushed a shade darker than the crest on his badge. "Righto," he said, straightening. "If you're happy with that, we should, uh, get going, then."

Claire hesitated by the bed. A part of her didn't want to leave, as if the moment she stepped away, everything would unravel again. Splitting up was not something that had ever been on the cards. Then she remembered they'd already been split up, at Katalyna's hand, and took a deep breath. "I'll see you in the morning," she murmured, brushing a strand of hair behind her ear and squeezing Emerald's hand.

Outside, the hospital lights were already beginning to glow, the sun dipping into the hills. Claire stepped into the growing dusk with Henry beside her, the air cool on her skin and her heart a tangled knot of confusion and something else she couldn't quite place. "So, Claire. Anything else happen since we last spoke? Tell me something about you that I don't know. I promise I'll tell you more about my time growing up. As uninteresting as that was compared to your childhood."

She smiled as he unlocked his police vehicle, climbing inside. "Well," she started as she buckled the seatbelt. "Almost two years ago, on my seventeenth birthday, I did a real-life message in a bottle."

His eyes lit with curiosity as he pulled out onto the street, and she continued. "It was the first time I honestly and truly thought Roxey was going to kill me. Like, for real. I wrote a diary entry outlining the tale of my abduction, stuffed it in an empty jar and rolled it overboard. I guess I hoped someone would eventually find it and she'd get caught or something. Seems silly now, I know."

Henry made a scoffing sound. "I don't think it's silly at all. Kinda cool, actually. Wonder if it'll ever surface."

Claire laughed half-heartedly. She found the rest of the drive much more pleasant than the trip to the hospital with Serenah and was effortlessly able to slip into a deep conversation with Henry. They became so immersed in the details that the short trip to his place felt like little more than a few blinks.

Claire expected Henry to live in a fancy neighbourhood. Maybe own a towering house and a well-kept, garden lined driveway, something that reflected the tidy shirt-and-gun holster exterior Henry wore so well. But as the car slowed in front of a plain-looking apartment complex, her expectations quietly reshaped themselves.

Pulling up in the carpark of a double storey building, he exited the car quickly and jogged around to Claire's side to open the door. He didn't say anything, just gestured for her to follow him around the side of the units. His unit was on the ground floor, tucked behind the main building, its modest entrance protected by a locked gate. The metal clanked softly as he unlocked it, guiding Claire toward his weathered timber front door. Inside, it was compact—definitely not flashy—but meticulously tidy. Not unsanitary like the traditional "bachelor's pads" she'd seen portrayed in films, or impersonal like a temporary rental.

Claire looked around, taking in the soft lighting, the warm woods and thoughtful splashes of colour. Somehow, it *felt* like someone lived here. Someone who cared. Almost like a woman's touch lingered in the décor.

As he'd promised, Henry pulled a tab under one of the couch cushions and the base sprung out flat to form a bed. Since about halfway there, neither of them had said a word, and the silence between them had become almost palpable. Claire couldn't take it anymore.

"Your home is lovely," she said quietly. "Love your taste in decor."

Henry, rummaging in a nearby linen cupboard, glanced over his shoulder with an awkward smile. "Uh. Thanks." He pulled out a folded towel and a neatly stacked set of floral sheets. Dropping the latter onto the edge of the couch, he handed her the towel.

As their hands touched during the exchange, Claire almost felt a flicker of electricity shoot through her fingertips.

Their eyes lingered on each other's faces, a little too long, too absorbed, before he cleared his throat and remarked, "If you like, you're welcome to take a shower while I cook us dinner."

The offer surprised Claire.

"You're gonna cook me dinner?"

He nodded, slowly and with an uncertainty in his eyes. "Er. Yeah. I hope that's okay?"

Claire took the towel from his outstretched hand, still blinking in surprise. "Are you kidding? That's…amazing."

In the bathroom, warm water rushed over her skin, and for the first time in what felt like years, Claire felt her shoulders begin to drop, real relaxation kicking in. There was something so much more satisfying about getting washed in Henry's shower. The pressure of the showerhead alone was like an inbuilt massage system. She scrubbed away the dust and dirt from crawling through the station vent, the steam wrapping around her like a shield.

She felt like she could stay there forever, but, before long, the most appetising scent overtook the smell of shampoo. She sniffed. Garlic, ginger, soy—something else rich in fragrance drifted through the crack under the door. Her stomach growled so loudly she cut her shower short, towel-drying with comical speed before dressing and practically floating down the hallway, pulled with her nose in the air like a cartoon character chasing a pie on a windowsill.

Henry was at the stove, stirring something that sizzled in rhythm with the hum of the overhead fan. He looked up. "Ah, that was quick," he said with a laugh as he tossed around what looked like the beginning of a chicken stir fry.

Claire hovered in the doorway, the scent pulling a contented smile to her lips. "Couldn't resist the smell of *that,*" she remarked.

He motioned to the stools at the breakfast bar. "Take a seat if you like. It's almost ready."

She wandered closer, choosing one of the centre barstools and sliding into it. From this angle, she could see most of the flat, the kitchen, dining and living room area combined as one. Sinking her face into the hand propped on the bench with her elbow, she began to admire his displays.

The decor was elegant, calming. Beautiful art pieces hung in balanced asymmetry across the walls, pretty little dancing statues lined the floating shelves. Claire was impressed with the thought behind every detail. Then her eyes caught something that made her heart jolt. She couldn't tell if it was pain...or jealously.

A photo frame displayed as a centrepiece in a shrine of items on the far edge of the bench. A gorgeous brunette woman with warm eyes and a dimpled smile stood beside a formally dressed Henry in an elegant wedding gown.

Chapter Twenty-Seven

Claire felt her stomach drop. Their faces posed so close together and the love in their eyes was unmistakable. "I, uh, I didn't realise you were married," she breathed quietly. Her clenched teeth barely let the words squeeze out.

Henry dropped the utensil he was using with a clatter, spinning around on the spot with a pained look on his face. In that instant, Claire realised why there was an ache in her chest and felt like kicking herself. She could have sworn there had been a stirring of feelings between them and now felt like an idiot. Either she'd taken his actions out of context, or for whatever reason, he was leading her on.

She gently kicked back her stool and stepped away from the bench, putting some distance between her and Henry. "Sorry, can I ask if your wife knows you're putting me up for the night? And why you didn't just tell me you were married when you almost kissed me? I may be new at this, but there were definitely…sparks between us, right?"

He stared at her with a blank expression, elevating Claire's annoyance.

"Where is she tonight, huh?" Her voice trembled with irritation—or maybe humiliation. But definitely hurt.

Henry raised both palms, his expression soft but serious as he walked toward her. "I'm sorry I didn't mention her before. I probably should've given you a heads up when I chickened out of kissing you. I had intended to tell you at some point in the near future, because yes, there is a definite spark between us. But I've been trying to stifle my feelings for you, trying to remind myself that this is a business relationship. Obviously, I couldn't."

He paused, touching Claire's shoulder as though trying to calm a bull. "I *was* married. Haven't been for a while now. She died, Claire."

The words struck her like a gust of cold wind. All the heat drained from her face, replaced with something far heavier. Gloom.

"Oh. Oh my gosh, Henry, I'm… I'm so sorry," she said, her voice small.

He stepped back slightly, giving her room. Then he nodded toward the breakfast bench. "Do you still want to stay here? You don't have to, but dinner's ready."

Claire nodded and returned to her seat whilst Henry resumed his position at the stove.

"Are you alright?" Claire asked. "I mean, how long ago…when did she pass?"

"It's getting better," he murmured. The stove hissed gently behind him, but Claire barely noticed the smell now. Henry followed her gaze and noticed her looking at the photo. He carefully picked up the frame and passed it to her. She studied it closer. He didn't look much younger than what he was now, maybe only a little lighter in the eyes.

"She's been gone three years," he said. His voice had shifted. It was lower, steadier. Sadder. "But it doesn't feel like it's been that long. Some days the pain's so fresh, it feels like it was only last week. But those moments happen less now."

Claire nodded. "How long were you married for?"

"Married? A year, roughly. But, believe it or not, we were together for seven years total."

"Seven years?" Claire echoed, louder than she meant. "How old *are* you?"

Henry looked mildly amused.

"I'm sorry," Claire blurted. "That was so rude."

He chuckled. "It's okay, we got that a lot. I'm twenty-four, she was the same age." He turned off the stove and pulled two plates from the cupboard, serving portions of food as he continued to speak.

"We had one of those rare stories, you know? Met in primary school. Started dating at fourteen. Married by twenty. We knew our future was with each other, despite what everyone else said along the way. We only saw each other."

He paused as he brought their plates over, closing his eyes momentarily as he set them down and slid into the seat beside Claire. "Didn't see losing her, though."

Claire swallowed, her airway compressed as though she couldn't breathe. She could see the pain in his eyes and placed her hand on his wrist as a gentle act of comfort. "What happened?"

"Long story short, she was being harassed by this guy at work. He kept asking her out and wouldn't take no for an answer. That day, I dunno, I guess he really scared her. Her colleagues said she left the building running and took off in her car. He followed, she wasn't paying attention and bam…power pole."

The room suddenly felt still. She couldn't speak, so she didn't try. Henry sat calmly, picking up his fork, but not eating. "Anyway. That's why I became a cop. Joined the force to keep busy. Needed a reason to get up and I liked the idea of holding people accountable for their stupid actions. Not that I could do a damn thing for her. Couldn't prove he's the one who ran her off the road."

Claire twirled her fork, trying to find any words that would help. "Bloody hell. I'm so sorry."

He shrugged. "Yeah. You wanna know the worst part though? No one believed her. She must've gone down to the cop shop four or five times to put in a complaint about him. It got to the point of stalking, even after I threatened him. Never enough proof to do anything about it, he was clever."

Claire suddenly felt like she understood. She knew why he'd believed her without so much as a question. In an effort to lighten his spirit again, she said, "So, I suppose *she's* the one who decorated this place, huh?"

He grinned, nodding with exaggerated flair. "Absolutely. Haven't moved a thing since she left. Taught me to cook, too." He pointed a forkful of food at her like it was proof.

Claire giggled. Several minutes passed in quiet chewing before Henry broke the silence.

"You remind me of her, you know."

Claire glanced up. "Oh?"

He nodded, the softest smile forming on his lips. "You're sweet, kind. Grounded. Humbly beautiful. You've got that soft warmth, but that hint of fire when you need it."

Claire felt her cheeks heat, a bashful laugh escaping before she could stop it.

Then he leaned in, slowly. And this time, he kissed her. Soft and tentative. The warmth of his supple lips sent a tingle through her whole body, unfamiliar but welcome. Her heart swelled with something she didn't quite have words for, but she knew what it was. Desire. She wanted more. But suddenly, it was over.

He pulled back as though he'd been zapped, a flicker of uncertainty in his eyes. "I'm sorry," he said, shaking his head. "I—I shouldn't have—"

Claire reached for his hand, threading her fingers between his. "I would've stopped you if it wasn't okay."

He searched her face, as though trying to decide whether she was serious. "It's just… I haven't been interested in *anyone* since my wife. And until I met you, I didn't think I ever would be again. I didn't think I was ever going to feel...that feeling…again. I feel like if I blink, I'll wake up. Like it's not real."

She leaned in, her voice barely above a whisper. "Henry, I've never been with anyone. Never known this feeling at all. But I know this *is* real."

He smiled and kissed her again, this time a little more passionately, gently pulling the back of her hair. She let herself fall into it, a little too much. Her body slid a smidge too far forward as she let herself go, causing her to slip off the stool completely. Her knees buckled and she used one of her feet to catch herself, simultaneously swinging out one of her hands autonomously to break her fall. Henry copped a flying karate like action to the chest.

He burst out with laughter as he grabbed Claire's shoulders to steady her. Claire was mortified, clasping both hands across her cheeks trying to hide her shame. He smiled, patting the stool beside him and resuming his meal.

After a light conversation, they finished eating, and Claire reached for the plates. Henry gently took them from her hands, shaking his head with a quiet smile. She felt a strange lightness in her chest—as if a weight had been lifted—and turned toward the couch.

Once the dishes were loaded into the dishwasher, Henry returned to find her sinking into the pull-out bed, blankets bunched in her lap. "Just so you know, I pulled the couch out for myself, right?" he said, his eyes swimming with quiet amusement. "I'd never expect you to sleep out here. You can take my bed. I'll survive on this lumpy thing."

Claire hesitated, touched by the offer.

He gestured to the space beside Claire and said, "If you don't mind though, I'd like to watch a little TV before bed. I usually wind down the evening with a good binge. Helps me sleep."

She patted the seat beside her and he sat down, leaving a polite gap between them. The show flickered on, casting soft light across the room.

As time passed, the distance between them seemed to close naturally—without effort, without thinking. Claire found herself drawn to the quiet warmth of his presence, to the steady rhythm of his breathing beside her. As midnight crept closer, a strange sensation resonated within Claire. She wanted him to reach out. Maybe put his arm around her and pull her toward him in an embrace. Maybe even resume their earlier kiss. To finish it before she could ruin it again.

She stole a sideways glance his way, her heart thudding in her chest as her eyes met his instantaneously. It was like he'd heard her thoughts. He leaned in, slipping an arm around her shoulders, pulling her gently into his chest. Claire didn't resist. The moment felt like something delicate, something neither of them wanted to break.

One of his hands found the side of her face, pulling her chin up to meet his. The other he placed on her thigh. She smiled and gave him a subtle nod. As if that was all he needed, his lips found hers again, this time more certain, more grounded in something mutual and unspoken. Claire melted into the kiss, letting herself feel every moment, the closeness of their bodies, the way everything outside the room seemed to fall away. But even as a lustful desire flickered between them, it was tenderness that anchored it—something gentle, healing, patient. A passion Claire had certainly only seen in her favourite romantic comedy movies.

With one arm wrapped firmly around her back, he drew her closer, anchoring her to the steady warmth of his chest. His other hand slid through her hair, slow and deliberate, his fingertips tangling for a moment before tracing the curve of her face Claire's breath caught as his touch drifted lower, skimming her jawline and gliding down until it paused at the delicate straps of her top. Her heart almost stopped when the hand on her back—also firm but trembling slightly—clenched around the clasp of her bra. He hesitated. Then, as if he'd gathered enough strength, he released the clasp, letting his fingers brush across her skin so gently it left her body teeming with goosebumps.

He pulled back just enough to meet her eyes, searching her expression, asking something deeper without words.

She bit her lip and wrapped her arms around his torso, her hands latching onto the back of his shirt until she lifted it over his shoulders and tossed it to the floor. His grateful smile was small, but powerful. Her heart thundered as he leaned in, pressing his lips to her neck and with a single fluid motion, he peeled her shirt upwards and flicked it away. Claire arched her shoulders to assist as he slowly pulled her loosened bra down her arms.

Gently, slowly, he guided her back, laying her flat against the lumpy mattress. His mouth followed, kissing her tenderly all the way down the centre of her chest until he hovered above her, his body shielding hers. The warmth of his skin against hers was startling, but the feeling of his bare chest against hers somehow so comforting. As he pressed down on her softly, she could feel his heartbeat—fast, like hers—and in that moment, there was nothing else. Nothing but the sense that this was safe. That she was safe in his arms.

He paused, eyes never leaving hers, his hand trailing down the contours of her sides, memorising every curve. When he reached the waistband of her pants, he stopped.

"Are you sure about this?" he whispered.

Claire nodded, admiring the restraint in his voice. "Yes," she breathed.

For the first time in her life, she wasn't afraid of surrender. She wasn't holding herself back.

She let go—of fear, of control, of all the lies that had kept her walled in—and gave herself over to the only thing that felt real. His trust.

Chapter Twenty-Eight

When, the morning light filtered softly through the curtains, Claire awoke abruptly. She blinked a few times, trying to make sense of the unfamiliar surroundings before her. For a moment, confusion swept over her—she was naked, wrapped in a sheet and sprawled across the lounge room floor. The faint sound of clinking dishes from the kitchen brought her back to reality when she looked up. Her mind raced through the events of the previous night, and then, as if on cue, a genuine smile curled at her lips, the kind of smile that came from deep within—untouched by the weight of the past.

"Morning." Henry's voice carried from across the room, light and steady as he walked toward her, a cup of coffee in each hand. He passed one to her, and Claire's fingers brushed his for a split second, a simple touch that made everything feel right again. A warmth spread through her chest, ignited by her healed heart.

"Morning," she chirped back. The awkward tension that had once lingered between them was gone now, replaced by a quiet ease that Claire welcomed, her soul finally breathing again.

Henry sat comfortably on the end of the couch. "I was thinking," he began, but before he could finish, his phone rang. With a quick apologetic look, he mouthed "sorry," and answered in a highly professional manner, speaking to someone Claire couldn't understand. She recognised the voice on the other end, though. His boss.

The conversation seemed tense, punctuated by moments of frustration as Henry's responses grew more clipped. When he suddenly said, "But Sir!" Claire crawled forward, her curiosity piqued as she pulled herself up beside him.

Henry pulled the phone from his ear, holding it between them and silently activating the speakerphone.

"It's done," the Commander said firmly, and Claire felt an odd chill run down her spine. "Now, do you know where the missing girl is?"

Claire held her breath, her heart pounding harder in her chest.

Henry glanced at Claire, studying her face for a moment. "No, Sir. No, I don't."

"Fine," the voice on the other end growled, sharp and threatening. "You can go and check the stations then. Bus, train. Have a look by the jetty too. We've got questions for her."

Henry nodded curtly. "Will do." As he hung up, his gaze locked onto Claire's, his expression unreadable for a long moment.

"Claire, they've got Emerald, Serenah, and Tayla in holding now," he said quietly, the words hanging in the air like a cloud of dread. "Roxey's gone and told my boss they're dangerous—she's claimed you all tried to kill her when she came to collect you. Apparently, that's why she's decided to turn you all over to the hospital. Now they're classed as a category three."

Claire's pulse quickened. "What does that mean?"

"It means they're classified as a danger to themselves and others," Henry explained. "It's why they're in lockup. They've just found Katalyna too. And Josie...Josie's been put into social services' care."

"Oh my god," Claire whispered, getting up. The sheet slipped from her shoulders, and for a second, she felt exposed, vulnerable. She stood, her legs weak beneath her, as she searched for her clothes, her mind spinning with the gravity of the situation. She suddenly felt small again, like that terrified girl trapped on the boat.

"Oh, sorry," Henry said, noticing her disorientation. He left the room momentarily, ducking into the bedroom. Returning quickly, he offered Claire what appeared to be a pretty sundress.

"It was Evie's," he said with a shrug. "But, I reckon it should fit you just right. I hope you don't mind, but I popped your clothes in the wash while you were still asleep..."

Claire took the outfit from him without hesitation, the fabric sleek against her fingertips. Whilst she was grateful for the fresh clothing, the heaviness of the situation lingered, gnawing at her insides and leaving her unable to feel much of anything else.

As she attempted to slip the dress on over her shoulders, she quickly realised it was actually a cute little romper jumpsuit. Henry politely looked away as she bent to step into it instead.

"So…what am I supposed to do now?" she asked, falling back onto the couch. "I can't run and leave them behind. But I can't voluntarily go back and join them. Back to that life. Or worse by the sounds of it." She leaned forward and grabbed the sides of her hair, tugging with frustration. "Ugh, I just need to get Roxey behind bars. This has to stop."

Henry sank down beside her, one hand moving in gentle circles across her back. "The diary," he said quietly, as if the words had only just dawned on him. "We can turn her whole story upside down if we can get that journal. If it's all written out like you told me, a confession, even in written form, could be the break we need. That's how we stop her."

Claire sat up straight. "It is," she murmured. "But, honestly? I'm starting to doubt she's dumb enough to have kept it. If I were her, it would've been burned the second we got away. And even if it's still stashed, there's no way I can find the ship, let alone get on it to look."

Her chest ached, and the helplessness brought a tear skimming down her cheek. She swiped it away with the back of her hand. "Ugh, wouldn't it be easier just to prove those mental health documents are all faked?"

Pulling a weird grimace, Henry shook his head slowly. "Yeah…I read those documents. They look as real as any official ones. You wouldn't know they were forged. Whoever did them sure knew what they were doing."

Claire exhaled sharply through her nose. "Okay…oh, okay then what happens if you type the name *Regina Johnson* into your little search database? Like you did for Michael. Just the general one, I mean, not the forgery one only your boss has access to."

Henry paused, deep in thought. "Let's see." He sprang to his feet and disappeared down the hallway, practically flying to his bedroom. A few moments later, he flitted back just as quickly with an already opened laptop in hand.

As he sat, he pulled open a tab using a shortcut bearing the same police crest Claire recognised from his uniform and badge. He clicked efficiently, his fingers flying over the keys as he opened a portal within the program. Claire leaned in, watching as he typed the name into the search bar. The screen blinked, processing. A rotating time turner spun in the corner as the database searched.

Henry began to tap his foot. Waiting with bated breath, Claire half expected the computer to turn up nothing. She expected Roxey to have chosen another false name tied to nothing. When the computer dinged, loading a profile page accompanied by a high-resolution ID photo and a full spreadsheet of records, her stomach clenched. It was the same doctor's badge from the forged documents that stared back at her.

Henry rubbed his chin, scanning the screen. "Interesting," he muttered under his breath.

"So… what does that mean? She stole someone's identity instead of making one this time?"

Henry shook his head and pointed to the screen. "Claire, look at this. Look at the photo. That's Roxey. Somehow Roxey…Sarah, what's her name, *is* Regina Johnson. The credentials, the identity. It hasn't been faked or stolen. It's real and it belongs to her."

Claire squinted, leaning in until her nose nearly brushed the screen. At first glance, it *was* Roxey. The crystal-clear picture outlined her sharp cheekbones, that haunting stare. But there was something off about it. Claire studied the image for a while, picking apart the tinier details until she figured it out. The woman in the picture was older. Defined age lines slightly heavier under her blue eyes.

Claire's gaze dropped to the doctor's birthdate. "Fifty-eight…" she murmured.

Henry cocked his head.

Claire frowned, mulling it over. "Roxey always said she was born in 1974, but it says here 1958. It can't be her."

Henry shrugged. "Unless she lied to you about her birthday?"

Claire shook her head and gestured. "Doesn't explain why she looks older here though. Look at her eyes. They're blue, for starters."

Henry scrolled further.

"Well, I'll be damned," he said.

Claire was intrigued.

He hovered the mouse over a sentence labelled "births."

She read aloud, "Two children listed…first born…Sarah Rose Twidale." Her mouth fell open. "What the hell? Okay, now how is that possible?"

Henry gave a low whistle. "My guess? This woman isn't Roxey after all. Or rather, if you want to be specific, Sarah. It's her *mother*. She's currently using her own mother's identity. Look at the line below."

Claire's eyes flicked back to the screen.

Henry clicked on the marital record to enlarge it. "Married to Jenson Twidale. Retained her maiden name to match her doctorate."

Claire blinked rapidly, trying to process the wave of information. "Wow. That means her mother gave birth when she was, what, fifteen? No wonder she can pass as her."

Henry nodded. "Looks like it. Being a teen mother didn't seem to hold her back though. She got her doctorate, married the father of her baby. Had another kid a few years later." He squinted. "*James.*"

Claire rubbed her temples.

Henry gave a wry grin and pulled a face as though a thought had just struck him. "Huh. I get where Chris created the name for her scrubbed identity from now. Rose Johnson. Her middle name combined with her mother's surname."

Claire nodded slowly, her mind spinning. "Makes sense. Well, is this helpful at all? Can you show this to your boss and get her caught? Nab her for some kind of identity theft?"

He made a face. "She's the spitting image of her mother. The credentials match. I doubt he'd believe it."

Claire stood up, throwing her hands up in irritation. "Then do a damn DNA test! Prove she's lying."

He stood up with her, calmly placing a hand on her shoulder. "I can't force her to do a DNA sample. I'd need probable cause, Claire. Looking older in a photo is not a good enough reason."

Claire felt her throat burning. "Of course. Well, what am I supposed to do then? I can't run; I can't fight her. I can't get myself locked in a psych ward with the others. Oh, and by the way, why didn't Tayla's parents stop them from taking her away? Surely they could have said something, right? Like, oh I don't know — hey, we didn't send our child to a mental health facility. I have no idea what you're on about doctor."

Henry's expression shifted. "Oh, right. Er. Claire," he said gently. "Tayla's parents are dead. There was a house fire last night. They perished trying to escape."

Claire felt her body involuntarily curl, like she'd been kicked in the guts. He pulled her into a hug as she let her weight collapse. Claire let out a frustrated cry as she buried her head in his chest. "Good God man, you're really good at doing that aren't you?" She lifted her head, looking him in the eye. "Leaving out the highly important details!"

He blinked a few times, saying nothing for a few moments. "The Commander told me earlier. I didn't want to pile it on you. I'm sorry." He loosened his grip and lowered his arms.

A wave of frustration crashed over Claire, and she let her head fall into her hands as she slumped back onto the couch.

"It gets worse," Henry said. "My boss…the guys at the station, they think Tayla started the fire. As revenge on them for sending her away."

Claire doubled over, like his words had winded her. "Are you *kidding* me?" she cried. "They think *Tayla* did it? She practically gags when she touches dirt. There's no way she'd have anything to do with setting a fire. If only they could see how squeamish she was."

She sighed. "Great," she muttered. "Roxey's made it all fall into place, hasn't she? It's all part of her 'new plan.' She knows we can't beat her."

Then, something sparked in her eyes. She straightened up, her eyes bright with determination. "Wait. Roxey's been talking to the police today, right? That means the ship has to be anchored close by. In one of the marinas. Close enough for her to return to. The journal. It all comes back to the journal. It has the written evidence of our personalities, our kidnappings."

Henry looked at her, his expression sharpening.

"I'll go to the beaches," Claire continued. "I'll check the docks. Swim out to the ship if I have to. I *have* to know if that diary still exists. If it's still there, this ends now."

Henry's voice was like stone. "I agree. And I'm coming with you. No way I'm letting you get back on that ship alone."

For a split second, Claire considered arguing, but the offer felt like a lifeline. She couldn't face this on her own. She nodded gratefully, feeling the weight of his presence beside her. "Okay," she murmured. "Let's finish this."

The drive to the boardwalk was quiet, the tension surrounding what was going to happen next tainting the air. Unspoken fear clouded Claire's brain. She was nervous. Terrified at the idea of purposely stepping foot on that ship.

When they reached the jetty, Claire recognised the first point of land she'd seen when they'd come in off the lifeboat in the first place. Ibis Isle. Walking along the beach, Claire squinted out onto the water, scanning the myriad of boats. Despite the selection, Claire knew exactly what Roxey's looked like. She's spent years studying it's every join, every beam. Then, through the mass of moored boats, Claire saw it. Roxey's boat—The Siren's Hearth—anchored just beyond the others, barely visible but unmistakable.

"That's it," Claire said quietly, pointing, her voice barely above a whisper.

Henry looked toward the boat, flicked his eyes at the boat hire stall, and then back at Claire, his face unreadable. "Do you think you could swim that distance?"

She narrowed her eyes at the water, picturing herself jumping off the jetty and swimming with ease to the boat. She nodded. "Yeah, I'd say so."

"Good," Henry said, his actions decisive as he opened the boot of the car and pulled out a thick, waterproof backpack. "Because that's how we're getting aboard. If she's nearby and sees a dinghy tethered, she'll come running. We have to be discreet."

Claire's chest tightened at the thought, but she knew there was no other way. The fear of what might happen if they were caught didn't compare to the urgency of stopping Roxey.

Henry clipped the straps of the backpack together across his chest to secure it and put his arm around Claire, guiding her toward the dock. As much as she wanted to turn back, to start running, she rerouted the fear into determination. She had to truly free herself. And her family.

The swim was harder than she expected, but Claire pushed through the exhaustion, focusing on the end goal. When she and Henry finally made it to the ship, they scaled the side, using ropes to assist with the climb, saltwater clinging to their skin. Ahead of Henry, Claire made to step on the deck, but he pulled her back and took rank, subtly stepping over the rail first. He scoped the empty deck, then reached out for Claire's arm, helping her up and over.

Henry called out suddenly, making Claire jump. "Hello! Is anyone here?"

"Her lifeboat is gone," Claire said, shivering as she nodded to the empty pulley nearby. "She's not here."

"You're freezing," Henry said softly, darting to her side. He quickly unclipped his waterproof bag and threw it to the ground. Rifling through it, he pulled out a slim puffer jacket and wrapped it around Claire's shoulders, running his hands all the way down to her waist. She pulled her arms through the sleeves, grateful he'd clearly thought ahead.

Motioning for Henry to follow her, she said quietly, "This way, her room is down here." Every bone in her body ached as they descended the stairwell into the belly of the boat. Every step deeper into the ship felt like a return to her past, to a place she'd desperately tried to escape. As they reached the door to Roxey's room, Claire stepped on a loose floorboard, the noise loud in the otherwise quiet space. Startled, she tripped over her own shoes and stumbled against the wall. Henry reached out to steady her, concern etched in his features.

"Are you alright?" he asked.

Before Claire could answer, a clanging noise echoed from somewhere below, sending an ice-cold chill through her. The sound of something—or someone— moving on the floor below.

"Henry," she whispered, her voice barely audible. "Did you hear that?"

Henry nodded, his expression darkening as he stood in front of her, calling out down the hall.

"Hello? Who's there?"

A voice answered, sharp and familiar, sending a shockwave of recognition through Claire.

"McLaren?"

Her heart skipped a beat. She knew that voice. And she didn't think before she started moving. She darted past Henry, her legs carrying her down the stairs as if moving with a mind of their own.

Reaching the bottom of the stairwell, she peered through the dull lighting, confirming her suspicion. His face peeked through the bars of the cage, a smile of relief spreading over his features.

"Michael?" Claire whispered, barely believing her eyes.

Chapter Twenty-Nine

"Hey, kiddo," Michael breathed, relief and concern etched into the lines in the corners of his eyes. His voice was rough and his eyes bloodshot and glassy. "What are you doing here?"

Claire crossed the room, grabbing onto the cage door bars. "Me? What are *you* doing here?" she cried, startled.

Michael gave a dry scoff and glanced over her shoulder as Henry stepped into the room. "Best guess? She lugged my unconscious ass all the way here." He gave Henry a nod. "Hey, McLaren."

Claire's brain worked quickly. "I *knew* it was weird you just vanished!" she exclaimed, the pieces clicking together.

Michael nodded grimly. "Yeah. She called me yesterday morning. Said she needed to speak with me urgently. And like a dickhead, I went to meet her. Thought she really wanted to sort things out."

Claire's heartbeat picked up. She bit the inside of her cheek, resisting the urge to cut him off.

"That's when she shot me, right in the neck." He rubbed his neck fiercely. "With a bloody tranquiliser dart," he muttered bitterly. "Didn't even see it coming."

Claire held her tongue until she was sure he had finished talking. Then the words poured out, colder than she intended. "What did you do to her, Michael?"

He stared blankly back at her. "What did I…? Er, what do you mean?"

Claire could feel her blood beginning to boil. She steadied her breathing, the memory of Serenah's words flickering to life in her mind like a warning light. "Joshua Locke left her at the altar. Logan Belford beat her. Chris Isaac murdered their children. We know she took revenge on them. She planned it out and stole their kids or close family. But you…" she lowered her voice and glared. "Why does she hate *you*? What did you do to her? Tell me the truth, were the two of you involved?"

Claire's questions were blunt and cold. Michael gripped the cage bars, fiddling with them as he looked away. His shoulders sagged.

"Alright Claire," he said finally, "Roxey…yeah. We were involved. And she's the reason your mother is dead."

Claire's breath caught in her throat. She'd expected it to be something like that, as though some part of her already *knew*. But hearing it out loud still made her chest cave. "What happened?" she whispered. Then, her voice gained steel as a wave of recently gained information clouded her again. "Oh, and by the way, don't leave out the part about my twin sister this time. Were you ever planning to tell me I was born with a twin?"

Michael winced and scrunched up his nose like he'd been slapped. "Do you think maybe we could get me out of here before we unpack all that? And off this ship altogether, preferably. You too, you shouldn't be on this damn boat either, Claire."

She hesitated, then nodded and began checking the room for the key. "I doubt she left the key here," she muttered, her eyes scanning the clutter as she moved junk out of the way. "She probably has it on her. But since we've got the time and all, you can keep talking while I look. Tell me, Father, why does Roxey hate you so much she murdered everyone in my life to later steal me?"

Henry, saying nothing, stepped up beside the cage and rattled the door, testing it for weakness. Michael sighed and leaned back against the bars.

"We met a short time after her cop husband, Chris, went to prison," Michael said. "She decided to run from her past and as fate would have it, blew her radiator. Just so happened to roll into my workshop that day. Obviously, I've never really been a policeman, Claire. Truth is, I'm just a mechanic."

He shot an apologetic look at Henry, then pushed on. "We hit it off. I really fell in love with her, Claire. But the thing was, I was already married. Had a pregnant wife at home. We had a fling, which I ended just after you and your sister were born."

Claire went rigid, fingers curling around a rusty wrench she hadn't even noticed she was holding onto.

Michael's shoulders dropped as he continued. "As you can imagine, she didn't take it well. Started stalking your mother and threatened you girls. When your mother went missing, I tried to get her convicted. But since there was no body, the police never believed me. She was just a missing person. Then the morning I found your sister, found Jasmine...well, I knew Roxey was responsible somehow. That's when I took you to that church. Like I said, I gave you up to keep you safe. And I suppose I didn't mention Jasmine because it hurts too much to think about losing her. Better you didn't feel it too, you were better off not knowing."

Claire stopped rummaging in the nearby clutter and slowly stepped back toward the cage, lured by Michael's gloomy tone. His eyes shimmered with tears, and the sight of it—this broken man behind bars, wrung out by regret, she felt his pain through her whole body. A stray tear rolled down her cheek, and she looked at the floor in an effort to compose herself and control her emotions.

She felt Henry step up beside her, resting his hand gently on her shoulder. The warmth of it grounded her and she felt strong enough to look up. Henry reached out and wiped her tear away with his thumb, brushing her cheek softly as his hand passed.

Michael's eyes flicked to Henry, then to her. Something in his expression shifted. His eyes lightened, the lines under his eyes forming a curious squint. He raised an eyebrow, pointing between them with an outstretched index finger. "Are you two—?"

A low, feral growl echoed down the stairwell. Claire didn't turn around. Her face fell.

"Rumble's home," she murmured. Henry's posture tensed as they turned to face the stairs together. There, half-veiled in shadow, stood the brute himself, his broad shoulders stiff and menacing.

"Any chance that big puppy listens to you?" Henry muttered.

Claire shook her head, barely moving. "None."

A slick, mocking voice floated down behind Rumble. "My, my. What have we here, boy?"

Claire closed her eyes. That torturous voice. Apparently Roxey was home now too. Roxey appeared in the gloom, carefully stepping down each stair like a queen descending from her throne. "Ah, my darling daisy," she purred. "Good to have you home."

Her neck tilted to Henry and she glared menacingly. "You, on the other hand, don't belong here." Before he could move, Roxey's hand shot to her jean pocket. She pulled out a tiny, seemingly homemade dart gun and pulled the trigger in less time than Claire could blink.

The dart hit Henry in the neck. He staggered, let out a frustrated cry, then collapsed to his knees.

Claire dropped beside him. "Henry!"

As the dart's sedative quickly overcame him, Henry curled into a ball on the floor like a dying spider. Claire guided him as he lost consciousness so he wouldn't hurt himself falling onto the hard floor. She grabbed his wrist, checking for a rhythm. His pulse was slow, but his heartbeat steady. She looked up, rage crystallising behind her eyes.

Roxey laughed, a low, coarse sound as she observed the interaction. "Ah, what's this? You *care* for him, don't you," she asked almost mockingly. "What a shame. His death will be such a tragedy."

Glancing behind Claire, Roxey checked the cage. "My dearest Michael. Good to see you're still exactly where you belong."

Claire rose to her feet, her fists clenched, fury making her shake. "Right, so what's the plan now, Roxey? Kill them both so we can play happy families again? Somehow, I don't think you'll get away with it *this* time. Everything's changed."

Roxey tilted her head, a chilling smile forming. "Why not? I've gotten away with it for this long. Soon everything will be back the way it should be. And it's changed for the better. Now at least you understand why we live out here, away from the world. Away from the people."

A familiar burn crept up Claire's throat, and tears brimmed in the corner of her eyes. "No, actually, I don't. I don't understand. And I don't *want* to. I don't want anything to do with you."

Roxey stepped forward, Rumble shadowing her movement. "But we're *family*, Claire. Family should always be together. And I can't live on the land…I always end up getting hurt. Better to be away from it all, to remove the temptation altogether."

Claire let out a disgruntled snigger. "You say family should be together, huh? What about McKenzie then? Why form a stolen, patched together family with all of us if you had an actual daughter out there all along?"

A silence stretched before Roxey responded. Her voice was quiet now, dangerous in its calm. "She mentioned that, huh…? Alright then. You want to understand? Fine. Because I didn't have her. Never did. My parents took her away from me."

She threw her nose in the air and began to pace, edging closer to the cage all the while. "I got pregnant when I was seventeen. My parents hated me for it, and they hid me when I couldn't conceal my growing body anymore. Made me drop out of school and everything. When I gave birth, they took Rachel from me. Said I was unfit to be a mother at my age, and she was better off without me. That my life would go nowhere if I raised her. They contacted the foster system and planned to give her away."

She crept closer, her once steely voice softening like silk pulled over a blade. "I knew if I had any chance of keeping her, I needed her father in the picture. To prove I had support and we could be a real family. But I still wanted to know if he loved me first, and wasn't going to just agree to a shotgun wedding out of obligation. I went to him and begged him to marry me, to forgive me for 'vanishing' on him. He agreed without knowing our baby girl existed. I tried to tell him about our daughter, but I was afraid I'd scare him off and opted to wait until after the wedding. But he decided not to go through with it at the last minute."

Claire's eyes widened as she realised what Roxey was saying. "Joshua..." she whispered.

Roxey nodded stiffly. "He told you all about it, didn't he? I figured he would. All I got was a phone call saying he was 'too young' to get married. And then he left. Just like that. My parents were less than impressed with my 'stunt,' as they called it and told me not to bother coming home."

She took a shaky breath. "They surrendered my daughter to the system, who soon changed her name after I kept showing up at every one of her foster family's doorsteps. After she was adopted, I lost her completely. I only found her again three years ago, when she was already grown up."

Claire swallowed, placing a curled hand over her mouth. "You're not kidding, are you? Emerald and McKenzie really share a father?"

Roxey's lips curved into a satisfied smile. "Oh yes. And here's the kicker—McKenzie shares her mother with someone you know too."

"Shut up, Roxey, I've told her what she needs to know," Michael suddenly snapped, his voice cracking as sharp as a whip through the heavy silence.

Claire whipped around to stare at him. "Okay…what's going on? What is it that I don't know?"

Before he could answer, Claire spun back and came nose-to-nose with Roxey.

"There's a lot you don't know, darling," Roxey said. Her voice was laced with condescension and amusement.

Claire hated how small she felt under Roxey's scrutiny, but her feet didn't move. She would stay grounded as long as it took to get some answers and end the game.

"For instance," Roxey went on, "did you know Michael and I were…*together*?"

Claire nodded stiffly, her jaw tightening. Roxey's eyes flicked with surprise, but her lips quickly curled into a wicked smile. "Oh, excellent, so we got that far. Well then—did you know he blames me for sweet baby Jasmine's death?"

Again, Claire nodded, though this time her stomach churned.

Roxey's eyes glimmered darkly. "Okay then, did you know, in fact, it wasn't me who killed her?" Claire's eyes snapped up, Roxey's statement striking her like a slap. Her gaze flew to Michael, but his confusion mirrored her own.

"Claire," Michael rasped, horrified. "No, if that's what she's getting at, it's not true. I didn't kill her."

"Bullshit!" Roxey spat, sidestepping Claire and striding toward the cage.

Michael grabbed the bars and shook violently, his fury evidently rising. "Don't you dare try and blame me! You murdered her, Roxey. You suffocated her in her sleep and blamed it on SIDS. Just like the babies you had with Chris!"

Enraged, Roxey forcefully slammed her hand into the metal bars, rattling the entire cage in a vivid shockwave. Claire felt something inside her jolt loose, like the wind had been knocked from her lungs.

Slowly, Roxey's posture weakened, and she closed her eyes, hanging her head silently. For the first time ever, Claire saw something in her she never thought she'd see. Guilt.

"You just had to bring that up, didn't you?" Roxey whispered, not to Michael, not to Claire, but to some aching ghost in the room with them. She turned around, her voice distant and dim. "Since we're on truth time now, the fact is…I'm the reason Christopher Isaac went to prison."

Claire staggered back. "Oh my God." She didn't mean to speak. The words just fell from her lips.

Roxey clicked her tongue and gave a bitter, quiet laugh to mask her pain. "Yeah, oops. Look, I loved Chris. I'm pretty sure I did. After losing my daughter to the system, getting rejected by her father and then ending up being thrown through windows by my first husband…I was sure Chris was my saving grace. Never imagined he'd find a whole new way to hurt me. When our son was born, I thought he'd be by my side. But he was never home. Chris was always gone, either working or 'out.' And I—"

She paused, swallowing hard. "I ended up with postnatal depression. It got so bad, one night, I lost control when Jesse wouldn't stop crying. And I shook him. Just one time."

There was a deep pause as the weight of her words sank in. "He stopped crying… and he never started again." Her voice cracked. "I couldn't face it and put him to bed, just laid him in the crib like nothing happened. Chris found him the next morning."

Claire's mouth was dry. Her body was trembling, but she couldn't move.

"When I gave birth to our daughter, I promised myself I'd do better. Get it right this time. But then… I found out Chris was having an affair. The worst part? With another man. With Tayla's father. I was destroyed. And then the baby was crying and—"

Roxey stopped, closing her eyes tight. "I didn't mean to, I just picked her up roughly. Too frustrated, too hurt to think."

Michael turned away. Claire felt her fingernails bite into her palms.

"When the hospital started questioning us and investigating why we'd lost another child, I panicked. I told them I'd seen Chris hovering near the cribs both times and found them dead the next morning. He got the blame. All this time, Bonnie's cousin's been locked up for something he didn't do."

Claire felt sick. Physically ill. "Is that why you went after Tayla? Took Bonnie? What, him being imprisoned for something you did wasn't enough suffering?"

Roxey's breathing became so heavy, Claire could see the rise and fall of her chest. Her fury bubbled to the surface, overcoming what had originally seemed like guilt.

"He promised me we'd be happy. That he would take my pain away. Prison didn't feel like enough. He'd been raising Tayla as his own. Not that her mother knew it, but the affair had been going on for well over a decade. And Bonnie, well she was a lot closer to Chris than she let on. They were like siblings at one point."

Roxey sniggered. "In fact, he was the one who encouraged her to get her qualification and 'follow her dreams.'" Roxey's voice dipped to a whisper. She looked at Michael, the softness in the lines under her eyes disturbing. "We were happy, weren't we? I really did love you."

Michael gripped the bars again, leaning close. Claire saw it immediately—the tension between them, not hatred, but something much worse. A thread of twisted love still tethering them like a sick joke.

Claire's stomach turned. She let her arms drop to her sides, hugging her own body as though trying to stop herself from being sick. Her arm bumped something inside the jacket pocket she hadn't realised was there before. Curious, she slipped her hand inside and carefully pulled the object to the edge.

Like an old phone, it was small and rectangular, with few buttons on the sides. She recognised it from the crime shows she'd seen on television. It was a simple recording device. Her eyes darted to Henry, who was still lying in the foetal position on the floor, breathing shallowly but steadily. She remembered him brushing her pocket earlier, when he'd helped her put the jacket she was wearing on. Had he slipped the recorder inside? Hope bloomed from somewhere deep inside her chest, sharp and sudden, but powerful.

Just in time, she looked up and caught Roxey leaning toward Michael, her breath warm and damning against his ear. "You have to believe me. I did not kill Jasmine."

Michael's face crumpled. "Rach, I found her that morning…with a blanket on her face. I thought you'd… I thought it was done on purpose."

Roxey's face twisted in shock, then horror. "I didn't… oh God. I didn't tuck it around her properly that night. I might have left the blanket loose near her little hands. She must've pulled it over herself. Oh no. My poor Jazzy."

Her voice laced with forceful accusation, Claire stepped forward. "Wait. What the hell are you talking about? Tucked her in? I thought you said you ended things with her when we were born. Why was she there to tuck us in? Did you get back with her after she killed my mother?"

Roxey turned on her, eyes narrowing. "Killed your mother? Ha! Is that what he told you?" She let out a shrill, unhinged laugh. "That's fantastic. What a cute little story."

Chuckling to herself, Roxey slid her hand through the bars, stroking Michael's cheek with false tenderness. He pulled back angrily. "Darling," Roxey said, facing Claire, her voice quiet but heavy. "I didn't kill your birth mother. I *am* your mother."

Claire stared between them, her blood turning cold. The world tilted, getting fuzzier by the second as though she were looking through somebody else's glasses. "No," she whispered, stepping back, shaking her head to pull herself out of the trance. "You're lying."

Roxey chuckled, walking beside the cage slowly, tapping each bar like an instrument. The ting of the metal as she clipped each one rang through the small room like a horrible song. "It's true. I met your father at his workshop just after I became *Rachel James*. I gave him my whole heart and in time, I told him the truth, all of it. And he didn't leave me, he married me. When I got pregnant, he suggested we name our daughter after a flower in honour of my birth name, Sarah Rose. Much to our surprise, we ended up blessed with twins. Two little flowers."

Claire's heart pounded violently. She wondered if she looked down, would her skin be green, or pale white? She couldn't decide if she was more sick or shocked. Roxey whimsically skipped toward her, stopping an inch from her face.

Stroking her cheek, she whispered. "We decided on Jasmine and Daisy. Of course, when your father handed you over to the system, they changed your name for your safety, with a little nudge from him."

Somewhere, deep in Claire's mind, something unlocked. She didn't want it to be true. But it fit. Horrifyingly, perfectly—it *fit*.

"But, you were born a flower and will always be, *my darling Daisy.*"

Chapter Thirty

Claire couldn't hold herself up any longer. Her knees gave way, and she crumpled onto the solid ground, the impact barely registering.

Roxey didn't flinch. She just stood there, looming, a satisfied smirk painted on her mouth. Like watching Claire break was some twisted prize she'd won. Claire's eyes found Michael, whose hand still gripped the bars of the cage. His expression showcased his disappointment and a single tear carved a line through the grime on his cheek.

"Dad?" she whispered. "Is she telling the truth?"

Michael nodded, his voice barely audible. "Yeah, honey. It's true. I lied before. I wanted what I told you to be the truth, an affair still sounds better somehow. But there was never anyone else, just her. Still, in a way though, she did kill your mother. The woman who gave birth to my children and the woman she became are two entirely different people. That morning…when I walked in and found Jas…when I saw how she died, I was devastated. I blamed her immediately. I figured…she was setting me up. That she'd planned it all, even plotted to send Chris to jail and was trying to do the same to me."

Claire's chest heaved, every word felt heavier than the last.

"She flipped out," he continued. "Said I was trying to sabotage our marriage. That's when she tried to set me on fire, Claire. I pushed her down, scooped you up, and I ran. For a few days, I kept you with me, tried to figure out how to keep you safe, but I knew she'd find us.

"In the end, I decided to take you to that church. Told them your mother was trying to kill you. Told them they needed to find you a home where she couldn't find you."

Claire stared at the floor, her voice flat, trembling with suppressed pain. "Well, look how that turned out for me. She found me anyway."

Roxey snorted—a sharp, cruel sound. "You really thought I was going to just let you go? I never stopped searching for the first daughter I lost, I don't know why he'd assume I'd just give up on you without a fight." She nodded toward Michael.

"Just got lucky with you, I suppose. I recognised you at the beach. Saw you playing with your…*adoptive* mother. You looked *so* like me when you were little, easy to spot."

Her voice softened for a moment, sickeningly fond. "I approached your parents at the church. Told them who I was and how much I wanted you back. They just laughed. Said I was insane. Said I needed help. I had no choice but to take matters into my own hands, you see. So, I showed them what insane really looked like."

Claire rose slowly to her feet, her movements stiff, deliberate. "Insane? You became a killer." Her eyes blazed. Roxey narrowed hers.

"Well, I figured… what was the point of resisting anymore? Every time I found fire, it turned to ash. Every time I tried to build a life, someone destroyed it. There was never going to be another option for me. I accepted the fact that I had to make my own happiness. And I did. Come now Daisy, I tried for years to be a good mother to you."

Claire let out a strangled laugh. "You're not serious? Is that really what you thought good parenting looked like? Trauma and obedience wrapped in a cult bow?"

Roxey ignored her and pressed on, her eyes reflecting something frighteningly close to heartbreak. "You don't remember the first few years we spent together? We had an amazing thing going, such a bond. But the second you walked into my room the morning of your tenth birthday, the day you *really* saw me…that was the moment everything changed for us. Forever. That's when I knew I couldn't let myself care anymore. Because things were never going to turn up good for me, no matter how much I tried."

Claire scrunched her nose up in disgust. "What are you talking about? I was reminded that you were the one who killed my parents, and somehow you're the one who got hurt?"

Roxey crossed her arms and glared. "Oh, you don't remember what you said to me, do you? Let me remind you. We fought, there were tears, I apologised and promised to make it up to you. And you still said, 'you're not my real mother' and threatened to throw yourself overboard. Said you'd rather that than have anything to do with me. You didn't even give me a chance to explain. I intended to tell you the truth back then. Maybe things could have been different for you."

Claire's face froze. She had forgotten how badly she'd reacted.

Roxey's voice cracked, just for a breath. "When I saw the look on your face, heard the hatred in your voice, I just stopped trying. After all the heartbreak I copped every time I thought I'd found happiness. After all the pain my former lovers had caused me. I started wondering why me, why *I* was always the one left to suffer. It wasn't fair. So, I started tracking them down, one by one. Their turn to feel pain, to have their family broken. And my chance to have a family that couldn't hurt me."

Claire's hand moved slowly inside her jacket pocket. Her fingers closed around the cold, lightly vibrating recording device. Like it was some kind of lifeline, clutching it gave her a euphoric feeling of gratitude toward Henry. Her pulse quickened. Maybe, just maybe, this was enough. This was everything she'd need, proof a thousand times better than the diary she'd come for. This was Claire's story, and Roxey's confession, recorded and provided in Roxey's *own* words. Her mind was a swirling mess, and she wished with all her heart she was strong enough to charge and tackle Roxey to the ground.

Rumble growled, and Roxey noticed Claire's hand moving around in her pocket, her eyes zoning in, locking onto the motion.

"What are you hiding, darling?" she asked in her falsely girlish voice, her stance riddled with suspicion.

Claire's hand clammed up and she opened her mouth, panic searing through her, but thankfully, the sound of footsteps rang out above them before she could think of an answer.

Claire turned toward the stairs, every breath held in her chest like a balloon about to pop. Tayla and Serenah appeared, side by side, followed closely by McKenzie. Her half-sister. Claire nearly collapsed all over again, this time from a mixture of relief and awe. "You guys!"

Serenah's eyes swept the room, assessing the danger like a meerkat with soldier-sharp instinct. Tayla's expression was blank and unreadable, but her eyes locked on Claire, wide with concern. McKenzie hesitated on the last step, hovering behind the girls, her face shifting between confusion and something that looked like guilt.

Roxey tensed beside Claire, her mouth tightening into a line. The moment stretched, taut and fragile. Claire took the opportunity to glance down at Henry, then back at her friends, her family, and adjusted her grip around the recorder.

"What the hell are you all doing here?" Roxey snapped.

McKenzie looked taken aback. "Oh, well, they wanted to come back. Convinced me they'd rather come home and cooperate than go to the hospital lockdown wards. I asked my boss if I could return them to their usual facility, and he thought it was a good idea. He's even going to contact the hospital and get some extra staff out to give you a hand here. You just need to sign some paperwork, and they can stay with you instead of going to the traditional mental hospital." McKenzie's enthusiastic disposition faltered as she observed Roxey's expression turning the longer she spoke. "I…I thought that would be what you wanted?"

Roxey blinked in surprise. Claire glanced between Tayla and Serenah, who both had a mischievous twinkle in their eyes. Despite Tayla looking as though she'd been crying for hours, their faces were composed. They didn't seem worried at all.

"Rachy, darling, that's great," Roxey started, but McKenzie cut her off.

"Mother, I told you—it's McKenzie. I was never even known as Rachel."

Roxey gave her a half smile. "*McKenzie*, we've already talked about this. I told you yesterday I'd decided not to bring them back here. I wanted them to suffer. They were supposed to be picked up by the ward nurses and locked in the bloody hospital."

McKenzie frowned, pausing as though deep in thought.

Then, out of nowhere, Henry leapt up from the floor and tackled Roxey around the waist, bringing her down hard. Rumble rushed in, growling, and latched on to Henry's leg. He didn't make a sound, instead focusing all his energy into snatching the tranquiliser gun out of Roxey's pocket. In a swift, clean motion, he fired, hitting Rumble in the shoulder. Never releasing his grasp on Roxey, he pinned her down as Rumble collapsed, whimpering, into a heap on the ground.

Checking the weapon's chamber, he noted the dart gun was empty and tossed it aside. With the same arm, he reached for his handgun, wrestling Roxey as she squirmed beneath him, attempting to free herself.

"No!" McKenzie cried, dashing across the room as Henry pointed the weapon toward Roxey's back. She drew a small handgun of her own and pointed it at Henry. "Get off her! McLaren, what are you doing?"

Roxey used the distraction to twist herself sideways, knocking the wind out of Henry with her knee as she lurched forward and snatched a pocketknife from McKenzie's belt. She whipped around, jabbing it just wherever she could reach into Henry's torso.

He yelped, collapsing off her as Claire rushed to fall down by his side. Tayla and Serenah sprinted across the room and the chaos exploded. Roxey wrestled with Serenah, while Tayla charged at McKenzie. An all-out brawl erupted as each party tried to take down the other. Claire checked Henry's wound, forcefully peeling back his fingers to see.

"It's not that bad," he whispered. "Or deep."

Just then, Claire caught a glimpse of something fly out of Roxey's pocket. It hit the wall with a *clink*. A key. The skeleton head key to the cage.

"Dad," she whispered. "I'll be right back," she assured Henry.

Crawling forward at first, she half stood to move faster, ducking just in time as Tayla's elbow whizzed past her face. Unable to avoid a collision, Tayla tripped over Claire instead, slamming into her side and sending Claire flying speedily forward. She broke her fall with her elbows, the recording device flying out of her pocket and clattering across the floor.

Mid fight, Roxey saw it. Despite the commotion she was battling, her eyes locked on it immediately. Summoning an almighty burst of energy, she caught Serenah's flying fist mid-air and slammed her own into Serenah's throat. Serenah dropped, clutching her neck. Roxey shoved her aside and lunged for the recorder.

Claire scrambled forward, half-running, half-crawling. At that moment, McKenzie landed a punch on Tayla, and she went down, falling into Roxey's path. Roxey almost tripped, but steadied herself, driving her heel into Tayla's belly without empathy, trying to move forward faster. Reacting to the pain, Tayla's foot flailed wildly, flinging the recorder straight under McKenzie's feet and sending Roxey tumbling at the same time. McKenzie bent down and picked up the device.

Picking herself halfway up, Roxey beamed. "Yes! Now put that on the ground and smash it, darling!"

"What?" McKenzie blinked, bewildered. "Why? I can't do that."

Roxey's expression hardened. She scanned the floor, found the knife, and retrieved it, rising slowly to her feet in a semi-threatening manner. "Rachel Jaymz," she hissed, "either toss it to me or you put that little box on the ground and stomp on it right now!"

"Everyone, stop!" a voice rang out.

Claire looked up. Emerald was coming down the stairs two at a time, a laptop cradled in her arms. Roxey's laptop, Claire recognised instantly.

Roxey's face flickered with concern at first. Then she appeared cocky. In the blink of an eye, she bent and grabbed Tayla's arm, hoisting her to her feet. Tayla struggled, but Roxey was stronger and wrapped her arm around her waist, holding her at knifepoint. The room fell still. Even the creaking walls seemed to pause, listening as Emerald made a simple, but powerful statement.

"Put the knife down Roxey, let Tayla go. Here's the deal. I've just scanned all the pages from your diary onto your laptop and attached them to an email. All I have to do is push this button" —Emerald motioned— "and the whole lot goes to the cops. Let us all go back to our lives, leave us alone, and we'll part ways amicably."

For a moment, Roxey froze. Then her mouth curved into something too calm, too controlled. She turned her head slowly toward McKenzie.

"Put the box on the ground, Rachel," she said.

Watching her mother tighten the grip across Tayla's torso, McKenzie crouched and very slowly laid the recorder down. The second she'd removed her fingers, Roxey's heel came crashing down. The vicious action caused the device to splinter under her shoe. Claire winced as if the blow had struck her.

In a shocking move, Roxey's next action came even quicker. Without warning, she yanked the knife around and drove it straight into Tayla's chest, aiming for her heart. Claire clapped her hands across her mouth, listening to the pained gasps of the group as Tayla screamed.

Roxey looked up at Emerald, cold and deadly. "Well, get on with it then. Press the button if it'll make you feel better."

Chapter Thirty-One

An eerie, pain-ridden quiet followed. Not even a breeze stirred the thick, suffocating air between the stunned figures frozen in the room. Emerald began to tremble, her knuckles whitening as she nearly lost her grip on the laptop.

Roxey carelessly let Tayla drop like dead weight, and she hit the floor with a sickening thud. "What's the matter? Didn't expect that now, did you?" Roxey sneered, her eyes glittering with satisfaction. "Thought you could outsmart me, huh? Please. I rerouted my email server weeks ago, when you girls first started getting restless. Every outgoing message goes straight to junk. And the junk folder needs a passcode to access."

Disheartened, Claire's eyes snapped from Henry to Tayla. She was still breathing, but barely. The tears that ran down her face mixing with the spreading pool of blood beneath her as she lay curled in the foetal position. Claire's limbs felt rooted to the floor, her mind consumed by helplessness. What could she do? Where should she move first?

McKenzie stood off to the side, her expression fractured with disbelief. She kept flicking her gaze from Tayla's trembling body to Roxey's stiff stance, her lips parting soundlessly like a fish out of water. Finally, her strangled voice emerged. "What is this?" she rasped, swallowing hard. "They were right, weren't they? You lied to me…You are *not* a doctor."

Roxey rolled her eyes, almost mockingly. "Don't be silly. I told you my methods were a little unorthodox, that's all."

"Unorthodox?" McKenzie repeated, her mouth left hanging open.

The momentary shift in Roxey's focus was enough for Claire. She took a cautious step forward, hoping to catch her off guard and knock her off her feet. But Roxey saw Claire's shadow and turned, snapping her head around like a predator sensing movement. She yanked her small pistol from beneath her shirt and levelled it with eerie calm.

"Don't you take another step," Roxey said. Then she sighed. Deeply. Like she was tired of the entire world. "Oh, girls. You've left me no choice now. I'm going to have to lower my numbers if we're going to move past this," she murmured.

Then, as if lost in her own deranged mind, she continued, louder now, and to no one in particular: "Well, it's going to have to be an accident, like my original plan…maybe the ship blows up…or sinks. Killed everyone on board…"

Fear slammed into Claire's chest like a hammer. She scanned the room: her father locked in the cage. Henry and Tayla slowly bleeding. Emerald, Serenah, and Katalyna too terrified to move or else risk being shot. But McKenzie—McKenzie was still free. Still mostly behind Roxey, still mostly trusted. If she were to take Roxey down from behind, she could knock the gun loose from her hand and spare a second for anyone else to rush her.

A lightbulb lit up in Claire's mind. She had buttons to push. But before she could speak, Tayla let out a ragged gasp and looked up tearfully. The sound tore through the room. She was trying to move, attempting to roll over. McKenzie dropped to her knees instantly, her hands pressing hard against Tayla's chest.

Roxey shifted, but didn't act—fascinated, perhaps, by her daughter's empathy.

Claire's voice cut through, calm but sharp, before anything else could happen. "McKenzie, you know in your heart she's not who she says she is, don't you?"

McKenzie's head turned slightly, listening.

"The only thing she didn't lie to you about is that she's your birth mother," Claire continued, "but did she tell you that she's my biological mother too? Or did she let that little detail slide?"

Roxey glared at Claire and gritted her teeth. "Now is not the time. Enough."

Claire ignored her. "No, it never would have been for you, would it? Mack, did she tell you she murdered my adoptive parents? The ones who protected me from her. Ask Henry."

From the floor, Henry nodded when McKenzie side eyed him, grimacing through the pain.

Claire shot a quick, involuntary glance in Emerald's direction, then back to McKenzie. "How about the fact that you've also got another sister? One you share a father with, who's life she destroyed alongside me in her little game. That's all we were to her, pawns in a game of revenge. Her mother was a doctor, and one of the many identities she's either stolen or created throughout the years. Think about it, with all the things she's been hiding, how much do you really think you can trust what she's told you?"

McKenzie took a deep breath, then seemed to stop breathing altogether. After a brief pause, slowly, she turned her head. Her tear-filled eyes swept across the room—lingering on Claire, then at Henry—and then something inside her snapped into place. Without warning, she snatched a handful of dirt and debris from the floor, stood up fast, and hurled it into Roxey's face. Exactly the way Tayla had done it to her.

The gun clattered to the floor as Roxey's hands flailed to clean her eyes. In the same heartbeat, McKenzie lunged. She tackled Roxey from behind, catching her off guard and easily slamming her to the ground, wrestling her into submission.

In one swift motion, she pulled a pair of handcuffs from her belt and locked them around Roxey's wrists. As though she'd just taken down a steer in a rodeo, she sat on her back, triumphant and breathing hard.

Claire stood still for a heartbeat, then broke into motion, rushing forward. Her intention was to check on Tayla, but to Claire's surprise, McKenzie opened one arm, pulling her in for a fierce, trembling hug. When she pulled back, McKenzie leaned down to feel Tayla's pulse and smoothed a hand across her paling forehead.

"Thanks for the inspiration," McKenzie whispered. She turned back to Claire. "I always *knew* something was not quite right with her background. I tried to ignore it, tried to rationalise her 'treatment methods.' But when your birth mother shows up right after your adoptive parents die..." Her voice faltered. "It takes a while to question it, I suppose. You just...you're just glad to have someone. I caught myself up too much in being happy to meet her, to have her in my life."

Claire's eyes widened.

"Your parents died...together?"

McKenzie nodded slowly, standing and helping Claire up. "Yeah, they died in their sleep about three years ago. Carbon monoxide poisoning. The, uh, stove had a gas leak."

Claire stared at Roxey. The malicious woman was slumped, silent and cuffed, on the floor with a blank expression, but madness still flickered in her eyes. Claire crouched and helped her sit up, coming face to face with her. "Their death wasn't an accident, was it?"

Roxey sneered. "Well, I had to do something drastic, so she'd need me. By the time I finally found her, she was already grown up. I intended to bring her back here like all the rest of you, but by the time it was settled enough to go back for her, Rachel was way too protected."

Claire glanced at McKenzie, who looked utterly shattered. "I—I joined the force right after they died. I needed answers, some kind of closure. But the cops kept saying they couldn't rule out foul play and wouldn't let me help. I became one of them to get on the inside."

She looked toward Henry, her eyes softening as she observed the pain on his face. "They put me and Henry together, cause he was also a rookie when I started. Henry, you alright there?"

Henry cracked a half-smile and stuck out his hand, flashing her a weak thumbs up. McKenzie pulled a pager from her belt and held it up, searching for a non-existent signal. "Alright, I'm calling this in. We'll get medics, backup… everything. Be right back."

As she stepped away, Serenah rushed to Tayla's side, whispering softly and pressing her jacket to her wound. Claire felt lighter. Not safe, but no longer drowning. She knelt beside Henry, brushing the matted hair from his forehead, getting lost in his eyes. Using his free arm, he stroked the back of her hand, and she began leaning toward him. Until Michael cleared his throat from inside the cage.

Claire looked up with a jolt, following his eyes to the skeleton head key still glinting, abandoned in the middle of the floor. A soft, tired smile crossed her face as she scooted to pick it up. Roxey's voice chased her, dangerously monotoned. "I was going to get rid of the others, you know. That's how it was meant to happen. Finalise the pain for my former lovers by staging an accident. Ensuring it made the news so they'd all see what I'd done. Should have done it years ago, but I couldn't. I chose a different path. Now everything's ruined."

A little while later, Claire sat in an interrogation room at the police station, just like she had only days before. But this time, it felt different. She felt at ease. Free. Unlike last time, no one believed her to be a mental patient. She wasn't being treated like a criminal. Emerald sat beside her, twiddling her thumbs, unusually quiet. Serenah had gone to the hospital with Tayla, who was still fighting for her life. Katalyna anxiously paced the waiting room by the reception area, her every step weighted with the desperate hope that the foster system would soon return her daughter. In another room, McKenzie was in a closed-door meeting with the Commander, while Henry was busy taking Michael's official statement.

When the ambulance had arrived at the docks, Henry had insisted they patch him up on the spot and let him go to the station. He'd refused to go to the hospital, adamant he needed to be part of what came next. It all seemed too quiet as the girls waited. They awaited the Commander's reaction. Waited to see if the tech team could salvage anything from the damaged recorder. Waited for Roxey's journal to be analysed, hoping it might finally clear the air and pin her for good.

After what seemed like hours, Emerald was the first to speak. "So…you and McKenzie are sisters, huh? That must have been mind-blowing to find out. And I heard you say something about her having another?"

Claire smiled, an unexpected bubble of laughter rising in her chest which she fought to contain. "Yeah, uh…Em, about that—"

The door clicked open. Henry stepped inside, moving carefully, his posture betraying how much pain he was still suppressing.

"Hey, ladies. Claire, could I borrow you for a moment? Emerald, McKenzie will be in shortly to see you."

Claire stood, sensing Emerald's curious gaze following her as she trailed after Henry. He led her into another room—the other interrogation room—where her father was already seated.

"Please, have a seat," Henry said, his voice shifting into something more professional.

Claire sat down, her nerves surfacing.

"I don't know how else to say this," he started grimly folding his arms firmly, "so I'll just get into it."

Claire clasped her hands together and held tight. "First off, my Commander doesn't think the journal will be any good to use as evidence."

Claire blinked. "What? Why not?"

Henry raised a calming hand. "Well, because it's signed 'Roxey Jenson' in every entry. The woman we have in custody is legally 'Regina Johnson.' According to the law, those are two different people. There's no clear way to tie 'Regina' to the actions of 'Roxey.'"

He used air quotes every time he said her name, which somehow made the sting of his words more powerful. Claire's stomach twisted.

"Which brings me to bad news announcement number two," he added. "The recorder's toast. She broke it well. Nothing on it is viable."

Claire opened her mouth, reeling, but Henry held up a finger. "At this moment, the only charge we have her on is the attempted murder of Tayla. If Tayla doesn't make it...it becomes murder."

Claire felt the room tilt slightly. Anger. Fear. Frustration. It all mixed together in a horrible, choking swirl. Then she turned her head and noticed something strange—Michael was smiling. She threw a palm down at the table. "Why are you smiling?" she demanded.

Glancing back to Henry, she frowned when she saw that he wore a small smile too. Michael reached into his pocket and placed a small, brick-shaped phone on the table.

"Guess it's a good thing your dad outsmarted her, hey," Henry chirped.

Claire frowned.

"When your mother darted me, she took my phone," Michael said, "but she didn't know I had a second one. A burner I bought, from when I was pretending to be a cop. The second I woke up in that cage, I realised it was still in my back pocket." He tapped the device as though patting it. "When she came down the stairs, I hit record on its radio app."

Claire's heart skipped.

"You recorded her…how much?"

Michael nodded. "All of it."

A rush of breath escaped her lips—part relief, part disbelief.

She threw out her arm, playfully hitting Michael on the shoulder. "I can't believe you." She turned to Henry, shaking her head with a teasing smile. "You seriously had me for a second, you know that?"

In a flash, she shot up and darted around the table, throwing her arms around his shoulders. Henry stood with a grunt, then wrapped his arms around her, holding her tight. Their lips met in a long, grateful kiss. Michael cleared his throat dramatically.

Claire grinned and pulled away, flitting over to wrap Michael in a grateful hug too.

Just then, the phone on the wall rang. Henry moved as quickly as he could and picked it up. After a brief conversation, he turned to them with a spark in his eyes.

"Josie's on her way," he announced. "She's being dropped off by her temporary foster carers. Katalyna's false records have been officially cleared."

Claire clapped her hands together with a small squeal. "That's awesome news!"

"And they're working on clearing Joshua and Logan. No concrete proof yet about Bonnie and Daphne's deaths, but things are leaning in the right direction. I reckon they'll be right."

With a smile, Henry opened the door and motioned for Claire and Michael to follow. They exited the room to find Katalyna beaming in the waiting area.

"Did you hear?" she asked, pulling Claire into a warm embrace. "Josie's coming back!"

"I did," Claire said, hugging her tightly.

Katalyna drew back, her eyes soft. "Claire…gosh, I want to apologise. You know I would never have left you all if I didn't think I had to, right? I had to make sure Josie was going to be safe."

Claire nodded, rubbing her arm. "Don't even worry about it. It all worked out."

Katalyna smiled, then her face dimmed a little like she'd just remembered bad news. "Oh, I uh…went to see Logan earlier."

Claire raised an eyebrow.

"Really? How did that go for you?"

She shrugged, pulling Claire onto a nearby pair of chairs. Michael politely stepped aside and went to pour a cup of coffee.

"At first, it was alright. But then…we got to talking, and he told me…some things that I really wish I didn't hear." She sighed and pulled a face. "Do you remember Sierra? The teenager Roxey murdered on the deck after her escape attempt?"

Claire nodded. She had no trouble remembering.

"She was Logan's daughter, Claire. Roxey kidnapped her the year before Daphne."

Claire sat up straighter and Katalyna continued, her voice laden in disgust. "And the reason he started dating Daphne? Because he missed Sierra. He missed having a younger girl in his life who idled him."

Claire coughed. "What?"

Katalyna nodded. "Yep. Oh, and worse than that, he remembers Roxey. Yeah, remembers beating her when she pissed him off. He said he lost his shit once because she wouldn't shut up about finding her baby. Said she talked about her night and day and left no space for him." She shook her head. "I always knew I stayed away from him for a reason."

Claire couldn't believe it. Katalyna took a deep breath. "Since he's such a dick, I've decided to let him take the fall for Daphne's death."

Claire blinked. "I'm sorry, what?"

"Yep. You heard me. He beat her too, remember?" Katalyna shrugged. "Roxey's already going down for so many other things once they're finished with her. Daphne deserves some justice too and they suspected Logan first. I told the cops I saw him hanging around the hotel right before those chocolates were delivered. He's exactly where he should be, honestly."

Claire held up a hand to her cheek. "Kat!"
The glass door swung open, and McKenzie stepped out, followed closely by Emerald—and to Claire's surprise, also by Joshua. Claire blinked.
"Well, here we go," she said quietly, watching the three of them walk toward her. It was so strange now, seeing them together, knowing she knew something about their family tie they didn't. And what a strange situation it was to be in. Emerald hugged her briefly, grinning.

"What's going on?" Claire asked as she pulled Emerald to the side, looking around her.

McKenzie spoke with a nod in Joshua's direction. "The Commander agreed the case against Joshua is too unstable now, considering Roxey's…history. For now. at least, we're letting him go until the new evidence has been assessed. As long as he doesn't leave town, he can go home and be with his daughter." She lowered her voice and spoke directly to Claire. "And speaking of family, now that we have some time, I'd like to get to know my little sister. If you're open to that, of course."

Claire smiled warmly. "I'd love that. But, first, now that you bring it up and all…I need to tell you about your other sister too."

McKenzie frowned. "We have another sister?"

Claire shook her head.

"Not exactly. I mean, I don't."

Emerald gently grabbed her father's arm and began to step away, as though believing she were leaving them to a moment. "Hold up," Claire said, stopping her. "This involves you too."

Both Emerald and Joshua froze, puzzled. Claire turned her attention to Joshua and gestured to McKenzie. "Joshua, I'd like you to meet your daughter. Your first-born daughter, that is. McKenzie and Emerald are sisters too."

A long silence followed, Joshua's face turning paler with every minute that passed. Claire took a breath and explained it all, beginning with Sarah Twidale's hidden pregnancy. Joshua took it amazingly well, considering. He stared at McKenzie for a long while, then slowly opened his arms. McKenzie, stunned but smiling, stepped into them. They embraced with tears, a reconnected family—both lost, now found.

Emerald stood still in the background, her hand wrapped across her mouth as she watched and absorbed the new information with wide-eyes. When McKenzie stopped crying, Joshua removed one arm from around her shoulders and pulled Emerald in, hugging both his daughters with pride.

Seeing the commotion, Michael cautiously stepped up beside Claire, as though sensing if he was welcome. Claire nodded.

Joshua laughed quietly. "Wow. You know, if Sarah had just been honest with me about getting pregnant, I would've gone through with it and married her. Wouldn't things have turned out so different? For everyone."

They all revelled in the idea for a moment, laughing to each other.

"Let's pretend that's not true," Claire said, scrunching up her nose. Behind the group, Henry appeared in the doorframe, catching Claire's eye. He smiled at her, an adorable twinkle in his eye. She tilted her head, returning the smile, a feeling of true happiness blooming inside her like a spring flower.

She looked around at all of them—her disjointed family, each carrying the scars of Roxey's lies, yet finally, slowly, finding the truth. Finding their peace.

Epilogue

Six Years Later

The car slowed until it halted beside the curb. Henry turned off the engine and quickly circled around to open Claire's door. She smiled as he bowed and took her hand, helping her step out of the vehicle like a princess from a carriage.

Turning to look at her father's house, she teased, "Okay, so are you going to tell me what this is all about now?" He closed the car door behind her. "Nope. Guess you'll just have to come inside and find out for yourself, huh?"

She sighed and grimaced, blurting, "Oh, sweetie. I already know. You're terrible at hiding anything from me. I know about the surprise party."

Henry's face fell, just a little. "Damn, I thought we had you this time. Aw baby, last time it was your birthday surprise party you spoiled, remember?"

Claire bit her lip. "I know," she whined.

"Damn, I'm so sorry. I know you wanted it to be perfect." He kissed her forehead gently and rested a hand across her perfectly rounded belly.

"It's already perfect."

They walked up the path together, and when Henry opened the door—

"Surprise!"

A roomful of people greeted the pair, erupting in cheers and blowing on horns. Claire gave a little jump, covering her mouth as if she were truly shocked, playing along with the excitement. Her head bobbed around, sifting between the smiling faces of her friends and family as they pushed their way in to the centre of the room.

The decorations were a beautifully even mix of pink and blue and everywhere she looked, there were more baby items jammed. Stuffed toys, onesies, bottles, and tiny socks layered every spare surface.

Claire's eyes darted from one warm sight to another. There was Katalyna, telling Josie off for swiping a finger across the iced cake. Emerald and Serenah stood in the kitchen, finalising a tower of bright yellow cupcakes, bickering all the way. Tayla chatting away with one of Claire's work friends, the deep-coloured scar on her chest visible above the low-cut neckline of her dress, worn with pride.

Michael approached the happy couple, kissed Claire on the cheek, and bent to hug her gently.

"I love it. Thanks, Dad," she murmured over his shoulder.

"Eh, your fiancé here did most of the work," he chuckled. Once he'd moved away, Claire glanced around again. "Hmm. No Mack?"

Henry scoped the floor and frowned. "I'll give her a call. I mean, I don't know of anything urgent going on at the station, but we'll find out." He slipped away with his phone already in hand. Claire moved deeper into the room, soaking in the joy and ready to mingle with her guests.

Her aunt, Serenah's mother, spotted her and came dancing over. She pulled Claire into an uncomfortably tight hug, pushing the baby deep into her bladder. "Woohoo! Not long now, huh?" she said, rubbing Claire's round belly. "Are you excited to find out what you're having?"

"Yep," Claire glowed. "Just three weeks to go. And it honestly doesn't matter if I have a boy or girl, that's why we chose not to find out. We just want our baby to grow up safe and loved."

To her surprise, Henry came jogging back in a hurry. She recognised the look on his face. Concern.

"Er, baby, can I borrow you for a sec," he said.

Worried, Claire excused herself and followed him to the kitchen, which had gone quiet and empty. Henry glanced around and spoke low. "Mack's on her way here now. And she said she has an update about your mother."

Claire felt her stomach drop in a way it hadn't in a very long time. Coldness crawled up her spine as she choked. "What?"

McKenzie was on the doorstep not five minutes later. A doomed look pasted on her colour-drained face, she spotted Claire and Henry in the kitchen, joining them.

Claire met her eyes. "Oh, Mack. What is it?"

"She's been downgraded, Claire," McKenzie said, monotoned. "Mother. Some paperwork was approved yesterday, and they've transferred her from the prison."

Claire reeled, grabbing the edge of the counter. "Huh? What kind of transfer?"

"She's gone over to the mental hospital. Into a low security ward." She slapped the counter in frustration as she spoke, enhancing the seriousness of each word.

Claire scrunched her face. "Oh, you're kidding. How is that possible? What does that mean?"

McKenzie hesitated, then replied, "What it means is that she can check herself in and out. For day leave. As long as she's compliant with treatment and her therapy sessions, she's basically free during daylight hours. Every day. Any day."

A knock sounded at the front door before another word was spoken. The three of them froze, their heads simultaneously snapping into place, staring toward the sound. From the loungeroom, Michael started toward the door, but Claire waddled quickly in front to cut him off, tailed closely by Henry.

Opening it, she came face to face with a nightmare. Standing there, like a ghost pulled from the past, was Roxey. She leant on the doorframe, as calm as ever. Her smile was soft, almost serene, and her eyes dropped to Claire's baby bump with an unsettling affection.

"I hear my darling Daisy's having me a grandchild," she cooed.

Claire, Henry, and McKenzie stood too stunned to speak, too horrified to move.

"Well," Roxey said, narrowing her eyes, but still smiling. "Aren't you going to invite me in?"

ABOUT THE AUTHOR

K.M. Tomkinson is an Australian author born in 1994.

Please feel free to keep in touch!

Social media links :

Facebook –
https://www.facebook.com/KmTomkinson

Instagram –
k_m_tomkinson

TikTok –
@k.m.tomkinson

Thank you for your support.